I

The Kempler Funeral Home overflows with Ellie's mother's friends and relatives. Some spill out the doorway into the cloudy April afternoon where her sister Jo has fled. Liz and Katie, Ellie's daughters, stand with her near the front of the room. The scent of the flower arrangements stirs up a slight nausea in her empty stomach. Instead of a casket, an easel holds her mother's picture. A memorial service will follow the visitation.

The buzz of voices fills the room. Occasionally, she catches a word or phrase but mostly, she tunes them out. It feels like déjà vu. Ten years ago, after her father was felled by a massive heart attack at work, she stood next to her mother, surrounded by flowers, greeting mourners.

Something akin to an electric shock ripples through her as she takes in the red hair, still luxuriantly thick, the green eyes, pug nose and freckles of the woman now standing before her. "Helen!" she exclaims.

"I'm so sorry about your mother, Ellie. She was always good to me."

"How are you?" Forgetting her daughters, who are talking to each other, she neglects to introduce them.

"Good." Helen smiles. "It's been a long time."

So long that she hardly knows what to say. "Did you see Jo?"

"Yes. Actually, I came with Nancy. They're outside, catching up on each other's lives. Joey looks good."

"She is." There was a time when no one knew if Jo would live to grow up. "Are you staying for the service?"

"Of course."

"Come to the house afterward. Just follow us."

"I'd like to but Nancy's driving. Maybe there'll be time to talk before we go."

"I hope so." As Helen disappears into the crowd, she turns to the next person, saying automatically, "Thanks for coming."

When Lyle Jensen and his wife finally make their way to the front of the line, she grasps their hands gratefully. "You were such good friends to Mom. Thanks again for everything."

Lyle nods solemnly. "Hey, she was a good friend to us. We'll miss her." He looks around. "Did I see Helen?"

It has been more than thirty years since he last saw Helen, and then for only one weekend. "You did. Come to the house after the memorial service."

Jo makes her way to Ellie's side when it's time to sit down. The J.S. Bach CD Ellie gave to the funeral director when she and Jo made arrangements plays quietly through the speaker system.

Jo leans toward her. "Will is here."

She thought he might come. He loved her mother. "Good."

Her cousin Steven takes a seat next to her daughters. The rest of her cousins and their children fill the row next to and behind her. Afterward, she hardly remembers the service although she, her two daughters and Jo spoke. Steven gave a moving tribute to his aunt while she twisted a wad of tissues and Liz and Katie and Jo cried quietly. She has managed to contain her grief but with each kind word the facade crumbles a little.

After the service, Will works his way toward her, his tall frame and broad shoulders weaving through those who are leaving. The girls hurry toward their father.

She likes Will. Their marriage lasted sixteen years, during which she loved him, not passionately but well. She still does in a disconnected sort of way. He strayed first. When she asked him why, he said the other woman loved him with a passion she never had or ever would have. It was true. Their divorce was as amicable as any can be, the settlement equitable. He paid child support regularly and chipped in more than his share of the cost of the girls' higher education.

He hugs his daughters before turning to her. "I'm sorry, Ellie."

She meets his eyes for a moment before nodding. "Thanks for coming," she says, as she said to everyone else.

"Of course, I came." He's not only good looking, but also fair and kind. She sometimes wonders if she was stupid to let him go so easily.

"Come to the house," she says.

"Yeah, Dad, there's lots of food," Katie urges.

Smiling, he shakes his head. "I have to get back." Putting an arm around each of his daughters, he says loud enough for her to hear, "Take care of your mother. I'll talk to you two next week."

Enveloping Ellie's hands in his, he kisses her on the cheek, then turns and leaves. Her vision blurs.

Steven takes her arm. "Hang in there, sweetie."

Before they leave, the funeral director hands them their mother's ashes, the memorial envelopes and the cards from the floral arrangements. He looks like a kind man and seems respectful of the dead who provide him with a living.

The weight of the container surprises her. Jo looks stricken. All of their mother's earthly remains lie in this rectangular urn. Steven and the girls come up behind them with some of the plants.

"We should go. No one can get into the house till we get there," he points out.

As if a spell is broken, she thanks Brian Kempler and invites him to the house.

"Thanks, but there's a family coming in soon." He walks with them to the door.

Rain has begun to fall. Steven drives Ellie's Ford Escort station wagon along the black roads. In the passenger seat, she cradles the urn as she once did her babies.

"I was surprised to see Helen and Nancy," Jo says from the backseat where she's sandwiched between her nieces.

"I was too. I never got a chance to talk to either," she responds.

"When I finished my thesis, I thought I was going to celebrate. Losing Grandma wasn't what I had in mind." Liz's voice breaks.

She reaches to clasp her daughter's clenched hands. "I know." Although her mother was seventy when she died, she seemed much younger than her years. If she knew she was at risk, she never let on. She took daily walks with her dog, kept a large garden, and drove elderly shut-ins to their appointments. Those people are probably still alive, she thinks with a touch of bitterness. She wasn't ready for the grief that followed her father's death after his third heart attack either.

Katie stares broodingly out the window, saying nothing.

"Are you all right, Katie?" Even as she asks it, she thinks it's a stupid question.

"No, I'm not all right. I want Grandma back." The sobbing this sets off can barely be heard over the drumming rain.

Steven glances in the rearview mirror. "You're going to ruin your mascara, girls, and there's company waiting. Beth would want you to look your best." Years ago he dropped the Aunt from Beth's name.

Jo remarks, "Mom wouldn't have wanted to live after a stroke like that. She knew it was time to die." More sobbing follows this.

"Even you have to grieve, Steven," Ellie points out quietly as the truth of Jo's words knife through her.

Her mother suffered a stroke. Shut outside, Bitsy, her mother's dog, barked at the Jensen's door across the road until Lyle opened it. Lyle discovered Beth McGowan lying face down on the braided rug Ellie's grandma had woven, her cheek bruised from the fall.

Their mother opened her eyes when Ellie and Jo arrived at the hospital, then closed them and slid into a deep sleep from which she never wakened. Ellie and Jo took turns sitting by her side, talking to her quietly. A sense of helplessness rendered Ellie nearly comatose.

When they reach the house, parked cars line the road and the driveway. The rain falls heavily, the sun obscured by the storm.

She unlocks the door and Bitsy leaps into her arms. Catching the small, black bundle of mostly hair, she holds him close, wondering if he thought he was abandoned.

Friends and relatives crowd inside behind her. Handing the dog to Katie, she goes to the kitchen to make coffee and put out food, much of it brought by these same friends.

Looking out the window over the sink at a grove of pines and not seeing them, she hopes Helen will show up.

Steven puts a hand on her shoulder, startling her. "How are you?"

"First Dad, now Mom." She shrugs and turns away from the sink. "Do you remember Helen?"

"Your best friend, the one who had to get married when you lived on Elm Street?"

"She was fourteen. I never expected to see her again."

Jo comes into the room with Ellie's daughters. "We better hustle. People want to eat and leave."

"Are Helen and Nancy out there?"

"Nancy had to leave and Helen rode with her. So no."

When everyone leaves except those few staying overnight, Jo takes drink orders. Ellie follows her into the kitchen.

"How was Nancy?" she asks.

"The same. She married a guy who works in the mill. She's a secretary in the mill's sales department."

"Nothing wrong with that." She pours liquor over ice.

"What did Helen say?"

"I told you I didn't have time to talk to her. You abandoned me. I had to greet the people standing in line."

"I was talking to those same people. I was just moving around. I couldn't stay there with Mom's picture among all those flowers. Don't be mad."

"I'm not. Just disappointed."

"Nancy told me Helen divorced her husband. She's a travel agent now and I guess she loves it."

"She'd be good at it. Wish I could remember her husband's last name. There's no way to contact her, even if I want to."

"Can't help you there. I don't think I even knew his first name."

"Donny."

Liz and Katie appear. "We'll get our own beer."

The four of them carry drinks into the living room where Steven is wiping his shoes on the mat as he closes the door. His hair glistens with rain. Cool air slips inside with him. "First I had to drag the dog outside, then he couldn't find the proper place to drop his load. Now we're both soaked."

Bitsy tap dances on her feet. The dog is a survivor, like herself, like her sister. "He wants a treat and he needs drying off."

"I'll do it, Mom," Katie volunteers. "Come on, Bits."

The phone rings as she drops with a sigh into one of the chairs. Her feet hurt, her body aches. Someone else can answer.

Liz puts a paper plate full of food on her lap. "Time to eat, Mom."

Katie hands the phone to her. "It's for you."

She tucks the receiver between her shoulder and chin. Heavy with grief and tired of talking about it, her emotions carry over into her voice. " 'Lo."

"We never got a chance to talk. I know it's been a long day, and it sounds like there are still a lot of people there. I can call back in a day or two."

She fails to recognize the voice. "Who is this?"

"Helen. I was at your mother's funeral."

"Don't hang up. I'm going to another phone." Her heart beats against the fist that holds it. She catches Steven's eyes. "Hang up when I pick up in the kitchen, will you?"

Leaning on the counter, sipping her drink, she says, "I hear you're a travel agent. Last I knew you were married with four little kids." The kids probably have kids of their own. Helen produced all of them before she turned twenty.

Helen laughs with a throaty sound that makes her smile. "That's how many years ago? I always stunk at math. I'm forty-seven. I divorced Donny seven years ago, when our last boy left home. I had my GED by then and I took some computer courses at the Tech. What about you?"

"I forgot to introduce my girls but they were standing next to me at the funeral home. They're both at UW-Madison. I divorced after sixteen years of marriage and took my name back." How long ago was that? Five years? She is lousy at math too but she realizes they both would have been forty when they divorced. "I'm an editor for a publishing house."

"Wow. You always had your nose stuck in a book."

She realizes what is different about Helen, why she failed to recognize her voice on the phone. It's her grammar. She hasn't used ain't or said don't in the wrong places.

"I read a lot of boring stuff. What about you? Your parents?" She holds her breath against the hope that Helen's father is dead.

"Mom died four years ago. My dad is still around. I look in on him once a week."

She feels sharp anger. She wants to believe there is justice in life and, if not, in death. She can't. Her parents would be the ones still alive, if there was. Silence falls between them.

Helen breaks it. "Maybe we could have lunch or dinner while you're here." She laughs. "I don't know where you live. Is it Milwaukee?"

"Yes." Close enough. "I don't know when I'm going back, though." She brought work with her.

"Well, good. Can we get together?"

She clears her throat. "Sure."

"Any day is fine with me. I'll give you my number."

"Tell me your last name."

7

"Ebertson. With all those sons, I kept it."

"Not a girl in the lot, huh?"

"Nope."

When she hangs up, she refills her drink, then sits down at the kitchen table and stares out at the night, at the falling rain visible in the light leaching through the windows.

II

Helen became Ellie's first best friend the summer Ellie turned ten, the summer her parents bought their first house, a Cape Cod on Elm Street. Her father had landed a job with a large paper corporation. Her mother worked part-time as office manager at a milk company. Helen, who was nearly two years older than Ellie, lived next door. Although it was an artery, the street was narrow, lined with elm trees the shape of wine glasses. Their branches laced overhead, creating a green canopy that housed hundreds of birds. When the starlings flocked, they made so much noise and littered the ground with so many droppings that people ran from shelter to shelter, covering their heads. That first August the police shot them out of the trees while Ellie and her sister Joey watched in silent alarm at how quickly life turned into something obscene.

Because the house was built into a hill, a basement door opened onto the small backyard. Immediately behind the yard ran railroad tracks on the other side of which stretched a large field divided

into garden plots for the employees who worked at the same company her father did—carrying on the victory garden concept after the victory.

Her family planted late that first summer in two plots just across the tracks from their backyard. She and her sister were expected to keep the garden weed-free but Joey quickly got out of that chore by claiming weeding gave her asthma.

The day after the move into the white two-story house, she was sitting on the front stoop when a girl with thick red hair, a pug nose and freckles cut across the lawn carrying a bag. The girl had breasts. Hers were nonexistent.

"Hi, I live there." The girl pointed at the gray clapboard house next door. "My mom made some bread. She does that when someone new moves in." She held out a paper bag. "My name's Helen Lindquist."

"I'm Ellie, short for Eleanor. Ellie McGowan."

"My dad hates Eleanor Roosevelt," Helen said.

"My dad says she should keep her nose out of politics, but my mom thinks she's a great woman." Mom had said that when arguing with Dad.

"My dad got drunk when President Roosevelt died. We had to step over him."

Shocked, she tried to reconstruct that day, but only remembered Mom crying.

"Ain't you going to take the bread inside?" Helen asked.

"Sure, come on in. My sister is sick but it's not catching. She has asthma and throws up a lot."

They walked into the entryway past the stairs that rose to the second floor, tiptoed through the living room where her sister slept on the davenport, a pail on the floor next to her, went through the dining room and into the kitchen where her mother was fixing Joey soft-boiled eggs and toast.

"Mom, this is Helen. Her mother made us bread. They live next door."

"Thank you, Helen. Would you girls like a piece?"

"Sure." She was always hungry. "I would."

10

"I gotta go. My dad gets off work at three. He wants me there when he comes home. See you later," Helen said.

"Ellie," Joey said when she tiptoed through the living room.

"What?" she asked impatiently.

"Want to play eights or war?"

"Not now. Maybe later."

"I'll play with you, honey," Mom said.

She hesitated before going out the door where the sun shone hotly from a clear sky. Even though her mother spent so much time with her sister and Joey got out of work because of her asthma, she didn't want to be her.

She rode her bike up and down the sidewalk, hoping Helen would come outside.

When she recognized Dad walking toward her, she was surprised that so much time had passed. He wore a dark suit and vest and a bowler hat. He'd loosened his tie and undone the top button of his white shirt. She rode fast toward him and he caught the handlebars when she braked.

"How's my sunshine?" he asked.

With the bike between them, they walked toward the house. She told him about Helen.

"She has to be home when her dad gets there but tomorrow we'll do something." She looked up at him and tripped on one of the cracks where the pavement had heaved in the winter.

"Whoa there, filly." He steadied her.

At dinner, Joey looked like a ghost, her face white as the milk she craved. Ellie couldn't understand why her sister was so thin, because when she was well, she ate like a horse, according to Dad. Which meant she ate everything in sight. Tonight she picked at her food and went back to the couch after a few minutes.

Mom asked, "Do you suppose it's the medication that makes her sick?"

"Ask the doctor," Dad said.

Ellie was wolfing down her mashed potatoes. She'd saved them for last, because she liked them best.

"Think they're going to run away from you?" Dad asked.

"What?" she said, gulping down her milk.

"Your potatoes."

She wiped her mouth. "Can I go out?" Summer evenings were the best. If there were enough kids around, they could play kick-the-can. If there weren't, she could ride her bike some more. Maybe Helen would come outside.

"After you help your mother with the dishes," her dad said.

"Can you call me when you're ready, Mom?"

"You just sit right there, young lady, and wait for us to finish." Dad was a stickler for manners.

When they got to the pots and pans, Mom let her go. She was a softy. She and her sister both knew it.

She raced outside, saw Helen sitting on her front steps and crossed the yard toward her.

"Are there more kids around here?" she asked.

"There's them kids down the street but my dad don't like me playing with them. He says they're trash."

She had never heard anyone called trash before. "Why are they trash?"

"They're dirty. Their noses run and there's holes in their clothes and their dad don't work."

She made a face at the picture Helen's description brought to mind. "Where does your dad work?"

"At the foundry. My mom cleans offices nights at KC."

A man opened the door a few inches. "Get inside, Helen."

"I have to go," she said.

Ellie and her sister slept in a bedroom that sloped at the street side. There were two windows, one looking out over the field of gardens, the other facing the house next door—not Helen's house, though.

Joey was already in bed when Ellie undressed and pulled the sheet up to her chin. She stuck her gum to the metal rung at the head of the bed. There was still a little flavor left and it was her last stick of Juicy Fruit.

Joey's eyes looked like bruises, huge and dark blue. She had three pillows under her head so that she could breathe. Ellie flopped back on her pillow, glad again that she wasn't Joey. "You feeling better?"

Joey nodded but she was having trouble breathing. Her shoulders lifted and ridges stood out in her neck from the strain and she was wheezing.

"Should I get Mom?"

Joey shook her head and reached for her atomizer on the table between the beds. It was a curved glass tube that widened into a bowl holding the medicine and ended in a red bulb. The adrenaline in it was brown. You could see the relief in Joey's face when she took a puff, but it didn't last long. That was the problem.

When Mom came in and kissed them goodnight, she took the atomizer with her. "If she needs me, will you come, Ellie?"

"Sure, Mom."

Her mother's hair was reddish brown, her eyes blue, her skin freckled. Ellie thought she was beautiful. Joey looked more like her than she did. Ellie's hair was black, her eyes brown and she didn't have any freckles—like Dad. Mom left the door ajar.

Next morning the air was thick with heat. Rain spattered against the windows and streaks of lightning cut through the clouds toward the ground, chased by rumbling thunder. She liked storms but she preferred them at night when they didn't keep her inside.

Mom was sleeping next to Joey as she often did when her sister was sick. Ellie got up and looked out the window at the rain falling. It blew in through the screen in gusts, dampening her.

"Hi, Ellie," Mom whispered, carefully getting out of bed so as not to waken Joey, whose skin was the color of her pillow.

"I didn't come get you because I didn't hear, Mom."

Mom smiled wearily. "I know."

Ellie grabbed her book from the small table that separated the beds. There was no reason to get up. She was reading *The Black Stallion Returns*, the second in The Black Stallion series. On the last day of school she'd been so immersed in *The Black Stallion*

Returns that her teacher had to tap her on the shoulder to get her attention.

Around eleven the doorbell rang. By then she was curled up in a chair with her book while Joey lay on the couch. She jumped up to answer. Helen stood on the stoop.

Mom came in from the kitchen. "You girls go ahead and play, just keep it quiet."

She showed Helen her room and they sat on the bed and talked. When it was close to three o'clock, Helen said she had to go home.

"Can I come with you?"

"You don't want to come over. My mom goes to work soon and it's just my dad and brother and me."

"So?" she said.

"You don't want to. Maybe tomorrow morning when Mom's home." She ran across the lawn to her house.

The first time she went to Helen's house when Helen's father was home was when Mom and Dad took Joey to the hospital later in that first week. They had finished eating dinner and were in the dining room, waiting for her mother to come downstairs.

Dad said, "Go stay with Helen, Ellie. Tell her mother we may be gone a few hours."

"But Dad, her mother's at work. Can't I come with you?"

"They won't let you in. You'd have to stay in the waiting room." She had to be twelve to go anywhere else in the hospital.

Joey's lips had turned bluish and her chest heaved with each wheeze. Her arms turned out at the elbows when she leaned on them. A panicky look came and went in her eyes. She was real good at not letting herself get too scared.

Dad looked scared, though, and called for Mom to hurry up. "I don't want to worry about you too, Ellie. Just do as I say."

"Okay, Dad, but Helen told me not to come over when her mother isn't there."

"Don't argue with me. I'm sure it'll be all right."

She shut up then but hung around till they left, hoping Mom would say she could come with them.

"Go next door now," Dad said as he got behind the wheel of the car.

Mom sat in the back with Joey. She'd given Ellie a quick hug and a kiss and told her not to worry, that everything would be all right.

In defiance, she went inside the house but it was so lonely with everyone gone that she found herself on Helen's porch, knocking on her door.

The door opened inward, and she looked up at Helen's father. He was tall and well muscled with red curls sprouting out of his undershirt. A cigarette hung from his lips and he squinted through the smoke.

"Well, girlie, you our new neighbor?"

"Yeah, Dad. I seen her next door." Helen's brother stood behind him in the dark living room.

"Helen's busy right now," Mr. Lindquist said and started to close the door on her.

She spoke fast, her voice higher than usual. "My dad sent me here because they had to take my sister to the hospital. She was having a bad attack of asthma."

"That you, Ellie?" Helen's hair was mussed, her face red.

"I told you to wait for me," her dad said. He turned to Ellie. "We're playing hide-and-seek." Taking the cigarette out of his mouth, he grinned, revealing stained, straight teeth. "Oh well, you might as well come in now you're here."

She slipped through the door, feeling trapped, wanting out as soon as she got in but she didn't know how to leave. She'd been saddled with manners, which meant you always had to be polite. You couldn't do and say what you wanted.

"Sit down, girlie."

She backed up to the couch and sat. The window shades were drawn, even though it was still light out.

"Dad, can we go to my room and play? Please?" Helen begged.

Her father thought this over. Finally, he said, "Okay. Just don't make no noise."

"We won't, Dad."

Helen's room was narrow with a single bed and a dresser and a table. One window overlooked the backyard, the other faced Ellie's parents' bedroom.

Helen ran her hands over her hair to smooth it and smiled at her nervously. "Is your sister real sick?"

She nodded. "I never saw her like that."

"Must be terrible not to be able to breathe."

"Yeah." She fingered a pencil on the table. "Do you do your schoolwork here?" she asked, wishing she had her own bedroom. She quickly took the wish back, because the only way she could have a room to herself would be if something happened to her sister.

"Sometimes. What do you want to do?"

"What do you want to do?"

They ended up playing cards till it was dark, then sat on the bed and talked until they fell asleep.

She remembered not being able to stay awake, the sleep coming over her, closing her eyes, her thoughts drifting into dreams.

She woke with a start, knowing someone was in the room besides Helen. She knew Helen was awake, too, pretending she was asleep. It was her dad.

"Helen," he whispered, his breath thick with smoke and a stale, yeasty smell that spilled over them. "I know you're awake. Come with me now, just for a little while."

The phone rang downstairs. Ellie jumped to her feet, her heart a wild thing in her chest. "That's my dad, I know it."

III

Ellie stands on the porch, watching the car carrying her daughters disappear down the road behind a grove of trees. Jo and Steven have gone back inside.

Before joining them, she fills the feeders. Bitsy sniffs around her feet while the birds wait in nearby trees and bushes. Between the garage and barn lies the remains of her mother's garden, the rows neatly laid out, the plants flattened. Beyond, last year's reeds and cattails stand broken, marking one end of the small lake. Every growing thing will green up in a week or two. There is color in the willow branches, the buds on bushes, the green shoots in the grass. No longer drab, goldfinches are molting their winter feathers for bright yellow ones.

Steven taps on the window where he and Jo sit at the kitchen table, drinking their second pot of coffee.

Pulling off her jacket and hanging it on the hall tree, she joins them. Both look unkempt as she supposes she does too. Steven's

fading blond hair, trimmed close to his skull, stands up in a series of waves. His cheek rests on a hand. Jo's reddish brown hair lies flat on one side of her head and stands out in a tangle on the other. The skin bags under her blue eyes, yet Jo looks younger than she does. Maybe she should color her hair too. There are nearly as many gray strands in it as there are black.

She pours herself a cup of coffee. The place seems empty, even with Jo and Steven there. She imagines what it will be like when they leave, peopled with ghosts. Perhaps she should go home, but there are things that have to be done. She was named personal representative in her mother's will.

"I wish you'd stay."

"Which of us?" Steven asks.

"Both. Either. I don't want to be alone."

"I'll come back on the weekend. We're at that crucial point of putting the magazine together." Jo is art director of her married lover's small monthly, *Sports Forever*.

"Give the dog a yummy, Ellie," Steven says gently, "and blow your nose."

Bitsy's toenails tap out a tattoo on the floor. She makes him sit. As he gently takes the treat from her fingers, she grabs a napkin and wipes her nose.

"How long are you staying, Steven?"

"As long as you need me or until tomorrow, whichever comes first."

Pouring more coffee, she sits with them at the table. "Why don't you move in?"

"And leave my boyfriend?" Steven says, his tone falsetto.

She laughs. "We could all live here together."

"Sure, Ellie," Jo says. "What would we do for money?"

"Ellie would edit, you would freelance and I would set up a law office in town," Steven says as if taking her seriously.

"Who am I going to freelance for? Pete?" Jo asks.

She and Steven exchange glances.

"I know what you're thinking," Jo says.

"Let's not go there," Steven cautions.

18

Steven believes, as Ellie does, that Jo's relationship with Pete is a dead end.

"I'll miss coming here and doing things around the place for your mom. We always had a good time. I remember when we went bird-watching at one of the trout streams on opening day. Of course, we didn't know it was opening day. We were the only people with binoculars. Everyone else had fishing rods." He grins wryly, drawing a smile from her and Jo. They have heard the story before.

She looks out the window at the birds swimming in her vision. Steven left work and drove two hundred miles to be with her and Jo the day their mother died. The three of them drank too much that night and reminisced into the early morning hours. He's the brother she never had.

"Thanks, Steven, for coming and staying this long." Her voice breaks. She's gone from numbly stoic to emotionally weepy.

"Aw, come on. Don't cry." He shifts in his chair. "Why don't you spend some time with Helen when we leave?"

She blows her nose in the napkin.

Jo remarks in an unsteady voice, "You can at least have lunch with her."

"She sees her father once a week," she says.

"So?" Jo asks.

There are things she has never told Jo or Steven or anyone. "I don't know if I can deal with that."

"If she can deal with it, why can't you? What did he do that was so awful anyway?" Jo inquires.

They both look at her with interest. "You don't remember, Jo, because you weren't around."

"Where was I?"

"Usually in the hospital."

"Come on. How long ago was this?" Steven says.

"Do you remember when the policeman brought me home that first summer when Helen and I rode our bikes down to the lake and went wading?"

"Yeah, sort of," Jo says.

19

"The next day Helen could barely walk or sit her dad beat her so badly. Her pedal pushers stuck to her legs."

"I remember how hot it was that summer. I could hardly breathe," Jo remarks. "It seemed like I had asthma all the time."

"When you went to the hospital, Dad sent me next door to Helen's."

"What happened there?" Steven asks, his gaze riveted on her.

"We played hide-and-seek." She remembers the old terror.

"What else?" he pushes.

"He came for her in the night."

That silences Jo and Steven for a few moments until Jo asks, "How do you know?"

"I was there."

"No wonder she married at fourteen."

She realizes she doesn't want to talk about what happened those two years she lived next door to Helen. She is having enough trouble dealing with her mother's death.

"What's going on at work, Steven?" she asks.

He grimaces. "I've been assigned a real scumbag for a client. The trial is in three weeks. I'm hoping he'll fire me."

"Remember when you thought you were going to save the poor?" Jo asks.

"And sometimes I do. That's why I'm a public defender." He sighs. "Never idealize the less fortunate."

"What *are* you going to do the rest of the week, Ellie?" Jo asks.

"I brought some manuscripts to work on and I have to go to the courthouse and register as personal representative so that we can settle Mom's estate."

"I thought we agreed to pay the attorney to do that," Jo says.

"Most of it, but not all."

While she, Jo and Steven are finishing off a bottle of pinot noir in the living room after dinner, Helen calls. " 'Lo," Ellie says.

"Hi. How are you?"

"Helen?"

"I wondered if you'd like to do lunch tomorrow."

"Hang on a minute." She covers the receiver with a hand. "When are you guys leaving?"

"Early," Jo says.

"Earlier," Steven adds.

"I guess I can," she says. "Where?"

Helen names a restaurant on Hwy 10 at the edge of town. "What time?"

"Eleven thirty, if you can make it. We'll beat the crowd. I'll take the afternoon off."

"See you then." She hangs up, already having second thoughts about her decision.

Mesmerized, as they all are, by the small fire in the hearth, she leans toward it. The flames supply the only light in the room. "Why do I want to see her after all these years?"

"Maybe she'll be boring as hell," Steven remarks. "People are almost never the way you remember them."

"Maybe." She holds out her glass for a refill.

She and Jo sleep in their mother's bed. There are only two bedrooms downstairs, and Steven is in the other one. The upstairs is heated through vents in the floor. They lie under a down quilt drawn up to their chins. The wind has picked up outside and it howls around the corners of the house. Bitsy lies curled into a tight ball in his small dog bed on the floor.

"I didn't like Helen's dad. There was something menacing about him," Jo admits, "and Junior was mean as hell. I remember that."

"Right on both counts," Ellie assures her.

IV

As soon as Joey was released from the hospital, Mom went back to work at Richards Milk Company. Helen's mother was home most of the day and Ellie and Helen spent that time together. Before Mr. Lindquist's shift ended at three, Ellie left if she was at Helen's house. If Helen was at her house, Helen went home. As long as Joey remained well, Ellie figured everything would be all right.

The heat rose off the pavement in waves, like in the desert in the *National Geographic* magazine pictures. The leaves on the elms withered, aphids ate holes in the garden plants and dust rose in puffs from the grass. She longed for water to swim in but the swimming pool was closed because of the polio epidemic.

She resented Joey tagging after her all the time. Early one afternoon when Mom came home, she snuck off to Helen's house alone in hopes that she and Helen could ride their bikes to the lake and wade without telling anyone.

She held her breath as they sped down Elm and crossed to

22

Walnut, the side street next to the corner grocery store. Once they were out of sight, she felt safe enough to taste the exhilaration that came with a sense of freedom.

The lake was visible as a distant blue haze when they reached the boulevard. The two of them rode side by side, their hair blowing in the hot breeze they created. The boulevard led downhill to the lake eight blocks distant. No one was at the turnaround, so they sat on the boulders at the water's edge. Green algae covered the rocks and bottles and cans rocked in the waves lapping the shore. Gulls screamed overhead.

"You gonna wade?" Helen impatiently brushed away the hair sticking to her face.

Ellie thought she looked grownup and very pretty. Mom braided her hair into two plaits, which loosened as the day wore on. She resembled an unkempt, little girl.

"I don't know." Although she was hot and sweaty, the slimy shoreline repelled her.

"Well, I am." Helen took off her tennis shoes and socks, surprising Ellie with a glimpse of her bright red toenails. Helen stepped carefully across the stones until she was calf deep in the greenish-gray water. "It's not rocky out here. Come on in, chicken."

Balancing carefully, she stepped over the slippery rocks into the lake. The water was cool, the bottom ridged with sand. They lost track of time, exploring the shallows, their shoes and socks and bikes on the rocks.

A squad car parked at the turnaround and a policeman called to them from the shore. "This is not a swimming place, girls. I'm taking you home."

Helen's eyes met Ellie's. Her face was burned and she looked terrified. "What time is it?"

She had no idea. She didn't own a watch. They made their way to shore and put their socks and shoes on over wet, sandy feet.

The cop stood above them, hands on his gun belt, lecturing on the dangers of swimming alone.

"But we weren't swimming," she pointed out. "We were wading."

"Wading, swimming, what's the difference? This is a dangerous lake."

She started to tell him the difference but Helen stuck an elbow in her side.

He put their bikes in the trunk of the police car.

"Boy, am I gonna get it," Helen whispered when they were in the backseat. "I hope my dad ain't home yet."

She knew she'd "get it" too. Her parents would probably take her bike away for a while. She'd be stuck playing cards and hop-scotch and marbles, and maybe roller-skating with her sister. Her skates had been languishing in the closet since she got the bike but she still liked to skate. Looking out the windows of the police car, she recalled with despair that wonderful feeling of independence.

The next morning Helen sat on her porch steps, chin in hands. Ellie's mother had gone to work. It was another hot, dry, dusty day and Joey tagged along after her.

"Did you get it?" she asked, knowing by then that Helen's dad had been home when the policeman took her to her door as he did Ellie to hers.

Her parents had taken her bike away for a week and told her not to venture any farther than the end of the block.

Helen turned away. "Yeah, I got it. I'm not listening to no more of your suggestions."

"Any more," Joey said, and Ellie punched her on the arm. "Ouch. Why'd you do that?" Joey wailed.

She ignored her and asked Helen, "What'd your dad do to you?"

"None of your business," Helen said angrily.

"Why are your pants stuck to your legs?" Joey asked.

"God, you two are nosy." Helen got up carefully and sat on the swing at one end of her porch.

24

"Just be quiet, Joey," Ellie said.

"I'm going home." In a huff, Joey marched across the yard to the house.

Helen carefully pulled her pants away from the backs of her thighs. The material looked wet.

"What happened to your legs?"

"What do you think?" She sat gingerly on the edge of the swing. "Don't your dad spank you?"

"Sometimes. I stuff things in my pants so it doesn't hurt."

Helen turned her head away. "He takes my pants off me. Go home, Ellie."

"I'm sorry," she whispered, horrified.

"What happened to you? They slap your hand? Take away your bike?"

Ashamed that her punishment had been so mild, she turned in time to see tears on Helen's face. "I'm sorry," she repeated.

"Too late for sorry," Helen yelled, sobbing now.

She fled for home, her heart an empty and desolate place.

She and Joey went to Helen's the next day when Helen called her over. Helen acted as if the punishment had never happened. Ellie had finished dusting, one of the chores that day. She still had to weed the garden. Somehow the weeds flourished when everything else shriveled up and died.

"Wanna play a new game?" Helen asked, taking them around to the back of the house into the room where boots lay in a pile and jackets hung from pegs on the wall. Helen's house was built into the same hill and this was part of their basement.

"I want to go home," Joey whined, looking around at the cement walls.

"Go ahead. I'll be there soon," Ellie said.

When they were alone, Helen told her to shut her eyes and lean back against the wall.

She did, and an odd kind of excitement took hold of her. When

she felt Helen's hand between her legs, her eyes popped open in surprise. The feelings evoked by the touch shocked her as much as the touch itself.

Helen was looking right at her, her green eyes bright, her hard breasts pressed against Ellie's flat chest. "That's what men do to women, only they put their thing inside you."

She was breathing hard, her legs so weak that she thought she was going to slide down the wall. She knew what Helen was doing was wrong and that letting it happen made her guilty too. Yet she made no attempt to stop her.

Helen stood back and gave her a sly smile. "You liked it, didn't you?"

"No," she lied.

"Yes, you did. I could tell." Her green eyes narrowed. "You better not tell."

She knew she'd never breathe a word to anyone. "Why do men do that to women?" She tried to picture Dad pressing Mom against the wall.

"They lie down." Helen shook her red hair over her shoulders. "Someday maybe we'll lie down and practice."

"I have to go home and weed the garden now." She slid toward the door.

Hoeing furiously in the hot sunshine, she chopped at the hard ground. The weeds had gotten away from her. Throwing the hoe down, she pulled their tops off at soil level, knowing they'd be back the next day.

When Mom got home, Ellie thought she could tell what she'd let happen.

"What did you do all morning?" Mom asked as she always did.

"I dusted and weeded."

"Good girl," she said, tousling her hair.

"I don't like going to Helen's," Joey piped up.

"Why is that?"

"She took us in the basement."

"Oh? What did you do there?"

26

"I left," Joey said.

Squirming under her mother's gaze, Ellie looked away.

"What did you do in the basement, Ellie?"

"Nothing, Mom. We were playing hide-and-seek."

"I'd rather you play outside when it's nice," Mom said. "I'm going to wash clothes this afternoon. Will you go upstairs and throw the towels and washcloths down the chute?"

Eager to get away, she took the steps two at a time.

V

Ellie parks in the restaurant's lot. The sun has finally come out of hiding and she welcomes its warmth, the promise that winter has finally released its hold. There are still pockets of snow in places that never see the sun. She stands for a moment, stretching her legs, looking around.

Not seeing Helen, she goes inside to get a booth or table in case there's a lunch crowd. First, though, she inspects her appearance in the restroom mirror. Brushing her hair back behind her ears where it curls under but refuses to stay, she studies herself with clear brown eyes. Except for the telltale lines exposed in the unforgiving fluorescent lights, she's aged well. Slender, moderately tall, with high cheekbones, black eyebrows and lashes, *she* is pleased with her appearance.

The waitress seats her at a booth next to a window through which she sees her parked car. She is looking out when Helen slides into the booth opposite her.

"I didn't hear you coming."

Helen's hair is swept back from her face and held in place with a clip. Not many women her age look good with longer hair but she is an exception. Her figure still makes heads turn. She isn't beautiful, though, as Ellie remembers her, but she loved her then.

"So here we are. I had so much I wanted to ask you, and now I can't think of a thing," Helen says with too much vivacity, as if she's nervous.

She knows the things she wants to ask Helen but not how to phrase them. She studies Helen's face. "Are you and Nancy friends?"

"We're friendly. Remember Janice, Nancy's sister? You know she married my brother, Junior. I guess we're family, only they're divorced too. Our kids are cousins, though."

"The trash." It slips out.

"They're really quite nice. It's Donny and Junior who aren't nice."

And her dad. He's the least nice of all.

"Your daughters are lovely. I always wanted a girl."

"I was so surprised to see you, I forgot to introduce Liz and Katie. I apologize. They went back to Madison." A little pride slips into her voice.

The waitress materializes next to their booth. Ellie orders soup, salad, bread and coffee. Helen says that sounds good enough for her. The waitress pours the coffee and leaves.

"Who was sitting on the other side of your daughters at the service?"

"Steven, my cousin. I don't think you ever met him. He came to Pine Hill but he wasn't there when you were."

"I thought maybe he was a boyfriend."

She laughs. "He's got a boyfriend of his own."

"Oh." Helen lifts one reddish eyebrow and smiles.

"There have been no serious boyfriends since my divorce. How about you?"

"Are you kidding? I'll never marry again. Donny was a bad experience. I think you know that. You hated him."

She had. "True. You said you see your dad once a week." She can't think of anything Helen might say to make her understand why.

"Yeah. He has Alzheimer's. Doesn't remember a thing. I don't know why I go see him. I don't love him. I don't even like him. Nobody does. Maybe that's why I go."

The explanation enables her to move past her dismay.

The waitress brings the food and fills their coffee cups before leaving.

"Tell me about your kids," she says.

"The two oldest boys took Donny's side during the divorce but they've drifted back. The two youngest told their father they'd kill him if he hurt me. It tore us apart for a while. Donny plays the victim well. When I left, I went to the shelter for abused women. I was afraid he'd kill me."

Not surprised, she asks, "Does he bother you anymore?"

"He did at first, but now he's with another woman. I guess they get along. At least, that's what my sons say."

The waitress appears again, asking if they want anything else. She puts the bill on the table and Helen snatches it.

"Oh no, you don't," she protests.

"Oh yes, I do." Helen gives her a mischievous smile that turns her heart over with its familiarity. "You drove a ways to get here. Besides, I want to do this again."

"We won't if you insist on picking up the tab."

Helen gathers her things. "Come on. I've got the afternoon off. I'll show you my place. It's not far from here."

She almost says she has too much to do but realizes whatever she was going to do today will wait till tomorrow.

Helen gives her a searching look. "It'll be like old times."

She knows it will never be like it was when they were young, nor does she want it to be. "I can't be too long. Mom's dog is at the house."

"You can always call Lyle. He'll take care of the dog." Helen smiles. "I loved your grandparents' place. I never forgot that weekend."

She hadn't invited Helen back because she'd spent too much time with Lyle. She still isn't sure what that jealousy was about.

A warm, fickle breeze has sprung up. She turns her face to it, sniffing spring on its current. It lightens her mood.

"Follow me." Helen climbs into an Oldsmobile Cutlass.

She slides behind the wheel of her Escort and trails the Olds to a small house across from a park. Helen pulls into the driveway and she parks on the street.

Inside, she looks through the bay window at the expanse of grass across the road. "Nice being across from a park."

"It is. Would you like another cup of decaf?"

"I've had enough, thanks."

"Me too. Let me hang up your jacket."

A cat, hiding behind the drapes, makes a run for the open basement door.

"Hey, there, Jocko, wait up." Helen snatches the cat and holds it to her shoulder, much like a baby. The black, tiger-striped feline purrs. "I never had a pet till I lived alone. I couldn't. Donny hated cats. So did my dad and Junior. My oldest grandson teases Jocko. Jocko doesn't understand teasing." Helen looks suddenly concerned. "You're not allergic to cats like Joey was, are you?"

"Nope."

Helen sets Jocko on his feet and he disappears down the basement stairs. "Want to go for a walk? We're not far from the lake."

"Love to."

They walk the few blocks to the lake where chunks of ice are still piled on the shore. Rafts of Canada geese float in the water and graze on nearby lawns. "You have to watch where you put your feet," Helen says, "or you'll step on their poop. They never seem to go anywhere anymore. What happened to migration?"

"They stick around as long as there's food and water." The breeze off the lake feels cool.

"Remember the cop?" Helen asks.

"Yes." How could she forget? That wonderful sense of freedom evaporated as soon as he appeared.

"Do you live alone?"

"Yep. My daughters have an apartment together in Madison. I live in a condo. We sold the house when we divorced." She glances at her watch. It's after three. "I should go soon."

"I want to see you again."

The excitement she felt when she laid eyes on Helen at the funeral home ripples through her.

"All these years, even when you still lived in town, I missed you. Donny didn't want me to have friends, didn't want me to have family outside of him and our boys. He made it so unpleasant when my family or friends came around that it was easier not to see anyone else."

"How lonely." Although appalled, she's not really surprised.

"It was but it's not that way anymore." Helen's green eyes glitter in the sunlight. "When you're a kid, you think your best friend is going to always be your best friend."

She nods, her gaze caught by Helen's.

"Come back, will you?"

"Yes, of course." How could she say anything else?

The wind is at their backs on the walk to Helen's house. "Next week for lunch. Same day, same place?" Helen asks as they stand next to the Escort.

"Sure."

The lines deepen around Helen's eyes and mouth and she startles Ellie with a hug. She smells of fresh air and something else. Soap? Cologne? "We were good friends."

"Best friends," she responds. "Thanks for lunch." Looking at her old friend up close, she remembers how the freckles blend into her lips.

Helen shades her eyes with a hand. "You look good, Ellie. I don't know if I told you that."

"So do you," she says.

Standing with one hand raised in good-bye, Helen becomes an increasingly smaller figure in the rearview mirror.

Ellie grocery shops before driving home. Warmed by the late sun beaming through the car windows, deep in thought, she fails to notice the landscape flashing by. Going over the afternoon in her

mind, she warns herself not to jump into another friendship with Helen. The two years they lived next door to each other were traumatic ones. She's committed to lunch next week. She'll see how that goes.

She spends the rest of the week either doing what has to be done to settle the estate or working on one of the manuscripts she brought with her. Finding something to do every waking minute keeps the grief and loneliness at bay. She banishes Helen from her thoughts. Nights are hard. She hasn't brought enough books and her mother's bookcase holds novels she has already read. Late one afternoon, she climbs the stairs into the attic and finds the Black Stallion books she loved as a child, along with *My Friend Flicka* and *Thunderhead*. She rereads them in the living room at night while a small fire burns on the grate.

Her daughters call during the week as does Steven. They worry about her being alone here. She tells them she's fine and thinks she is.

When Jo turns into the driveway late Friday, Ellie is filling the feeders, dressed in a sweatshirt and jeans. Bitsy runs toward the Grand Am, snapping at its tires.

Slamming on the brakes, Jo jumps out. "Damn dog! He's going to commit suicide under the wheels of someone's car. Down, you filthy little beast." Pushing the dirty paws off her jeans, she bends over to pat him. "He has no manners."

"You'll hurt his feelings." Ellie grins. "I was afraid you weren't coming." She's used to being alone but not here. The silence at times is unbearable and she wonders how her mother endured it.

"Lonesome, huh?" Jo hugs her.

"It's so quiet, Jo. You can't believe how silent. I think I would go nuts without Bitsy." When she's alone, voices follow her from room to room—her mother and father, her grandma and grandpa. She talks to them.

She carries Jo's backpack inside. "Did you bring me something to read?"

"Yep." Jo picks up one of the Black Stallion books lying on an end table. "You read these when you were a kid."

"I know." As a child, she desperately wanted a horse and was forced to settle for an imaginary one, on which she galloped through the gardens and alongside the car when they went somewhere.

"I made chicken chili, which you better like. It was a lot of work."

Jo follows her into the kitchen. "Have I ever complained about a free meal? Smells good enough to eat but I'd kill for a drink first."

She checks the chili simmering on the stove. "How was the rest of your week?"

"Not so good." Jo looks around appreciatively. "I love this house." The white kitchen walls, the polished maple floor, the window over the table with a view of the feeders, the one over the sink that looks out on the grove of towering Norway pines. Their mother updated the kitchen with new countertops, new cupboards and new appliances after their father died which was when she moved in. "Mom had an eye for interior design. She was a bit of an artist."

"Like you. Let's go into the living room. It's still cold enough at night to build a little fire."

They walk on oak flooring through the dining room into the living room. Above the wainscoting on the walls, tiny morning glories twine toward the ceiling on a white background. She helped her mother paper these rooms. How many years has it been? Long enough to need repapering or painting.

Jo stretches out on the couch while Ellie settles in the chair nearest the fire, where the heat soaks into her jeans. The dog lies on a rug in front of the flames.

"Why was your week not good?" she asks.

"I never knew I could live without Mom."

She looks away from the fire to Jo. "I know," she whispers.

"When are we going to spread her ashes?" Jo asks. The urn rests on the mantel.

"When the ground is dry and it's going to stay warm out."

"Yeah, she might get cold."

She turns away from Jo's grief to hide her own.

VI

Joey stood with hands on knees, chest heaving.

"We better go home, Joey," Ellie said. The attack had come on suddenly while they were skating.

They were near the end of the block and all four of the trashy kids watched from their porch. The smallest one, a boy, stood spread-legged with a hand thrust inside his pants and a finger up his nose.

"What's the matter with her?" the biggest girl asked.

"She's got asthma," Ellie replied.

"I do not," Joey snapped breathlessly. She became furious whenever anyone told someone new that she had asthma. "I just have to sit down."

"You can sit here," the girl said, pointing to the porch steps.

Joey skated over, sat down and unscrewed her skates. She conserved air by not talking much. Ellie slung the roller skates over her shoulder.

"My name's Janice and this here is my sister Nancy and them are my brothers Bob and Tommy. Tommy, get your hand out of your pants and stop picking your nose." She smiled apologetically. "He's pretty disgusting."

She looked Janice over, saw she wore a clean shirt and shorts. "I'm Ellie and this is Joey."

"You wanna do something sometime?" Janice asked.

"Maybe." What she meant was when Helen wasn't around and wouldn't find out.

Someone hollered from inside the house.

"That's my ma. I gotta go inside now and help," Janice said.

"Yeah, we have to go home too. Come on, Joey."

It seemed like forever before they reached the house. Joey would take a few steps, then stop and lean on her hips or knees to catch her breath before taking a few more, and pause to start the process all over again. Finally, Ellie held the door open and Joey sat down on the stairs inside with a thump.

"I'll get your atomizer," she said, dashing up the steps two at a time, grabbing the atomizer out of its box in their bedroom, and thudding down the stairs so fast she nearly fell.

Joey inhaled. She watched her carefully, hoping the door would open and Mom would be there. Immediately after the puff, Joey began to shake. She asked what time it was.

Ellie went to the kitchen to look at the clock and heard the car in the driveway and the front door opening. She ran back to the stairs. Mom had set a bag of groceries on the floor and was kneeling in front of Joey, brushing the hair out of her face with her hands.

"Why didn't you call me, Ellie?" she asked.

She picked up the bag. "We just got home. It came on real sudden."

"Come on, sweetheart, I'll give you some medicine. You'll be just fine," Mom said to Joey.

But she wasn't okay. Ellie woke in the night to the murmur of voices. Mom was making up a story for Joey who couldn't sleep

because she had to sit up in order to breathe. When Mom dozed off, Joey woke her up.

"Come on, Mom, finish the story."

When Ellie wakened again, it was morning and she wondered if she had dreamed her mother's presence in her sister's bed. Joey lay sleeping alone, propped up on two pillows, her mouth slack, her breathing labored.

She unstuck her gum from the rung and popped it in her mouth. Then she twisted her head until she saw what kind of day it was—sunny, hot. Fresh air poured in the open windows, carrying the smell of cut grass. She detected a whiff of rank weeds from the field. No matter how often she pulled them out, they always sprang back up within a few days.

Mom stuck her head in the door and with a finger to her lips, beckoned her.

Dragging her clothes behind her, she crept out of the room. "What?"

"I just didn't want her to wake up. She only went to sleep a couple hours before daylight. Listen, Ellie, I have to go to work for a while this morning. Can you keep an eye on your sister and call me if you need me?" Mom looked so worried that she became anxious.

"Sure, Mom."

She ate two bowls of Wheaties with cream and sugar on them before going back upstairs. Tiptoeing into the room, leaving the door open, she sat as quietly as possible on her bed. Opening her Black Stallion book, the third in the series, she nearly forgot all about Joey sleeping in the bed next to hers. Once when she looked over at her sister, she thought she saw the color of her eyes through her closed lids.

She told Helen later that day as they stood in the shade of the elms. "I met the kids down the block."

"The trash?"

"They didn't look like trash to me." She was still puzzled as to why they were unacceptable.

"Well, I can't play with you if you play with them."

"I didn't say I was going to play with them. Janice asked me, though."

Helen tossed her red hair. "Want to go to the basement?"

Her legs went weak. "My sister's sick again."

"Come on," Helen said.

It smelled damp. Daylight streaked through the dirt on the only window. Helen told her to lean against the wall again.

"Close your eyes," she ordered.

She did, only to feel Helen's tongue pushing between her teeth. In her surprise, she nearly bit it. Her eyes popped open.

"That's how men kiss women," Helen said.

"How do you know?" she asked, wondering why her parents would do this.

"My dad told me but you have to promise not to tell anyone I showed you."

"I won't," she said, ashamed to be disappointed that Helen hadn't done what she did the last time they'd been down here.

"You want me to do that other thing, don't you?" she asked.

"What? No. I have to go."

Helen touched her there again and the strength went out of her legs just like the last time.

They both heard Helen's mother coming down the basement steps at the same time because Helen stiffened, too. Helen grabbed her hand and pulled her behind the furnace.

"You down there, Junior? Helen?"

She promised God that she'd never go in the basement with Helen again if He saw to it that Helen's mother didn't find them. It was one of those bargains made under duress that even at the time she knew she wouldn't keep.

She went home, worrying that Mom would notice something different about her. However, Mom seemed distracted and distant. She ladled tomato soup into a bowl, while Ellie fixed herself a peanut butter sandwich.

"Where's Joey?" she asked.

"In bed."

"Is she throwing up?"

"No, but she still has asthma." Mom put a hand on her back, brushed her hair out of her face with the other and sighed.

She swiveled in her chair so that she wasn't facing her. She was sure Mom was onto her, that she knew what had happened in Helen's basement.

When Mom cupped her chin in her hand and turned her face toward hers, her heart thumped anxiously.

"Thanks for watching your sister this morning. You're such a help."

"Really?" she said in astonishment, suddenly willing to do anything for her mother. She was sure she would die if Mom found out her shameful secret and she vowed as before to never go into Helen's basement again.

VII

When Jo leaves Sunday morning, the silence closes in on Ellie again. She takes Bitsy for a walk and works on one of the manuscripts. When Lyle shows up at the door and invites her to dinner, she goes gratefully.

Lyle and Harriet's large kitchen with its yellow walls and linoleum, its white countertops and cupboards cheers her. She doesn't understand why she's bothered by the quiet, the absence of people, because she never is at home. Of course, at home her friends are close by.

"Don't be such a stranger," Harriet says, giving her a hug. She's a dumpling of a woman, round and pleasant looking.

"I don't feel like a stranger. I used to spend a lot of time here when I was a kid, helping milk the cows and put up hay, or at least thinking I was helping." She laughs and Harriet does, too.

"How are the boys?" she asks.

"They've got their own lives, you know. It hurt Lyle that they

41

didn't want to farm." Lyle is out in the barn. "You can't expect them to follow in your footsteps. Farming ties you down."

"I know," she agrees and turns as Lyle takes his boots off in the mudroom.

A smile breaks the somberness of his face as he comes into the room. "It's always good to let the cows out of the barn. Happy cows make better milk."

"I believe that."

"Too many places keep them inside all the time."

"Let's not get on the subject of mega-farms," Harriet says. "Not tonight." Opening a beer, she hands it to Lyle.

The two women are drinking the wine Ellie brought over.

The meal is plain but good. Comfort food. They talk about the property and what it means to each of them. The buildings and land, which have come down through her family, are as much her heritage as Lyle's farm is his.

"I can't get used to the silence," she says before leaving.

Harriet hugs her. "Next time it's too quiet, come over."

"It won't be quiet long. The frogs will keep you awake nights and the birds will start in before first light. They already have," Lyle says. He pulls on his boots. "I'll walk you home."

She protests but he insists. When they step outside, they hear the frogs. "Nature is noisy. It's just a different kind of sound." He leaves when she opens her door and shushes the dog's barking.

The answering machine is flashing. Helen. She calls her.

"Hi. I had dinner with Lyle and Harriet." Hearing the TV in the background, she asks, "What's on the tube? Anything good?"

"Noise. Don't you ever turn on the TV when you're alone just to hear voices."

"I guess you're a little lonesome, too."

"Want some company?"

Yes, yes, yes, she thinks, but says, "Don't you have to work?"

"I can take a day off. I'd love to come and see the place again."

"It's supposed to be nice tomorrow," she says, hiding the excitement she feels, and gives Helen directions.

That night, she lies awake listening to the incessant chorus of frogs and a couple of barred owls hooting back and forth. When the birds wake her at first light, she's unable to fall asleep again. She almost calls Lyle to tell him he's right, that she only has to open a window. She knows, though, that the silence that gets to her is of those who once peopled this house.

At nine o'clock Helen knocks on the front door. With her hair still wet from the shower, Ellie flings it open.

"We didn't talk about time. Should I go away and come back in an hour?" Helen asks with a big smile. "Did I catch you at a bad time?"

"No. Want some breakfast?" She leads the way to the kitchen.

"I wouldn't turn it down. I was in such a hurry to get here, I forgot to eat."

"Coffee?" She refills her cup and pours one for Helen.

"The house is just like I remember." Helen stands in the middle of the room, looking around her.

"Mom redid the kitchen and repapered the other rooms." She puts bacon in a pan, her back to Helen.

"Coming here and living next door to you when we were kids showed me how things should be."

She turns. "What things?"

"Families. It made me want a family like yours. Marrying Donny was like jumping from the fire into the frying pan, but I didn't know that."

"Isn't it supposed to be the other way around?"

"No, not even Donny was worse than my dad. You should come with me sometime to see him."

Her heart pounds angrily. "I don't ever want to see him again."

"But he got what he had coming. He's being punished."

"He doesn't know it, though, does he? That's the difference."

"Oh, he knew it when it began to happen." Helen smiles wryly. "You're angry with me, Ellie. I did the best I could."

She flushes. Is she so rigid? "Maybe it's not you I'm mad at. Maybe it's your dad."

"You ignored me all these years."

"I couldn't deal with it, Helen."

The bacon is crisp. She pours the excess grease out of the pan and breaks four eggs on the surface, then pushes down the toast lever.

"Can I help?" Helen asks.

"You can slice a tomato. That'll speed things up."

Sunlight splashes over them as they sit at the table. "When the leaves come out, it won't be so sunny," she remarks.

Helen momentarily slips into an old speech pattern. "It sure feels good, don't it? I can't remember a colder winter, although cold is good for business. People travel to warm places in the winter." Helen looks at her. "Why did you divorce your husband?"

Startled by the change of subject, she says, "He wanted the divorce."

"Sorry. I shouldn't have asked."

"It's okay. I wasn't who he thought I was."

"Who is?" Helen asks.

She feels the need to defend Will. "He was a good friend and a wonderful father. He still is."

Helen's toasted muffin with the egg and bacon and tomato lies on her plate, untouched, along with the hash browns.

"Eat," she urges. "Your food is getting cold and so is mine."

After breakfast and cleaning up the dishes, Helen suggests a walk. "I brought boots. It's soggy out, and I want to see everything—the barn, the woods, the lake, even Lyle's farm if he don't mind."

"He won't mind. He recognized you at the funeral home."

"I know. We talked for a few minutes. I met his wife. They fit well together."

"Don't they?"

"He said to come over if I was ever here again." Helen lifts a brow. "I never thought I would be."

She flushes a little. "I never thought you would either."

Outside, the ground is a giant sponge. A warm breeze carries the hint of growth. Bitsy sniffs the air.

44

"Where do you want to go first?"

"The barn," Helen says.

The snow has melted away from the double doors. She slides one partway open. Bitsy goes in first. It's cold inside and smells faintly of hay. Dust motes float in the dim light.

"I thought I was brave to climb the ladder to the loft," Helen says. The ladder is vertical, pounded into a post supporting the trusses.

"Me too," she admits, although she spent a lot of time in the loft when she was a kid. "It's coming down that's scary."

"Joey got a bad attack of asthma that day."

"Dust. She had to stay out of the barn after that."

"I'm going up," Helen says, climbing the ladder. At the top she wiggles on her belly before standing up and brushing off her sweatshirt and jeans. "Are you coming?"

Ellie starts up the flat one-by-fours, using them to pull her to the next step. At the top, Helen takes her arm and helps her to her feet.

The dog leaps at the ladder, barking. "It's okay, Bitsy," she soothes.

A few bales of hay lie in a far corner. Vents at both ends admit fresh air. The window-sized door at one end is large enough for bales. After cutting, someone threw them on a portable elevator that carried them to the loft where they dropped through the opening and were stacked by whoever was up there.

Her grandpa never used the loft to store crops or the barn to house animals. Lyle's dad sometimes laid up excess hay or straw in their loft. Now Lyle harvests large round bales of hay that have to be moved by a loader tractor with forks and stored undercover outside.

She and Helen sit on the edge of the loft, swinging their feet. A chain and pulley hang from one of the trusses over the open area. She remembers taking turns swinging from the pulley with Lyle. One would hurtle across space and be pulled back to the safety of the loft by the other, wielding a rope.

She tells Helen about this feat and Helen wants to try it. She

45

shakes her head. "We thought we were Tarzan and Jane. I can't do it now. The rope is gone anyway."

When they start down the ladder, she holds Helen's hands till Helen can take hold of the top step. Then Ellie slides on her belly, digging her fingernails into the cracks between the boards on the loft floor. Helen guides her feet and steadies her legs till she can grab the top step.

Closing the large door behind them, she feels the sun on her head and shoulders. "Where to next? The lake?"

"If you promise there won't be any snakes."

Although not sure, she says, "It's too cold for snakes. They're curled up together in balls underground."

Helen shivers. "I hate snakes."

"The snakes around here aren't poisonous and they eat rodents. The farmers welcome them."

They stand at the edge of the small lake, thirty-five acres of rippling motion with a wetland at one end for overflow. With the ice gone, the blue water glitters in the sunlight.

"You and Lyle and Joey caught snakes and frogs and turtles like it was a sport or something."

"We always let them go." A frog plops into the water near her foot. Helen jumps and she laughs. "Frogs can't hurt you."

Bitsy noses the amphibian, making it jump again.

"I know. I'm a sissy that way."

She reaches down, catches the sluggish frog and holds it palm up to Helen. "Some frogs freeze solid in the winter. Want to hold it?"

"No, thanks. I heard frogs are disappearing."

She's read that too. Loss of habitat, more pollution. "Want to walk along the shore?" She hasn't done that yet this year. She lets the frog go and calls Bitsy away from it.

The towering white and Norway pines on a hill toward the end of the lake gave the place its name—Pine Hill. "This was a good spot to hide when we played spread. It's also a nice spot to watch the water."

They sit side by side on the thick mat of needles. The aroma of the pines takes her back to her childhood when she ran through the trees and lay at their feet. The little pines coming up between the older trees give the woods a fairyland appearance. Bitsy lies at her side, panting.

"My youngest son," Helen pauses and steals a glance at her, "is gay. He tries so hard to hide it, it breaks my heart. His two oldest brothers would beat him silly if they knew."

"What's his name?" she asks, wondering why the confidence.

"Chris. He was supposed to be my girl. That's what I would have named her. He's Christopher, of course. She'd have been Christine."

"My cousin Steven is gay. He's like a brother to me and Jo."

"He's lucky to have you two. Chris has only me to come between him and the rest of the family."

"What about his next older brother?"

"Randy. Chris and Randy are about as close as two brothers can be but he hides it from Randy too. Donny left his mark on the boys. Men are supposed to be tough. They don't cry and aren't gentle. They swagger, drink beer and talk tough."

Helen lies back on the soft cushion of needles. Her hair splays around her.

She resists a sudden urge to touch it. "How do you feel about Chris being gay?"

Helen turns her green gaze on Ellie. "I love him. He's the sweetest of my boys, but I worry about him. He's so ashamed."

"He talks to you about it?" she asks with surprise.

"He doesn't have to. It used to come up in conversation before I divorced Donny. The older boys would talk about beating up fags, and Chris would grow quiet. Once he said some people were just that way, and why did they have to be bothered. His dad said he'd whip sense into him if he ever caught him with someone like that. His oldest brothers said they'd kill the guy. It's hard to be different in a family like ours." Helen grimaces. "I never talked to anybody about this."

She remembers the brief affair she had after Will strayed, with someone she met at the Y. A woman. Their few attempts at love-making in the woman's apartment left her breathless with excitement, and ashamed. They were both married. The other woman's husband traveled on business. She never told anyone about the woman, not even Steven.

Helen rolls onto her side and rests her head on her hand, her elbow buried in the pine needles. "Do you remember, Ellie?" she asks, as if reading Ellie's mind. Her face is flushed, either from the sun or her thoughts.

"Remember what?" Picking up a needle, she tickles the dog with it. Her casual tone belies her thudding heart.

"Do you remember our experiments?" Helen says in a soft voice. "Do you think all kids do that stuff?"

Unnerved by the question, she doesn't reply.

Helen pulls herself up on the palms of her hands, her green eyes questioning. "I never thought much about it, till I realized Chris was that way. Then I remembered us, and thought maybe I was too."

She looks away, her throat so thick she's still unable to speak.

"Ellie, you shouldn't be ashamed. It was my doing, not you."

She'd liked it, though, and couldn't admit even that much.

VIII

The doctor came to see Joey that night. He gave her a shot of adrenaline. She turned ghostly pale and her pupils grew till they blackened her eyes. Her voice and hands shook but the telltale wheeze disappeared.

In the hallway, Mom and Dad talked to the doctor in low voices but Ellie got the drift of their conversation. If this didn't work, Joey would have to go back to the hospital.

"Joey," she said.

"What?"

"I'll teach you to ride my bike." Her sister didn't own a bicycle yet.

"Thanks, Ellie." Joey looked like she was trying to hold herself together, that any minute she'd fly apart. Her eyes were shadows in her thin face.

"Can you sleep now?"

"I'm wide awake."

Ellie fell asleep quickly, dreaming the Black Stallion was hers. She rode him fearlessly through the field out back while everyone looked on admiringly.

The next afternoon Joey was bad again. Mom stayed home from work. Joey sat on the edge of the bed, leaning on her hands, struggling for each breath. She'd been sleepless for most of two nights now and two days.

Ellie went in to cheer her up. "You want to play cards?"

Joey shook her head, not having any breath to waste on talk.

"Should I get Mom?" She wondered what it was like to sit hour after hour, waiting for the asthma to go away. She knew it wasn't going to disappear by itself. Joey must have too because she nodded.

When Dad got home, he and Mom took Joey to the hospital and sent her to Helen's house for the night. This time Mom called and asked Helen's father if she could stay there.

"Come on in, girlie," he said, when she knocked on the door.

"Can't we play outside till dark?" she asked.

"Please, Dad," Helen begged.

Her eyes darted around the living room. She felt smothered in that house with the shades drawn. Junior was sitting on the couch.

"You want to play kick-the-can, Junior?" she asked, even though he gave her the creeps too. His hair was the color of Helen's, only cropped short. He also had a pug nose and freckles but he wasn't like his sister. He didn't seem to have any friends and did everything as if it was a chore, including play.

"I guess. Okay, Dad?"

It wasn't any fun. She wanted to be at the hospital, even if she had to sit in the waiting room. Mom had said she was better off at Helen's.

They went inside when they couldn't see the can anymore. Helen's dad was sitting in his underwear on the couch, listening to the radio and drinking a bottle of beer.

"About time," he grumbled.

"It just got dark, Dad," Helen said.

He grabbed for her, catching her by the shorts and pulling her onto his lap. "Gimme a kiss and I'll forgive you."

She tried to squirm away. "You're all bristly."

But he kept shoving his face in hers, making smacking noises. Ellie backed into a corner and bumped into Junior, who poked her in the ribs.

"What're you staring at?" he sneered. "You want a kiss too?"

Shaking her head, she moved away from him.

When Helen escaped from her dad and took Ellie up to her room, she wiped her face with her arm. "What're you looking at?" she asked, like her brother.

"Nothing."

"Don't your dad kiss you?"

"Not like that." He gave her pecks on the cheek. She seldom sat on his lap anymore, although Joey sometimes did.

"Don't he love you?"

"Of course he does." It was something she never thought about. His love she took for granted but now she began to doubt it, even though she didn't want him to kiss her like that. In anger, she shot back, "He doesn't beat me like yours does."

Helen bit her lower lip and looked at her through narrowed eyes. "He just hits me because he's worried I won't grow up good."

But she didn't want to fight with Helen. She felt alone and scared, fearful that any minute Helen's dad would burst into the room.

"You girls go to sleep now," her father yelled up the stairs.

Junior stuck his head in the room. "Sure you don't want more kissing?" He smirked and shut the door quickly when Helen threw a pillow at it.

"What's going on up there?" her dad hollered. "I'm coming up if I hear any more noise."

It was shortly after nine. "Where am I going to sleep?" she asked. There was only the single bed.

"We ain't too big for this bed. We can practice kissing."

She remembered her promises but her legs betrayed her excitement. "When does your mom get home?" She didn't think she'd sleep until another grown-up was in the house.

"Eleven thirty," Helen said, pulling off her shirt.

She saw Helen's breasts before she jerked a pajama top over her head. They were small and pointy.

"What do you wear to bed?" Helen asked.

When it was hot, she sometimes only wore underpants but she had brought summer pajamas with her for the night. She put them on, hiding her flat chest from Helen.

They got into the bed and lay there, their sides touching. Then Helen climbed on top of Ellie, who kept her eyes on the door, sure any minute Mr. Lindquist would open it.

"Don't you like kissing?" Helen asked, drawing back, her eyes slits in the dark room.

Not wanting to hurt her feelings, she nodded. She didn't think Helen liked it much either, because she slid off her. After a while, she fell asleep.

Ellie wasn't sure how long she slept but she woke with a start, knowing someone was in the room besides Helen. Terrified, she tried to lie perfectly still. Her heart pounded so hard she was sure it would give her away.

"Helen," her father whispered, the mattress rocking a little as he shook her. "I know you're awake. Come on now."

"I don't want to, Dad, not tonight," Helen murmured.

"It don't take long," he said.

She squeezed her eyes shut tight, pretending sleep. The bed lifted slightly as Helen left it. Their feet moved across the wood floor, hers a patter, his shuffling. The door closed quietly.

Lying rigid in the dark, trying not to bolt from the bed and flee the house, she breathed in the night smells until once more sleep overcame her.

When the door opened again, she awoke enough to know it was only Helen. As Helen slid in next to her, she noticed a funny odor

that she couldn't identify, a smell that Helen hadn't given off earlier.

In the morning she couldn't wait to get out of the house. Sneaking out of bed without waking Helen, she put on yesterday's clothes and held her breath until she stepped outside on the porch. Dew trembled on the grass.

Her parents' car was in the driveway. Thinking she was safe, she stretched and yawned. The screen door squeaked behind her and a hand closed over her arm.

"Where you going, girlie?" Helen's dad asked.

She thought she screamed, someone did, and he let go of her arm. Backing away from him, she said, "Home. My mom and dad are there."

He laughed. "You're scared of me, ain't you?"

"No," she said, shaking her head, nearly tripping down the porch steps in her hurry to get away.

"See you later, girlie." He disappeared into the house.

She ran across the yard, opened the door and bounded up the stairs to her room. Joey's rumpled bed lay as she'd left it. She slumped on her own, her breath coming in gasps.

"Hey, sunshine, you're up early." Her dad stood in the doorway in his pajama bottoms. He looked tired. "You okay?"

"Yeah." She knew she'd jumped. "How's Joey?"

"Resting easier." Motioning with his head toward his bedroom, he said, "Your mom's still in bed. Why don't you get in with her?"

Only when she was against her mother did she feel safe. Mom shifted her weight and drew her into her arms, murmuring, "What is it, Ellie?"

"Nothing. I missed you." She closed her eyes and felt her body grow heavy.

"You get the short end, don't you, honey?"

"Let me go with you next time, Mama." She hadn't called her Mama since she started school.

"Maybe there won't be a next time."

She couldn't remember when Joey didn't have asthma. Her attacks were getting worse, not better. Even though she knew her mother was being wishful, that she was worried, she didn't want to talk about Joey. She snuggled closer.

Mom kissed her on the forehead. "My big baby," she whispered.

Dad came into the room, smelling of aftershave. He bent over and kissed them both. "Are you going to work, Beth?"

Her mother sighed. "I have to, Larry. I'll go to the hospital this afternoon. What about Ellie? We can't keep sending her next door."

Wide awake now, she said, "I'll go with you, Mom. I can read in the waiting room."

Dad said, "She'll be all right here during the day. One of us can stay home tonight."

She didn't know a day could be so long. Not wanting to see Helen, she stayed inside. The doorbell rang off and on all morning but she sat on her bed and finished the Black Stallion book. After she put it down, she didn't know what to do. The next time the bell sounded, she opened the door.

"Where you been?" Helen asked.

She shrugged and backed away so that Helen could come in.

"Is your sister still in the hospital?" Helen looked around as if expecting to see someone else.

Her heart beat faster and she looked around too. "Yeah."

"Are you coming over tonight?" Her green eyes darkened.

She shook her head.

"You don't like my dad, do you?"

"Why does he come get you at night?"

"You was just pretending to sleep, weren't you?" She walked into the living room and sat on the davenport. "Don't your dad ever come get you?"

"No. What for?"

"To teach you about stuff."

"What stuff?" she asked.

She looked scornful. "Never mind. You're such a baby. You wouldn't understand."

"I'm not a baby." She had an idea. "We could bike to the lake."

"All right, but we have to be back before my dad gets home."

Helen's mother came outside before they left. She was real nice with kind eyes and a friendly smile. "Don't go far," she called.

"Does your dad come get you when your mom's home?" she asked.

" 'Course not and don't you tell her nothing. Dad would get you."

"My dad would get him then." But she knew she wouldn't tell anyone.

They biked past Janice and her sister and she nearly lost her balance waving.

As they crossed Elm and started up Walnut toward the boulevard, she waited for that exhilarating sense of freedom to come over her. Instead, she felt sneaky and wanted to get where they were going and back as fast as she could. What if Mom came home and found her gone, not to be trusted?

On the way back, she studied the homes they passed, some of them two or three times as big as hers. What kind of people lived in these houses? What did they do with so many rooms? Who cleaned them?

She lagged behind Helen who was half a block ahead. Helen never looked to see where Ellie was until she got to the corner of Walnut where she braked and waited.

"What's taking you so long?" Helen asked impatiently.

"I was looking at the houses."

"What for?" Helen asked. "You ain't never gonna live in one of them."

Sometimes she wondered if Helen was her best friend or just her only friend. Joey was right. She did have terrible grammar. "How do you know?" she asked.

Helen shrugged. "Maybe you will. I won't. I'm gonna leave home soon as I can."

It was the first time Helen had said something like that. She rode after her. "Why?"

"Then he can't come get me," she said, biking furiously down Walnut toward Elm. The further they got from the lake, the more modest the houses became.

"Where were you this afternoon, Ellie?" her mother asked when she got home. "I called for at least two hours and no one answered."

"Riding my bike with Helen," she said guiltily. "How's Joey?"

"Better."

When Dad walked in from work, she asked, "Are we going to visit Grandma and Grandpa Poole soon?" Most summers they spent weekends with her grandparents at Pine Hill. Dad's parents lived so far away they only saw them once or twice a year.

"Soon as Joey's home and well," Dad said, fixing a sandwich. He was going to the hospital while Mom stayed home with her.

"Can Helen come with us?" she asked.

Mom and Dad looked at each other over her head. She searched their faces, trying to read their thoughts. Dad shrugged.

IX

She brushes off the pine needles and holds out a hand to Helen. "Let's go to Lyle's. I don't want to get there any time around noon. Harriet will insist we stay for lunch."

Helen takes the helping hand and jumps up. "I'm sorry I brought up that stuff. We were just kids when it happened. Forget it."

Forcing a smile, she nods. She's never forgotten the excitement Helen's touch generated but she's never talked about it either, not even when she went to counseling after the divorce, just as she has never mentioned her brief affair with the married woman.

Bitsy bounds ahead. She calls him back when he nears the road. Lyle's family has always owned a golden retriever, which runs to greet them when they near the farm.

Guessing Lyle will be cleaning up after milking, she looks in the open doors. He's climbing onto his John Deere tractor at the other end of the barn, ready to spread manure on the fields, when she calls his name.

He pauses, one leg on the running board, before jumping down and walking toward them, his homely face lit with pleasure. He takes Helen's hands in his. "Are you staying long?"

Helen shakes her head and laughs. "Just for the day. You still look like you did all those years ago, doesn't he, Ellie?"

"You look wonderful," he says, "don't she, Ellie?"

"Yes," she admits, remembering the old jealousy, no longer at sea about where it was directed.

"Come on in the house and have a cup of coffee. It's always on." He takes Helen by the arm, as if afraid she might escape, and leads her toward the house.

She follows, a little put out at bringing up the rear.

Harriet is stirring something on the stove. Wiping her hands on a towel, she hurries toward them. "Helen, is it?" She puts an assortment of coffee cups on the table. "Can you stay for lunch? Beef vegetable soup."

Ellie shakes her head. "Thanks, Harriet, but I've got a pizza ready to put in the oven."

"I suppose you're catching up on old times. We don't want to interfere with that."

"Sure we do." Lyle sits down next to Helen. The smell of cow manure radiates from his boots in the mudroom. Getting up, he puts them outside.

The talk turns to farming, to Helen's job at the travel agency and to Ellie's editing. Small talk. Harriet puts cookies on the table and Ellie dips one in her coffee.

"Want more?" Harriet jumps up to fill their cups.

"Not for me," she says, "but thanks." She glances at Helen, asking with a look if she's ready.

Helen nods. "Thanks for the coffee and cookies. They'll keep me going till lunchtime." She shakes her hair away from her face. Lyle watches. "We don't want to interrupt your day."

"You're not," he says.

Ellie carries the cups to the sink. Hugging Harriet, she says softly, "You're right. We've got a lot of catching up to do."

She and Helen cross the road again with Bitsy in the lead. The

dog runs to the front porch and stands at the door, waiting. It's damp now and clouds have begun to obscure the sun. The breeze no longer feels warm.

She lights the paper and kindling in the fireplace and takes the chair nearest the fire. Public radio is playing a Bach Brandenburg concerto. Bitsy lies on her feet.

Helen stretches out on the davenport. "Great music. My boys are into country. I listen to anything else. Want to play paper dolls or cards or marbles?" she jokes.

Ellie smiles. "What two-handed card games do you know?"

Helen shrugs. "Gin, but I'm too comfy here. I'd rather talk anyway."

"Okay. What do you do for fun?"

"Go to movies and out with friends. Watch TV. I belong to a card group. We play sheepshead. What about you?"

"I belong to a card group too. We play bridge, though. I also belong to a book group and go out with friends for fish almost every Friday. Once in a while I see a play or concert. More often I go to a movie. In the winter I occasionally go on a cross-country ski weekend with Jo and the girls. Usually here."

She recalls her mother joining them on the trails, falling on the steep hills but gamely getting up and continuing. Liz always hung back and accompanied her.

"This is suicide hill. It's too steep to go down, Grandma," she hears Liz say. "Take your skis off."

"Private joke?" Helen asks, seeing her smile.

She shares it.

"That's wonderful. My two younger sons might take care of me like that. The older ones would laugh. It's not that they don't love me. It's that they think showing any softness is unmanly."

Ellie murmurs something, meaning to sound comforting yet not condemning.

"My oldest grandson, Sonny, wants to be as tough as his dad, even though he's only six and sometimes forgets. His younger brother, Scott, feels he has to pretend he doesn't like the cat but Jocko knows. He winds himself around Scott's legs, purring, till

59

Scotty picks him up. Then Sonny tries to jerk Jocko away, and I have to step in and tell the boys to knock it off. If Scott stays over by himself, Jocko sleeps with him."

"Do you like being a grandma?"

"I love it, although I don't want to be a permanent babysitter. I just wish one of the boys would have a girl, although I remember being glad I didn't have one, even though I wanted one."

"Because of your dad," she says knowingly.

"My dad and Donny. I didn't trust either one."

She has no comment. Instead, she asks, "Ready for lunch?"

Adding cheese and onion, she pops the pizza in the oven. "How about a salad to go with it?"

"Sure. I'll help."

"They're already made." Taking two glass bowls out of the fridge, she puts them and the salad dressing on the table.

"You're damn efficient."

"Not really. I do a lot of procrastinating. I fixed the salads when I probably should have been working on a manuscript."

"Maybe you'll write a book someday," Helen says.

She laughs. "I don't think so. I'd be scared to death I'd bore somebody."

Helen's green eyes darken. "You could write about us."

"I don't think so." And relive the sheer terror? Not likely.

"Was divorce hard for you?"

"For both of us, I think. No one understood. We seemed like the perfect couple."

"You put a good face on things, huh?"

"It was a pretty functional marriage for the most part."

"I did a lot of pretending too."

Were she and Will pretending? "He had an affair, then I did." She sees the woman from the Y as clear as if she's in the room. Brown eyes in an olive-skinned face framed by unruly dark hair, a slender body with brown nipples and black pubic hair.

"I was too scared to cheat on Donny. It was afterward that I found out I didn't want another man. Too confining. My boys wouldn't stand for it anyway."

60

"Are you afraid of them?" She was, and she hadn't met them yet.

Helen leans on her hand, her fingers buried in her thick hair. "No, but they're a little possessive."

"Your hair looks the same," she says, still wanting to touch it.

"I color it. You don't do that. You're so sure of yourself."

"Not really. Black never looks real, unless it is." She pulls the pizza out of the oven and sets it on a platter on the table.

Outside the sun disappears behind clouds. "We've lost our nice day."

"You'll have to invite me back for the next one."

After lunch, they stand next to Helen's car. Helen has to work that afternoon, and says, "Why don't you spend the night next time?"

She smiles to hide her confusion. "We'll see. I do have to go home sometime, you know."

The ache that only goes away when someone is around to distract her returns as Helen's car pulls out of the driveway. A chickadee scolds and falls silent. She fills the feeders before going inside.

Sitting near the fire, she works on the manuscript but puts it down after rereading the same sentences. Her thoughts return to the woman she met at the Y, to how they began talking and somehow ended up in the woman's studio apartment where she was so jittery with excitement that she didn't trust herself to speak. There were two more meetings at the Y that ended up in the woman's bed. She never saw her after that, even though she went to the Y three times a week and always looked for her.

After spending hours reliving those few acts and what they meant, she usually ends up with her hand between her legs—not even a close second to the deed itself. She knows now that, as a child, Helen was acting out the sexual abuse she experienced with her father. However, her reactions to Helen's touch all those years ago and to the affair with the woman at the Y raise questions about her own sexuality that she isn't ready to face.

X

When Helen asked her mother for permission to go to Pine Hill, her mom said yes without even talking to her dad. Helen told Ellie her dad was mad about it but she was going anyway.

When they drove out of the driveway, Mr. Lindquist was out of sight, which was nothing unusual. He was probably in his underwear drinking beer. Junior swung idly on their front porch swing and raised a hand when Mom waved.

Helen had told Ellie the startling news that she'd seen her brother kissing Janice after dark the other night. She'd confronted him in front of Ellie and he'd said Janice was no more trash than anyone else. He had gone on to say at least Janice didn't let her dad mess around with her. Helen had run off before Ellie could ask how he messed around with her. She didn't like Junior enough to ask him but she looked at him in a different way.

Helen sat between Joey and Ellie, who were keeping a running tab of the horses they saw during the hour and a half trip. On the

last leg of the drive, when Dad turned onto the sand road that led to Pine Hill the old Chevy's tires caught in the ruts and he slowed down to a crawl so the car wouldn't be dragged into the ditch.

She and Joey unrolled their windows all the way and stuck out their heads. She loved the smell of the sun on the sand and the pine trees and the clean air. Her dad said this area was once a forest of white pines and she thought it must have smelled great. Her braids whipped around her face.

Grandma and Grandpa were standing on their porch with their dog, Midnight, as if they knew she and her family would be there any minute. She spilled out of the back door and took turns hugging them and the dog. They were all heavyset, even Midnight. Grandpa was bald and his voice warbled. Grandma always wore a dress and knotted her long, gray braids at the back of her head.

Mom gently pushed Helen to the forefront and said, "Aren't you forgetting someone, Ellie?"

She introduced Helen, who ducked her head shyly when Ellie's grandparents solemnly greeted her.

They carried their bags upstairs where she and Joey always slept. The windows looked out over a grove of pines, Grandma's garden and the weathered barn and outbuildings.

"We'll have to sleep together," she told Helen happily.

Helen shrugged. "We done it before."

After supper, Grandma excused them from the dishes. Grandma and Mom wanted to talk, they hadn't seen each other in so long. She and Helen and Joey hurried out into the warm evening.

Grandpa and Dad were already heading for the lake to fish, so they went to the barn. The building was swept clean because of Joey's allergies but in the light flowing through the open door, dust motes danced and she hesitated before going in. A chain and pulley, accessible from the loft, hung from the open rafters. Although she wouldn't admit it, it scared her to dangle over the barn floor and she only did it on a dare. They climbed the built-in ladder to the haymow and sat with their legs hanging over the

edge. From there they looked down at the stanchions lying in shadows.

Outside of the dog, her grandparents had no animals. Grandpa delivered mail. His parents had farmed the place, homesteading the land. Most of the original land had been sold.

They were talking about Junior kissing Janice when Joey began wheezing.

"You better get out of here, Joey," she said.

"I don't have to," Joey replied stubbornly.

"It's the dust," she told Helen.

"Let's all get out of here," Helen said.

By the time they reached the house, Joey was in the middle of another attack.

Mom took one look at her and said, "Oh, honey," in a sad and sort of desperate voice before going for Joey's atomizer.

She and Helen stayed on the porch. The screen creaked shut behind them. Daylight faded slowly, coloring the sky with pinks and purples. They were sitting on the steps when Lyle Jensen, the neighbor boy, came over.

She had been wondering when he'd show up, because he always did. He was her age and skinny with a big head and ears that jutted out and thick, dark hair.

"Hi. Heard you was coming," he said. Lyle helped her grandparents. He mowed their grass and shoveled their snow. Last summer he'd painted the house with Grandpa.

She introduced him to Helen. He looked her over with so much interest, she said, "She's older than you."

That didn't seem to make any difference, though. He tried to impress her anyway, asking her if she'd like to ride on his tractor tomorrow.

"Sure," she said, tossing back her red hair.

Lyle hung around as the day faded into night, taking the colors with it. Lightning bugs flitted around the yard. She suggested they catch them in a jar with holes in the lid to make a temporary lantern but he and Helen just kept talking like she hadn't said anything.

Grandpa and Dad returned from the lake, surrounded by fireflies. The dog put on a show of trying to catch the flickering bugs.

"How are you, Lyle?" Dad asked when he and Grandpa got close.

"Good, Mr. McGowan. Catch anything?"

He showed us the five bluegills he and Grandpa had pulled from the lake. They flopped in the basket and she wanted to set them free.

"Where's your sister?" Dad asked.

"Inside. She had an attack in the barn."

He and Grandpa hurried past, Grandpa pausing only to put a large hand on her head. The screen door slapped shut behind them. Midnight stayed behind, lying on the porch floor panting, his long red tongue dripping.

Joey came out with Mom and Dad, who were taking her to the hospital in town for a shot of adrenaline.

"Time to come in, girls," Grandma said.

"See you tomorrow." Lyle put his hands in his pockets.

She and Helen played hearts with Grandma and Grandpa under a pool of light at the kitchen table till Mom and Dad came back with Joey. Joey breathed easier, although she looked wildeyed from the shot of adrenaline.

In bed she never heard anything after the first calls of a pair of barred owls. Grandpa said those were the only owls that hooted in the summer. She fell asleep, smelling fresh-cut hay on the breeze that blew in the open windows and woke with her arms and legs tangled up with Helen's. She lay very still in the morning light, not wanting Helen to move away from her.

When Midnight was sent upstairs to wake them, he licked her on the nose and mouth, his breath hot and smelly. She hugged him in an excess of joy, and asked, "You all right, Joey?"

Joey nodded, her face pale, her pupils huge, and Ellie believed her because she heard no wheeze.

The day was brilliant with sunlight. Grandpa was gone on his delivery route. Had Helen not been there she would have accom-

panied him as she'd done in the past, putting the mail in the boxes for him. Afterward, they'd stop for pancakes in town.

Lyle came to the door as they were helping Grandma clean up after breakfast. Annoyed with him for butting in on her day with Helen, she ignored him. He didn't even notice. He and Helen went off on his old John Deere tractor, putt-putting around the Jensen's hay fields. Helen stood on the running board, leaning against the vibrating fender. Ellie thought they'd be back before long, but they were gone the rest of the morning. Even her mother was annoyed when the green tractor chugged up the driveway.

"Don't you have work to do, Lyle?" Mom asked. He caught the hint and left, and she turned to Helen, "We can't let you go off like that again, Helen. We're responsible for you."

After lunch, Joey and Ellie waded into the lake, the sand swirling around their ankles, but Helen hung back. Grandma sat on the shore in a lawn chair, waving away insects.

The small trout stream that fed the lake meandered off into a field someone else owned. Grandpa and Dad had built a raft that floated in the middle of the water. She and Joey swam to it with Midnight in their wake. Mom waded out slowly, her arms above the surface as if she were cold. Then she plunged in and the dog swam circles around her.

"Come on in, Helen," Ellie called as she and Joey rocked the raft.

Out of the blue, Lyle showed up in his swim trunks, carrying an inner tube. He ran into the water and swam out to the raft. Climbing up the ladder, he chased Ellie and her sister off and, arms wrapped around knees, jumped in after them.

Helen waded daintily into the water and sat on the tube. Lyle swam over and began pushing her around. She laughed at something he said.

Ellie got out and stood in the hot sun with a towel wrapped around her, thinking that she'd not bring another friend with her again.

❧

Later that day the three girls and Lyle walked over to the wetland at the far end of the small lake. Cattails rose from the hummocks of grass that dotted the shallow water like tiny islands. Lily pads floated on the surface, some with white flowers.

The swamp fascinated Ellie. Frogs and turtles abounded and snakes lurked among the grasses. She and Joey caught and released the frogs. Sometimes she managed to grab turtles by their shells as they scurried off their sunning logs. Today she picked up a pencil-sized red-bellied snake that she nearly stepped on.

Helen screamed.

Not to be outdone, Lyle found a garter snake that was about two feet long and draped it around his neck. The one good thing about Lyle, he wasn't cruel. He'd shown her how to catch a snake by quickly grabbing it behind its head, so it couldn't bite. He'd told her to support the rest of its body, not to let it dangle.

Helen screeched again and Joey jumped into the muck in pursuit of a turtle. Joey only pretended an indifference to snakes, really putting distance between her and the reptiles.

Lyle released his snake, placing it carefully in the grass. Ellie set hers down once his had crawled away.

"I want to go back to the house," Helen said, but she didn't move, only stared at the ground around her in terror.

"It's okay," Lyle said. "I didn't mean to scare you."

They escorted Helen to the yard where the mown grass couldn't hide surprises. Her face was white and she looked mad. She clutched Ellie's hand and refused to let go, which was just fine with Ellie. At least, it wasn't Lyle's hand Helen was holding.

At supper that night Grandpa asked if they wanted to go see the outdoor movies in town. Between Memorial Day and Labor Day, unless there was rain, the town showed movies in the small park by the millpond on Saturday nights. Westerns were usually the choice. The audience sat on benches set into the hillside. Popcorn and pop could be bought at the drugstore across the street.

Migrant workers gathered in town for the movies—swarthy, sturdy people who spoke the language of Mexico. This was veg-

etable country and the migrant workers traveled from state to state, picking whatever crops were ready. They filled old trucks and cars with their many children who helped in the fields. She had heard it said in town that these people were all pickpockets who would knife you for a few coins. Grandma and Grandpa told her that wasn't so, that they worked hard for the little money they earned. She thought the kids were beautiful with their dark eyes and skin and hair. Grandpa had pointed out the shacks they lived in on the farms where they picked. She had seen them stooping through the fields, dragging burlap sacks.

Mom and Grandma stayed home. The rest of them got into the old Chevy and drove to town. Grandpa bought them popcorn and orange pop and she found seats with Helen and Joey in the front row while Grandpa and Dad sat in the benches farthest from the screen.

Mosquitoes descended as dusk fell, about the time the movie flickered onto the screen, which was when Lyle found them and squeezed in next to Helen. Ellie sat between Helen and Joey, surrounded by dark, lithe children, talking a language she couldn't understand.

Lyle whispered, "Keep your eyes on your money."

She didn't have any money to keep track of, so she wasn't worried. But one little girl watched her shovel popcorn into her mouth with such intense interest that she held out the bag to her. Grabbing a handful, the girl gave her a dazzling white smile. She smiled back.

Lyle leaned over and whispered loudly, "Don't give them none. You might catch something."

"What?" she asked worriedly.

"Lice," Helen said, running light fingers over Ellie's head, making her shiver with pleasure.

She handed the little girl the bag. She took it eagerly.

"You can have some of mine," Joey whispered.

❧

68

She got real tired of Lyle appearing all the time and taking over Helen like she was his girlfriend or something. She'd looked forward to showing her around, not to sharing her with him.

The next day he asked her when they were coming back and she said with a shrug, "I don't know."

"Maybe Helen can come with you again," he suggested.

She shrugged, knowing she wouldn't ask her.

They left mid-afternoon. Lyle stood in the yard with her grandparents, waving. For the first time ever, she was glad to be going home.

Joey fell asleep as soon as they turned off the sand road that led to Pine Hill. She stared out the window, pretending she was galloping on the Black Stallion beside the car. Helen sat silently between Joey and her.

"It's awfully quiet back there," Dad said. "You girls have a good time?"

"Oh yes," Helen said. "I wish I could live there."

She turned to look at her with surprise and said meanly, "But you can't."

Helen took her hand and squeezed it. She whispered in Ellie's ear, "I like you better than Lyle."

Ellie's angry resolve melted a little but she knew she wouldn't risk losing Helen to Lyle again.

XI

Ellie watches Helen's car disappear behind trees. The ground chills her feet, radiating up through her body to the dull ache in her chest. Momentarily, she longs to go back to those early years, with two loving parents, no adult responsibilities, no real failures and a first best friend. She can't quite recapture the essence of being that young but knows it comes with Helen.

Helen phones when she gets home. "Thanks, Ellie. I had a great time. Why don't you come and stay overnight Thursday?"

She hedges, "I've got so much to do," and glances down at Bitsy. "What about the dog?"

"Bring him. I don't want to wait a week. Thursday is my day off. He won't eat the cat, will he?"

She laughs and thinks of the reasons to say no—the manuscripts she has neglected, the estate that has to be settled.

"Come in time for lunch," Helen adds.

She hesitates before saying, "All right, but I can't stay overnight."

"Pack your toothbrush, just in case."

Steven calls that evening. "How are you, sweetie?"

"The truth is I'm not getting much done. I've finished one manuscript. All I've done with the estate is be named personal representative, pick up some death certificates and open a checking account."

"Sounds like progress to me. Do you want company this weekend or not?"

"I do, I do. How many? I'll pick up some food."

"Just me. Have you heard from the girls or Jo?"

"I'll call them."

She does after she hangs up. Her daughters have other plans for the weekend and Jo is attending a conference with Pete.

"Why isn't his wife going?" she asks, indignant for the woman.

"It's business and she's out of town anyway."

"Or so he says."

"You always talk about him as if he's a creep," Jo says.

She jumps into the opening. "He's cheating on his wife and kids, Jo. Chances are someday he'll cheat on you."

Jo's voice turns stony. "I have to go now."

Remorseful, she calls Jo to make things right and gets the answering machine.

"I'm sorry, Jo. I'll try to keep from running off at the mouth." She hangs up, feeling better.

The next two days she works on the second manuscript mornings and evenings and on her mother's estate during the afternoons—posting death notices in newspapers, sending death certificates to her mother's insurance companies and Social Security, canceling credit cards and subscriptions, paying bills. Bitsy crowds close when she sits on the floor, going through her mother's papers.

Thursday morning she ships off another manuscript. It will return for final editing before going to a proofreader.

The sun rides high in the sky, making her almost giddy with its warmth and the smells it coaxes from the earth. She throws her backpack in the backseat. It holds her book and personal items—shampoo, toothbrush, toothpaste, deodorant, clean underwear, anything she might need in case she is stranded. Bitsy sits on the passenger seat, his ears perked, his eyes straight ahead.

A four-wheel drive truck, splattered with mud and sporting running boards two feet off the pavement, is parked in Helen's driveway. She knows it belongs to one of Helen's sons, another reason not to stay overnight.

Reluctant to meet the owner of the truck, she stays in her car, listening to the news on public radio, stalling for time. Finally, she climbs out, clips Bitsy's leash to his collar, waits as he pees on a tree and rings the bell.

Helen opens it, looking worried or annoyed or both. "Come on in, Ellie. Jay here is leaving soon."

"Why can't you, Ma?" a male voice says from inside.

"Because I have plans."

She steps hesitantly into the small foyer. Bitsy hugs her side.

"Ellie, this is my son, Jay, and these are my grandsons, Sonny and Scott. Ellie was my best friend when we were kids."

Jay grunts. He's short and wiry and looks like his dad did when young. Two little boys stand next to him. She understands the situation in a glance. The boys take a few steps toward Bitsy, who backs away.

"Why didn't you say your grandsons were coming to visit? That's great."

"See, Ma, she don't care if they stay."

"Of course, I don't," Ellie says. "I've been wanting to meet these two."

"We won't be no bother, Grandma," the younger boy promises. He looks at Ellie. "Can I pat the dog?"

The older one promises, "We'll stay out of your hair."

Helen laughs and strokes each boy's cheek. They lean into her touch. "You're no bother. It's just that I have company, but if she doesn't mind . . ."

"Why would I mind?" Ellie says, sensing the boys' need to be wanted. She pulls Bitsy out from behind her and hunkers down to the children's level. "Come say hello. Let him smell you before you pat him."

The boys do as she says. Bitsy relaxes a little and nervously licks her.

Scott giggles as his small hand comes between the dog's tongue and Ellie. "He likes me," he squeals.

Bitsy edges toward the smaller boy, perhaps sensing a friend.

"I'll be back for them tomorrow morning," Jay says, heading toward the door. "Nice to meetcha." He nods at Ellie, friendly now that his mother has agreed to watch his sons. He puts money into Helen's hand. "Go out to eat."

Helen tries to hand back the two twenties but he won't take them. "I make good money, Ma." He squeezes her shoulder and goes out the door.

The change in the boys is instantaneous. They head for the basement stairs. "Come on, Bitsy," Scott shouts.

They thud down into the basement, the dog scrambling after them, and the cat appears at the top of the stairs, running. Helen scoops him up. "The cat is off limits, guys. Come on, I'll fix lunch."

The boys thunder up the stairs. "We want a Big Mac," Sonny announces.

The smaller boy smiles winningly at his grandmother and she caves.

Helen looks at Ellie. "Sorry. They're at that demanding age, the one that never ends."

"Let's go. I don't know when I last had a Big Mac."

The two boys jump up and down, echoing, "Let's go."

"We'll take my car," Helen says.

Bitsy sits between the boys in the backseat. They feed him pieces of their hamburgers and fries.

Later that evening when the boys are tucked into Helen's bed, watching the TV in her room, the two women finish off a bottle of Shiraz.

Ellie feels mellow. "Where's their mother?"

"Jay gets the boys once a week and usually brings them here. He's a lousy father. He and Candy separated last year."

Getting up, she puts her glass in the kitchen. "I should go."

"Why don't you stay? We drank the whole thing." Helen holds up the empty bottle of wine.

"I can't . . ."

"I'll sleep on the couch. You can have the bed."

She decides to get up early and leave before Jay finds her there. "Okay."

Helen's face lights up. "Let's see what's on the tube, or do you want to go to sleep?"

"No. Turn it on."

Falling asleep during a commercial, she awakens to find Helen standing before her with bedding clutched in her arms. "Okay, I can take a hint. Show me the bed."

Helen has carried the two boys to twin beds in the other upstairs bedroom. Jocko is asleep on Scott's bed.

Murmuring something about putting Helen out of her bed, she tosses her backpack on it. Bitsy lies on the pad she carried upstairs for him.

"It's queen-size," Helen says, assessing her with her green eyes. "You won't even know I'm there." Seeing Ellie's reaction to this, she quickly adds, "Never mind. I'm all set downstairs."

"I don't mind sleeping on the sofa."

Helen squeezes her arm. "I mind. I wouldn't sleep knowing you're on the couch."

In the night, she wakens knowing someone is in the room. For a moment her heart jumps around frantically as if Helen's father has somehow returned. When Helen slides in beside her, she turns her back and is drawn into sleep again as if drugged.

When she wakes up in the morning, Jocko lies near her on the bed. He lifts his head and opens one green eye. She thinks of Helen's eyes and remembers with a hot rush Helen getting in bed with her. Hearing voices downstairs, she sits up. One is deep, male.

Knowing it's probably Jay retrieving his kids, she dresses slowly, brushes her teeth and her hair, before making the bed and shoving her things into her backpack. Bitsy is nowhere in sight, so he must be downstairs, giving away her presence.

Instead of Jay, a taller young man stands in the kitchen, drinking coffee and talking to Helen. Like Helen he has red hair, green eyes and freckles. The boys hang from his free arm and belt loops.

Bitsy barks twice and she shushes him.

"Ah, there you are," Helen says. She introduces the young man.

"Come on, Uncle Chris, let's go," Sonny says.

"Chris is taking the boys for the day," Helen explains. "You guys love Uncle Chris, don't you?"

"Yeah," Scott shouts. "I love you too, Grandma."

"But your uncle is more exciting." Helen grins. "He's taking them out for breakfast and then to an indoor water park."

"Sounds exciting," Ellie says, trying to sound sincere.

"Want to come?" Chris asks with a wink.

"I forgot my suit but thanks for asking," she replies, charmed.

He grins. "Okay, you guys, go get your things."

Helen hands her a cup of coffee and she wraps her hands around it. Feeling Chris's eyes on her, she squints at him through the steam. The sun pours through the dining area patio doors, framing him in an aura of light. His hair blazes as if on fire.

Helen reaches out and touches it. He doesn't flinch. "Thanks, Chris. I don't usually mind babysitting."

"Hey, no problem, Mom. Anytime." He glances at Ellie, catches her gaze and drops his.

The boys race into the room with their paper sacks of clothes, their jackets open. The dog barks.

"Give me a hug and a kiss," Helen demands. As each move to do so, she zips pants, re-buttons shirts and runs her fingers through their unruly hair. "What do you say to Ellie?"

"Nice to meetcha." They speak in unison.

Ellie leans forward and shakes their hands. "Nice meeting you too."

Chris moves out of the light and offers his hand in a firm grip. "I've heard about you from Mom. Nice to put a face to a name."

When they're gone, Helen starts frying bacon. "Sit down," she says. Bitsy lies at Helen's feet, near the food.

As bidden, she sits at the table in the sunlight. Calling the dog to her side, she fills his food bowl. He ignores it, sniffing the air.

"Chris looks like you," she says.

"Yes, he and Randy both. Jay and Jack look more like Donny. I didn't really look at your girls. Do they take after you or their dad?"

"Liz, who's named after Mom, resembles my side of the family more than Katie does. I used to think Jo and I bore no resemblance to each other, though, that she looked more like Mom and I looked like Dad. As we get older and the hair colors fade, the underlying facial structure comes through and now I see a likeness."

"My brother and I always looked alike." Helen flips the bacon onto a paper towel on a plate. She begins an omelet and puts the toast down when she adds peppers, onions and cheese to the eggs.

"Where is Junior?" she asks.

"He lives in a shack on the river and works in the mill with Donny. All he cares about is hunting and fishing. He's been arrested for poaching."

"Does he have kids?"

"A boy and a girl. Fortunately, Janice left Junior when the kids were little and took them with her." Helen seems to read her mind. "I couldn't leave Donny and raise the boys. I didn't have any money or education."

She eats quickly, hoping they'll get through breakfast before another one of Helen's sons shows up.

"Any place you want to go?" Helen asks.

"I should grocery shop and go home. Steven is coming tonight."

Helen nods. "I have to go to work at one. I've only got the

morning. I'll shop with you. That okay?" Without waiting for an answer, she says, "I have to shower first."

"I'll do the dishes," Ellie volunteers.

When Helen comes down, dressed in tan slacks, a kelly green blouse and loafers, she looks stunning. A gold chain nestles between her breasts. It's the simplicity, the contrast between the red hair and green shirt. She feels shabby by comparison in her jeans, tennis shoes and blue pullover.

In the grocery store, she's distracted, feeling pressured to hurry, but Helen goes off by herself to find some of the things on Ellie's list.

"I can't pick out a birthday card for you, though," Helen says as they stand at the racks of cards, showing each other the funny ones. "Who's this for?"

"Steven." She holds out one with a poem about losing one's teeth and hair and wits. "What do you think?"

"Perfect."

Before she checks out she picks out a bottle of merlot.

XII

Ellie's birthday was coming up. At dinner, her mother asked if she wanted a party with friends but Helen was her only friend. Still, it was the first time anyone had suggested such a thing, so she thought it over carefully. She considered inviting Janice and Janice's sister, Nancy, but if she did, Helen probably wouldn't come. She said she'd just invite Helen.

She wanted a radio for her room so that she could listen to her programs but Dad said she might disappear into her room forever.

"No, I won't. I promise." She pictured herself lying on her bed listening to the radio with Helen.

"I think we should weed tonight," Dad said, looking out the dining room window at the gardens. Theirs had taken off now that he was watering it in the evenings.

"Aw, Dad," she said.

"I'll help Mom do the dishes," Joey offered. No one liked to weed.

Crawling down the garden rows, swatting mosquitoes with her free hand, she looked up to see her father staring at Helen's house. Following his gaze, she saw Helen silhouetted behind the white shade in the window of her bedroom. Her dad loomed over her. She could hear their voices, hers pleading, his urging.

"What the hell," Dad muttered. "Is that Helen's room?"

As she nodded, Helen's dad moved away and the light went out, making it impossible to see in the room and then their voices also vanished into the dark house. She shivered.

"Is something funny going on over there?" he asked.

But she didn't know what he meant.

Mom invited Helen over for dinner for Ellie's birthday. It was only two weeks before school started. Ellie had searched the garage and house looking for a present big enough to hold a radio and found none.

While Joey helped Mom fix dinner, she went outside and sat on the stoop, waiting for Helen to come over. The starlings raised a ruckus in the trees overhead, pooping on passing cars. A police car parked across the street and a cop got out. He pulled his revolver from its holster and began shooting into the trees. She stared in horror as the black birds fell to the pavement. Some of them flopped around before they became still.

Mom called her inside and shut the door.

"Why is the policeman shooting birds?" Joey asked, and wailed, "Make him stop."

Mom took her apron off and put it over her head. Telling them to stay put, she marched across the yard and into the street. She talked to the policeman, gesturing at the trees, the houses and the dead birds. He put his gun back in the holster and drove away. As she hurried back to the house, her face hidden by the apron, Ellie's heart swelled with pride.

Before dinner, though, more policemen parked out front and this time used rifles to shoot the starlings out of the trees. The

neighbors gathered to watch from their front doors or porches. They waited till the shooting stopped before eating.

It was her favorite meal of hamburgers, mashed potatoes and corn on the cob from the garden but it was spoiled by what had gone on in the street. She fought down nausea. When her mother brought out the chocolate cake and everyone sang "Happy Birthday," she got over it.

She opened her present from Joey, which she guessed from the shape and weight was a book, another in the Black Stallion series. Really pleased, she thanked her. Helen thrust a package at her. Unwrapping the paper, she stared at the unveiled comic books. Her mother forbade reading comic books. She looked at her for guidance.

"Aren't you going to thank Helen?"

It was the manners thing. It was more important to be polite than to be honest. She paged through the *Wonder Woman* comic books. She would read them that night. She smiled at Helen and thanked her.

Then out of nowhere appeared a big box, wrapped in gift paper. She opened it slowly. It was a radio just the right size to put on her dresser.

Looking at Mom and Dad, she asked with amazement, "Where was it?"

"Aha, I knew you'd look for it," Dad said.

"Can I listen to it?"

"Sure, plug it in."

She twirled the knob till she found some music and sat back down at the table to eat her cake.

After dinner, she and Helen took the radio to Ellie's room, where they lay on her bed and listened.

"Wish I could stay here forever," Helen said.

Ellie's hair stood on end where her arms and legs touched Helen's. "Wish you could too."

❧

Summer ended when school began. Roosevelt Grade School, a two-story brick building, stood on the corner of Elm and Hickory streets, the paved and graveled grounds enclosed by high fencing. Ellie walked there with Helen and Joey the first morning. They went to their separate grades once they were inside.

Her teacher, Miss Albertson, seated them in alphabetical order, putting her in the desk behind a boy named Richard McGinnis. The entire school smelled of musty old books as if no one ever let in any fresh air, but Miss Albertson opened the windows the first day. A leafy breeze blew through them, making her long to be outside.

Miss Albertson was on the large side. Her black hair, peppered with gray, was pulled back from her face and curled in a tight row around her creased neck. Her black eyes shone bright. Ellie was to notice she missed little.

At recess the students were released to the bleak playground. Instead of trees, there were a couple of swing sets, a jungle gym and a set of basketball hoops. Grass struggled to grow along the fence.

Helen leaned against the brick building, surrounded by girls in her class, among them Janice. Ellie walked over to the small group.

"I use tampons," one of the girls said, looking around as if she'd admitted some big secret.

She listened, only understanding from the way they were speaking that the subject was hush-hush.

Helen noticed her. "Ellie don't know what we're talking about. She don't have the curse yet."

Rather than appear bewildered, she wandered away and Janice followed to explain. "The curse is something girls get when they're old enough. They bleed down there once a month. Ask your ma."

She frowned. It sounded crazy. Then she remembered the mysterious box in the bathroom closet and things wrapped in stained toilet paper in the wastebasket.

Joey wandered over.

"You like your teacher, Joey?" she asked, her eyes on the little clique. Janice hung around the fringes again, looking in.

"I hate school," her sister said with such vehemence that she caught Ellie's distracted attention.

"Why?" she asked.

"You can't even get a drink of water when you want to."

She nodded, looking at Joey with interest. She too disliked having every minute of the day planned by someone else. "I know." She sometimes got so thirsty she daydreamed about having a bubbler next to her desk.

All afternoon Richard entertained her, passing her notes, making soft, rude noises when Miss Albertson or someone else talked. Toward the end of the school day, she took out the Black Stallion book Joey had given her for her birthday and opened it in her lap. The desk hid it from Big Al's view.

When the final bell rang and the kids clambered down the stairs to the schoolyard, she took her time. She knew Joey would wait for her and she wanted to give Helen plenty of time to get a good start if she was going home without them.

Helen was waiting with Joey at the bottom of the steps.

"Come on, Ellie," Joey said impatiently.

"Don't you have any homework?" she asked Helen as they walked under the elms toward home. The leaves rustled dryly. Some had already fallen.

"My dad don't like me to bring any home," she said. "You want to come over?"

Her dad would be there and Ellie had a chapter of history to read and math problems to do. She opened her mouth to say no but Joey spoke first.

"Sure."

"Don't you have any homework either?" Ellie asked.

"No." Joey spread her empty arms wide.

When they banged through the front door, Mom was waiting. "So, how was school?"

"Mom, can I go to Helen's? I don't have any homework," Joey said before Ellie could get in a word.

"Why doesn't she come over here?" Mom patted the sofa on either side of her.

"Don't let her go, Mom. I've got homework," she said.

"Well, I don't see why she should have to stay home just because you do."

"But Mom, Helen's mother is at work."

"Her father's home," Mom pointed out.

She couldn't tell her that was the reason Joey shouldn't go there.

"But I thought you wanted us to play outside when it's nice."

"I do. Stay outside, Joey."

"But Mom," Joey protested.

"Now that's enough. Tell me about your day."

Ellie went upstairs to do her homework. Later when Joey came looking for her, she was finishing the last story problem.

"I don't like Helen's dad," Joey said, throwing herself on her bed.

"I told you not to go there without me."

"He wouldn't let Helen go outside. Why does he go around in his underwear all the time?"

She shrugged. "How should I know?" Then she remembered something she wanted to ask her mother. "You stay here. I've got to talk to Mom." She found her in the kitchen.

"Mom, Janice said girls bleed once a month."

Mom stopped peeling potatoes and looked at her for a long moment before answering. Then she told her all about the curse, which she called periods. "You get your period once a month and that's what tampons and Kotex are for, to soak up the blood."

"But why, Mom?" she asked, horrified.

Mom explained how something called the womb gets lined with blood in case there's a baby and that if there's no baby, the blood is expelled from the body.

Increasingly disturbed, she stared at her. "Where does the blood come out of?"

Her mother told her it came from the same opening as a baby would. Her face reddened as she said that people made babies

when the man put his penis inside the woman he was married to. She realized that Mom and Dad must have done it twice, once for her and once for Joey. Everything Helen had said was true. Dad put his tongue in Mom's mouth and his hand between her legs. He shoved his thing inside her. She wanted to ask if Mom's legs went weak when he touched her. Of course, she didn't.

She caught sight of Joey leaning against the buffet in the dining room and knew she was listening. She jerked her head at her sister so Mom would know she was there.

"Come on in, Joey. You need to know these things too."

Joey slunk into the kitchen and leaned against the table. "I want to be a boy," she said.

Mom pulled her against her hip and smiled. "It's not always easy to be a boy either." She pushed Joey's tangle of reddish-brown hair off her forehead.

"Boys get to do everything. Girls have to cook and have babies and bleed inside."

Mom hugged her closer. Ellie could see she was trying not to laugh. "Having babies is wonderful and it's something only women can do."

It didn't sound wonderful to Ellie. Something that big coming out of you must hurt terribly.

"I'd rather play baseball," Joey muttered into Mom's apron, which was absurd because the few times they'd tried baseball she'd ducked from the ball and struck out.

"You would not," Ellie said derisively.

"I want to be able to play baseball," she said.

That was a different matter, one she understood.

"Why don't you two go outside now and enjoy the rest of the day?"

They sat on the stoop, a little stunned by the disturbing information. Ellie watched Helen's house, hoping she would come outside, but the shades were drawn.

XIII

It's early afternoon when she gets back to the house. Across the road, Lyle pulls a plow behind his John Deere. Crows and gulls peck at the ground behind him, white and black scraps against the dark soil. She waves and he returns the gesture.

After putting the car in the old garage, she stands in the sandy driveway, soaking up the lingering heat of the sun, noticing the signs of spring around her. Leaves so new they're translucent, green grass as soft as moss, a pair of mallard ducks bobbing on the blue water. Returning to her condo in Shorewood becomes less and less desirable.

Inside, she signs Steven's card and wraps the book she bought for him—*More Tales of the City* by Armistead Maupin. Then she bakes a chocolate cake.

Steven's Mustang convertible drives past the kitchen window. He gets out and stands in the early evening, his hands in his jacket pockets, his gaze toward the pond. She knows from his stance that

something is wrong. He and Leonard? It has been a shaky relationship for a long time.

"Hi, birthday boy," she says when he walks in and tells the dog to shut up.

"Noisy little bastard," he remarks mildly. "You'd think I was a murderer."

"How can he know you're not till he sees you?" she asks, so glad he has come.

She gives him a hug. He pecks her cheek and sets his bag on the floor.

"It smells great in here." Striding into the kitchen, he spies the cake on the table.

She sings "Happy Birthday," continuing even as he raises a palm in protest.

"And a bottle of wine. Shall we partake?" His eyebrows arch in question.

"After dinner. I'm taking you out," she says.

He suddenly looks forlorn and heaves a sigh.

"What is it, Steven?"

"Leonard is in love with someone else."

"Is he having an affair?"

Again Steven's eyebrows rise. "Of course. I am so devastated, and I don't know why. I'm not sure I love him but I hate the thought of him sneaking around fucking someone else, especially when I've been faithful."

She snorts a laugh.

"Leonard and I don't have sex anymore," he says.

"Well, no wonder he's cheating. Whose idea was that?"

"His," he tells her.

"Oh," she says, deflated.

"It's pretty much over." He splays out a hand as if to say it's hopeless.

"I like Leonard," she says.

"I like him most of the time too, just not right now. I dread the

thought of boxing up my things and moving. I dislike even more admitting failure." He looks at her out of deeply set blue-green eyes. "That's what keeps us together, I think."

"How do you know he's strayed? Did he tell you?"

"I caught them in our bed with their pants down."

"Oh," she says, trying to look horrified when the image makes her want to giggle. "That must have been disturbing."

"To say the least," he agrees with a wry smile.

"Let's talk about this over dinner. I'm starving."

They drive to the Lakeside Hotel next to the millpond in Cedar Creek. It's a bit cool to sit on the porch, so they take a table next to the windows. On the drive there, they discuss whether Steven should leave Leonard or stay till they're so bored neither cares.

Their drinks arrive and Steven asks, "How was your week?"

"Well . . ." she starts and then pauses, not knowing where to begin.

"What?" he says.

In a low voice she asks, "Do you think it's normal to fool around with someone when you're a kid?"

He looks surprised but recovers quickly. "Boy or girl?"

She hesitates. "I never told anyone this before."

"Helen?" She doesn't answer but he can tell. "We're all sexual, Ellie, even as kids. I abused myself regularly. Helen was probably acting out what she learned from her dad."

"It was so exciting," she says softly, belatedly looking around to see if anyone's listening. "My legs turned to mush."

A broad grin crosses his face. "Hey, it would have sent me into orbit if she'd been a he."

"That's what I'm asking. Do you think I'm"—she leans forward and lowers her voice even more, but is still unable to use the defining word—"like you or that she is."

He slugs back his beer and holds out his glass. "I can't answer that. Only you can, and she." He waits till the waiter leaves. "Did something happen this week?"

"Not really. She came here for a day and I went there overnight. She climbed into bed with me but it was the only bed and we just slept."

"You never told anyone about the stuff that happened when you were a kid?" he says.

"I was so ashamed. I thought Mom could tell by just looking at me."

"Ah, guilt. That's how parents keep their kids in line. You probably did the same with your girls."

"It's called conscience, Steven. What kind of monsters would we be without one?"

"Conscience, guilt, you can call it what you want. You're too hard on yourself. I always thought you were a lesbian." He laughs when she shushes him and looks around furtively.

"Did you really think that?"

"No, although you were pretty macho as a kid. Picking up snakes and all."

"You were no sissy."

"I had something to prove."

That evening while consuming the wine and cake in the living room, Ellie says, "There's something else I should tell you about Helen, or rather her sons. I think the two older ones are a lot like her ex, bigoted and possessive."

"Maybe you better find another woman."

"I'm not looking for a woman."

"Who was it you had an affair with in retaliation for Will's infidelity? You never said."

"Promise you'll never tell anyone?"

He crosses his heart. "Unless I'm being threatened with torture or death."

She feels a flush of heat as if she's making a huge confession. "No one you know, or I. We didn't exchange last names or phone numbers."

"What happened?" he asks, staring at her.

"I met her at the Y in the locker room. I'd been swimming.

She'd been running or something." They started talking, and went out for coffee. From the restaurant they drove separately to the woman's studio apartment. "I think she kept an apartment in order to have sex with women."

"How many times?"

"Three. I knew her as Barb."

"You amaze me, Ellie. You're full of secrets. What was the sex like?"

"I was so nervous I was afraid to touch her at first." Barb put Ellie's hand on her breast and then guided it between her legs. Their breathing was the only sound as they quickly climaxed. Barb wasn't interested in Ellie's personal life. She didn't want to know her. "It was the most exciting thing that ever happened to me," she admits quietly.

The next two days and night they discuss Leonard and Helen as they walk through the fields and woods and down the road. It's the first time since last October that Ellie goes outside without a jacket. It has been a cold winter. The warmth itself makes her euphoric. Elated to be free of secrets, she talks and talks.

When Steven leaves on Sunday, she does some serious thinking. It's one thing to discuss her indiscretions. It's another to know where to go with them. She decides to let the friendship with Helen play out. She can always end it at any time.

"My turn," Helen says on the phone that night. "I have the day off tomorrow."

Ellie calculates how much she can get done in the morning. She is only two chapters into the third manuscript. Her boss e-mailed her, asking if she is ready for another. She decides to work on it that evening and early next morning. "Come at noon," she suggests.

"Should I pack a bag?"

"If you want to."

"Do you want me to?" Helen persists.

"Sure."

"Don't sound so enthusiastic."

"Steven left this afternoon. I didn't get anything done over the weekend."

The brightness goes out of Helen's voice. "I forget that you need to work."

"I'll get it done. I always do. I want to see you," she says, realizing she does.

She spends the next few hours working on the manuscript. When her eyeballs feel dry and raw, she goes outside and waits for Bitsy to find just the right spot. In the moonless night, the zillions of stars provide the only light. The dog is a shadow moving across the yard.

Inside, the phone rings and she runs to answer. It's Liz, asking if she's lonely.

"No. I haven't had time or been alone long enough," she says honestly. "Steven was here over the weekend and I saw Helen a couple of days last week. Are you coming?"

"I can't. I got another teacher's assistant job but it includes a Saturday morning lab. Katie is doing research for a professor who's writing a book on corporate greed. I'll let her tell you about that. I just wanted to know how you were. I called the condo first. When are you going home?"

"Maybe never." She laughs.

"Aunt Jo said you were lonesome."

"When did she say that?"

"We went out for pizza with her last night."

"Was Pete there?"

"No."

Liz is working on her master's in wildlife management. She has always been the environmentalist. She talks about her thesis on the causes and effects of non-point source pollution.

"Want to talk to Katie?"

"Love to."

"Hi, Mom." Katie is working toward a double major in business and journalism.

90

"Tell me about this new research job. What's it like?"

"There's so much out there, Mom."

"Corporate greed? It could be a book of epic proportions."

Katie laughs. "I told Dr. O'Connor my mom is an editor."

"Yeah? Was he impressed?"

"He said maybe I was following in your footsteps. We could start our own literary agency."

"Whoa, girl. I like my job."

"Have you no ambition?"

"Not right now. We'll see what comes down the road."

"Mom, have you ever thought of writing a book?"

"I don't have time or inspiration. What's going on in your life besides the research?"

"That and school take up all my time."

She doesn't probe. Her daughters spin in their own orbits now and she isn't their sun. Sometimes she misses the years when she was their main dumping ground, the recipient of their wishes and woes and fears, the one who was expected to make their lives better.

She thinks they lost some of their faith in her when she and Will divorced. If she couldn't repair the marriage, what could she fix?

Helen arrives exactly at noon. The warm breeze ruffles her hair as she gets out of her car. She carries a bottle of wine.

From the open kitchen window, Ellie watches her walk toward the porch. She wipes her hands on her jeans and goes to the door.

Her feelings toward Helen bounce off each other in conflict. The past merges with the present, making it difficult to dump the baggage of their earlier friendship. Sometimes, like now, she thinks she should tell Helen to let it go but once Helen is out of sight, Ellie finds she wants to see her again.

"Right on time," she says.

Bitsy bumps her leg in his hurry to greet Helen. In an exorbitant display of submissive pleasure, he rolls on his back at her feet. Helen bends down to scratch his small chest.

"If I get a rub on the leg from Jocko it's usually because he wants food." She looks up at Ellie, her green eyes glinting in the light, a big smile on her face.

She wonders why Helen wants this friendship. It's not as if they're next-door neighbors anymore. There are fifty miles and over thirty years between them, a span she doubts they can close.

During lunch, she mentions going home.

Helen's expression becomes unreadable. "What about Bitsy and your mom's estate?"

"I can't stay here permanently."

"Why not? Why can't you live and work here?"

She frowns. "I own a condo. The dog can come with me."

"He'll hate it after running free."

"He doesn't run free now. He chases cars, so I have to go out with him."

"I don't want you to go."

An unexpected thrill ripples through her. "Why? It's not like you haven't lived all these years without me around."

Helen opens her mouth and closes it. She gives a little shrug and slides to the front of her chair. "I tried, Ellie. I called. Rejection hurts."

"I know. I'm sorry." She is.

"Wouldn't you like to move back home?"

"Where I live now is home," she says, although she thinks she might want to stay on at Pine Hill, at least through the spring and summer. If she does, she'll have to go home long enough to get her mail, pack and make some arrangements for being gone.

Helen stands up. "Let's go for a walk."

"Why don't we finish eating lunch? We've got the rest of the day."

"It's too nice to be inside. I'm cooped up in the agency most of the week. I can't even see outside because we're in the mall."

"Okay." Ellie grabs her sandwich.

Bitsy runs ahead, his ears pinned with joy, his tail straight out behind him.

Little yellow flowers bloom underfoot. Her mother would have been able to identify them. Around the lake, reeds bend in the wind. The surface of the water blows across the pond. She thinks how her mother would relish this day and wonders if the bitterly cold winter had a hand in her death.

Helen pauses when they reach the lake. The sand, pushed up by melting ice, forms a ridge along the shore. Pale red lashes shade her green eyes. Her freckles are darker, brought out by the sun.

That evening after dinner, she and Helen sit on the porch chairs while daylight ends in a burst of color. Lyle sprawls on the steps, drinking the beer she offered him, while his dog and Bitsy lie side by side on the sandy driveway. It could be thirty years ago with different dogs and without the liquor. The three of them talk till Harriet comes to look for him.

"I wondered where you were," Harriet's features are unclear in the dim light.

He gets up and calls the dog. "Next time let us know when Helen's coming and we'll have you to dinner."

"We'd love to have you anytime," Harriet says to the two women, but adds, "Maybe they want time together, Lyle."

"What for?" he asks.

"Girl talk," she answers.

When they're out of earshot, Ellie says quietly, "He's still interested in you." She glances at Helen but can't see her expression. "I was jealous that weekend you were here."

Helen reaches over and puts a hand on her arm and Ellie's hair rises under it. "I was jealous because this was your place, not mine."

They go inside when the wine is gone. It has made her tired. When it's time to go to bed, she retires to her mother's room and Helen to the guest room.

In the night, the bedroom door opens. Bitsy growls softly. Her heart thumps with alarm till she recognizes the shadow in the doorway as Helen.

"There are strange noises outside."

"The frogs or an owl."

"Can I sleep with you?" Helen asks, sounding panicky.

"Sure, as long as you don't snore. You did last time."

Helen slips into bed. "Snore?"

"Sleep with me. I meant to ask you why."

"I was lonely."

It's amazing how much easier it is to talk in the dark. "Do you do this with everyone who stays over?"

"No, but we slept together when we were young. I had a single bed. Remember?"

"How could I forget?" Those scary nights are forever etched in her memory.

She has trouble falling asleep and searches her luggage for her tiny portable reading light. Beside her, Helen sleeps quietly, her hair spread in waves across the pillow. She longs to feel its thickness but looks away instead.

XIV

When Joey became sick again, Ellie was sitting on her bed reading. She heard a thin wheeze and looked over. The sound came when Joey exhaled.

"Have you got asthma again?" she asked. It seemed to have come out of nowhere, unless it was from something blowing through the open window. Ellie smelled weeds and cut grass and some overpoweringly sweet flowering plant.

"No," Joey snapped.

She turned back to her book. Out of the corner of her eye she watched her sister.

"Don't look at me," Joey hissed.

"I'm not but I hear you wheezing. Where's your atomizer?" She didn't want to have to go over to Helen's for the night.

"In the drawer."

Swinging her legs over the side of the bed, she handed it to Joey. Please make it go away, she begged silently, watching Joey

take a puff. But once asthma set in, it never went away on its own. She knew that and so did Joey.

"I'll get Mom," she said.

"No. Not yet." Joey sounded fierce.

They sat on their beds, pretending to read. After a while, she fell asleep and wakened when her mother took her clothes off and helped her under the sheet.

They didn't take Joey to the hospital till the next night. She begged to go with them but Dad was impatient with her. It was dark outside.

"Do you want me to walk you over there?" he asked.

"Yes," she said, hoping Helen's dad would be in his underwear and Dad would change his mind.

He delivered her to Helen's door, which Mr. Lindquist opened, dressed in slacks and undershirt, a cigarette dangling from his lips.

"Thanks for letting her stay over," Dad said. "We'll be late."

"Any time." Mr. Lindquist smiled through the smoke. "Come on in, girlie."

Helen sat on the couch in the living room with Junior.

"We're playing hide-and-seek," Junior said. "Dad's it."

Mr. Lindquist shut the door and put his cigarette out in the tall ashtray. "I'll close my eyes and count to fifty. You go hide."

"Take your shoes off," Helen said under her breath.

She responded to the urgency in Helen's voice and pushed her tennis shoes off with her toes.

When he began counting, Helen grabbed her hand. "Come on," she whispered. "Quiet, though. He's listening."

They started upstairs noisily while Junior headed for the kitchen. But as soon as Junior was out of sight, Helen pulled her silently and slowly down the steps and into the walk-in closet under the stairs. Her dad was only up to thirty-two as they wormed past winter coats and jackets, over boots and shoes. They huddled in the far corner under a pile of blankets, suffocating from fear and heat.

"Ready or not, here I come," Mr. Lindquist yelled. The words should have sounded funny coming from a grown man. Instead, they terrified her.

Crowding close to Helen, she put her lips to Helen's ear but Helen covered her mouth. After that, she didn't try to speak. Her heart thudded whenever his footsteps came near the closet and her mouth was so dry her lips stuck together.

Helen had been right, Mr. Lindquist had been listening because the first thing he did was gallop up the stairs. His stocking feet slithered overhead, and through the floor and closet door they heard the running monologue he carried on. "I'll find you." He threw a door open and switched on a light. "Maybe you're under the bed." His knees hit the floor.

She squeezed her eyes shut as if she was under the bed about to be caught. She desperately wanted to ask Helen what would happen when he found them but Helen again clapped her hand over her mouth.

"Guess I'll have to keep looking," he said, going to another room and flinging open that door so that it banged against the wall. He talked loud and walked heavily, so that they knew where he was, until he went into the attic.

There were a few moments when she thought he was safely out of earshot but Helen wouldn't let her speak. Then he clambered down to the first floor where they were hiding. Instinctively, she shrank closer to Helen, huddling under the musty smelling blankets.

The door to the closet opened and crashed against the wall. The string that switched on the overhead bulb clicked as he pulled on it. She saw the illumination through the weave of the blankets. He cursed. Then fingers of light flashed into the corner where they lay hidden.

She held her breath, afraid the thudding of her heart would give them away or that she would scream her terror. The door slammed shut and his footsteps moved toward the kitchen.

"You'll have to come out sooner or later, you know." His voice moved away with him and his footsteps faded down the basement steps.

Helen took her hand and pulled her toward the closet door and the thin line of light under it. Pushing it open, she dragged Ellie, blinking, into the living room. They ran quietly across the wood floor toward the front door.

The night was cool after the stifling closet. They streaked across the porch, free, safe. She wanted to run home but no one was there and she knew she'd be scared wherever she went. At the bottom of the steps, he jumped out at them.

"Aha, caught you," he yelled.

She screamed and wet her pants, paralyzed by terror.

He grabbed Helen, who also screamed.

"What's going on?" The neighbor across the street came down his front walk toward them.

"Nothing," Helen's dad said. "This is my kid. Stay out of it."

"I'm not his kid," she yelled.

"We're playing hide-and-seek. You know how girls get scared."

The man paused. "What's your name?" he called, uncertainty in his voice.

"None of your business." Mr. Lindquist turned toward her. "Come on in now. I won't hurt you none."

Reluctantly, she followed him and Helen inside, where he told them to go to bed. She went gladly.

In Helen's room, she asked her, "Do you play hide-and-seek a lot?"

Helen nodded, her face so white and her eyes so dark she looked like a ghost. Something tapped at the window. She threw it open and gulped air.

"That you, Junior?" Unlike them, he apparently had gotten out safely.

"Yeah. I heard him catch you. Throw me a blanket, will you?"

She thought of the blankets in the closet.

Helen took one off her bed, pushed the screen out at the bottom and let the bundle fall silently into the backyard.

"Where you going?" Helen whispered into the night.

She heard no answer. "What did he say?"

"Nothing." Helen tossed her a clean pair of underpants. "You can wear these tonight."

She blushed and changed out of her wet clothes while Helen's back was turned. Scared to go to the bathroom alone, she asked Helen to go with her.

They got into bed together and lay with arms and legs touching. Her mind flew in all directions, so that she couldn't concentrate on any one thing. It kept coming back to when Mr. Lindquist jumped out of the bushes at them. She shivered uncontrollably.

"Are you cold?" Helen asked, putting an arm over her. Her breath warmed Ellie's cheek.

She didn't know what she was. "No."

"Don't tell no one about this."

"I won't," she promised. "Does your mom play hide-and-seek with you?"

"No. Saturdays and Sundays are different. Stay over one of them nights."

She said nothing, but she swore to herself that she'd never spend another night in Helen's house. If Junior could sleep outside, even though it'd be spooky, she could stay alone in her own house.

Helen's dad came for her in the night. Instantly awake, Ellie heard the door open, his footsteps pad across the floor, his low imploring voice. Strung so tight she thought she'd fly apart. She pretended to sleep but stayed awake and jittery till Helen returned alone with that funny smell clinging to her.

She awoke to daylight and Helen's mother calling them downstairs.

"Your mom's home," she said and Ellie shot out the door with a quick good-bye.

XV

In the morning, as before, Helen is gone from the bed. Rain splatters the sill and Ellie closes the window. She pulls on her clothes, smelling coffee in the making. Helen and the dog look at her as she enters the kitchen.

"I took him out," Helen says.

"Thanks." Pouring herself coffee, she sits at the table with Helen.

"Are you coming over Thursday?"

"I'm not getting much work done, Helen, and I need to go home, collect my mail and make arrangements if I'm going to stay here any longer."

Helen's face brightens. "You're coming back?"

"I'll come back but I don't know how long I'll stay." Thinking they're skirting something important, she says, "Helen, you have a family and I'm sure you have lots of friends . . ." She leaves the sentence hanging.

"I know, but something's missing. I thought it was you."

"Why would it be me?" she asks.

"I don't know." Helen squints at her through the steam. She feels a little shock of connection.

Helen's eyebrows arch in question. "I can go away and never see you again but I don't think that's what either of us want."

"What do we want?" she asks.

Helen looks away. "Forget it. It's a stupid idea."

"Are you going to tell me what it is?"

"Maybe when I see you again. We'll see. Thursday? Overnight?" Helen says.

"Okay. I'll leave for Milwaukee from your place on Friday."

After finishing with the third manuscript on Wednesday, she calls Helen and leaves a message on her machine, saying she can't come the next day, she's leaving early for home.

On Thursday morning, while packing a few things for the trip, the doorbell rings, sending Bitsy into a barking frenzy. Looking through the small, oblong window expecting to see Lyle on the other side, she's shaken to see Helen instead.

Briefly, she considers pretending she's not home but how can she with Bitsy making so much noise? She opens the door and looks at Helen through the screen. The dog shuts up and the silence seems as loud as the barking.

"Can I come in?"

"I'm packing."

"I thought so." Helen opens the screen and lets it slap shut behind her. Never breaking eye contact, she shuts and locks the door before gently backing Ellie into the nearest wall.

The wainscoting cuts into Ellie's hips as Helen presses her against it. Her legs lose their strength. Her arms lie uselessly at her sides. She is once again ten years old.

Helen's green eyes seem to ask permission as she slowly leans forward. Her lips are pliable, her tongue almost a query.

101

Ellie's heart beats wildly in her throat. She feels as if she's melting into the wall. She can't breathe and develops a sudden headache. If this is excitement at its most extreme, she will die from it. She pushes Helen away enough to free her mouth. "I can't—"

"Come on." Helen takes her hand and leads her to her mother's bedroom.

"No. Not there."

"Then here," Helen says, turning into the guest bedroom across the hall.

It is different than it was with the woman from the Y—gentle yet intensely personal. Helen undresses her, stacking her clothing on a chair. She shivers and covers her breasts as Helen piles her own clothes on top of the others. They stand for a moment on one of Ellie's grandmother's braided rugs as if unsure what to do next.

Helen raises one eyebrow and asks, "What can't you do?"

"I couldn't breathe." Afraid to look lower than Helen's neck, she sees her anyway. The porcelain skin that has always been covered, the breasts she envied as a girl, the pale nipples, the red, curly pubic hair. She turns her head away.

"I've never done this before," Helen whispers and kisses her on the cheek.

Ellie barks a laugh. "You could have fooled me."

"I think you're cold. I am." Helen takes her hand again and Ellie feels foolish at having to be led to the bed.

Once under the covers, she loses some of the paralysis that overwhelmed her when Helen came through the door. She lies on her side, legs drawn up, arms still crossed over her breasts.

"Turn over. I'm good at massages."

Helen kneads her neck and shoulders, working her way down her body till she reaches her thighs and calves. Worming under the covers, Helen rubs her feet. She talks quietly as she does these things.

"For a while I thought I'd be a masseuse. I even took some classes. How am I doing?"

She mutters something affirmative, but she is less relaxed than she was before Helen started the massage.

"It's true. I never did it with a woman. I was waiting for you. I thought we could finish what we started all those years ago. I thought you liked it. You acted like you did." She slides a hand between Ellie's legs. "You feel like you do." She snuggles closer, her breasts soft against Ellie's arm, her fingers moving slowly.

She shudders at the touch, spreading her thighs a little, and Helen laughs quietly into her ear. The slow teasing movement elicits an almost painful pleasure. She raises her hips off the sheet.

"Turn over," Helen whispers.

She does. Desire makes the rest easy. Helen's hair falls on her face and she threads the fingers of one hand through it, kissing Helen as if it's the natural thing to do. With the other she explores Helen's body—the warm skin, the full breasts and hips, the curve of belly. There she pauses for a moment before slipping her hand between Helen's legs, her fingers already in motion.

Afterward, they quietly hold each other before shyness sets in and they fall away to lie on their backs. She realizes the sounds she heard were the two of them as they gave way to passion. Her heart still hammers wildly.

"Wow," Helen says after a short silence. She says it again and throws an arm over Ellie. "I never guessed it would be like that. Did you?"

"No." She knows she could do it again, right then. She looks at Helen, whose hair lies on her shoulder.

Helen meets her eyes and smiles. "You're something else."

"Me? You started this."

Helen's hand begins to move. "I think I need practice."

When they finally get up and dress, it's afternoon. Ellie is starving. They eat lunch at the kitchen table, eyeing each other over the sandwiches.

"You've done this before, haven't you?" Helen asks.

"A few times. That was the very brief affair I had after Will had his. It was a chance thing."

"Tell me," Helen demands, and she does.

They spend the night, arms and legs entwined in an intimacy Ellie has never known. Nor has she slept so deeply and dreamlessly since she was a child. In the morning, when she opens her eyes, the first thing she sees is Helen, who is watching her.

"I took the dog out," Helen says.

"Thanks."

"I don't want to go home."

"Neither do I, but I must."

Her condo seems alien to her, the air stale. She turns on public radio and opens the patio door to the small balcony that overlooks the green space between the buildings. Bitsy presses his nose to the screen and sniffs. This is all new to him.

She calls Gloria Barnham, her closest friend, the one who brought a carload of friends to the funeral. "Are you really home?" Gloria asks.

"Long enough to forward my mail and pack."

"I'm sorry we couldn't come to the house after the service. I've always wanted to see the place."

"You can visit this summer. It was good of you and the others to attend Mom's funeral."

"When are you coming home for good?"

"I don't know. I felt so lonely there at first with Mom gone and no one else around. Now the condo doesn't feel like home anymore."

"Maybe you just have to stay somewhere long enough for it to feel like you belong there. Am I going to see you?"

"Want to go to out dinner tonight? I don't have anything to eat." Gloria is divorced, her children grown.

"Sure. The corner restaurant?" The one they often go to for fish. It's Friday.

She can't leave the condo without Bitsy. He dogs her footsteps, bumping into her leg when she stops moving, abandonment anxi-

ety in his eyes. She will leave him in the car with the windows cracked. The nights are cool enough near the lake.

The city lights block out the sky, the traffic is stop and go. She is forced to squeeze into a small parking space. These things seemed like the norm once. Now they are annoyances. She tells the dog to be good and locks the door. His barks echo in her ears as she walks away.

When she throws her purse on the seat beside her and sits down with the noise of other diners around her, she realizes how isolated she has been. She orders a glass of wine while waiting for Gloria. Helen has replaced the woman from the Y in her fantasies. She hardly remembers the drive here. When Helen left that morning, they embraced beside her car. Didn't all women hug? Their last kiss was inside the house. Ellie breathed in Helen's scent to take with her.

"Drive careful," Helen called from her open car window.

"You too."

She will call from the condo tonight. She refocuses when Gloria sits across from her.

"You look good, girlfriend." Gloria is short, a little on the chubby side, with wonderful skin, beautiful brown eyes and a lovely smile.

Ellie once was attracted to Gloria. It has always been there, that tug toward women. She just refused to admit it to herself. "So, what's new?"

"Same old, same old. What about you?"

She looks at her friend for a silent moment. Should she tell her? The urge to confide passes when the waitress appears to take Gloria's drink order and ask if their minds are made up about dinner.

"Fish fry," they both say, and add, "Please."

"Our bridge substitute thinks she's permanent." Gloria gazes at Ellie over her wine glass.

"Will the person with the gray Ford Escort please come to the check-out counter?" someone says over the loudspeaker.

Ellie realizes with a jolt that she owns a car of that description. "I'll have to go see." Maybe Bitsy is stuck in the window opening.

"I'll go with you," Gloria says.

They thread their way through the tables to the front desk. "I own a gray Ford Escort," she tells a young man with soulful eyes and acne.

"I'm sorry," he apologizes, "but some people have complained about a dog being left alone in the car. It's barking and they're worried about it getting too hot."

Her face grows hot with embarrassment and she looks around for the complainants. None comes forward. She has never been accused of animal neglect and finds herself explaining. "I brought him because I didn't want to leave him alone in a strange place. The car windows are cracked and it's not really hot outside."

"Let's go and take a look," Gloria suggests. "Don't let anyone clear our table."

Bitsy doesn't at first recognize her and throws himself at the window, fiercely barking when she taps on the glass. "Hey, cut that out."

Unlocking the door, she lets him out. He pees on the car's tire and she puts him back inside. Starting the engine, she turns the air on low. "He should be all right now."

"Let's get take-out and go to your place, Ellie."

"Good idea. We can pop a cork there."

At the condo, they finish their dinners and sit in the wicker chairs on the deck, drinking the wine. The sounds of the city are intrusive—horns beeping, loud voices, laughter and shouting, music. No frogs or owls here, not that she could hear if there were. The lights from the streets and buildings and cars create a twilight effect. No sky filled with stars that she can see.

"You're quiet, Ellie," Gloria remarks.

"Am I? I've got a lot to think about."

"Tell me."

She shifts in her chair but when she opens her mouth to talk, nothing comes out. "It's too early," she says eventually. "Give me a little time."

"Have you met someone?"

"Maybe."

"No fair. You're going to leave me hanging?"

She laughs. "It might be nothing, just a passing whim." The truth is she can't wait to get back to Pine Hill, to Helen.

When Gloria leaves after ten, she calls and Helen picks up on the first ring as if she's waiting by the phone. "I wondered when I'd hear from you."

"I went out with a friend. Sorry it's so late."

Helen's voice is hushed. "It's good you didn't call earlier. Jay was waiting when I got home and left the boys here. He wanted to know where I was last night."

"What did you say?"

"That I was at a friend's overnight. He asked if it was you."

"And?"

"I said yes. I couldn't think where else I'd be."

"What did he say then?"

"Does it matter? He can't tell me who I can see and where I can go." Helen sounds annoyed.

"Did you tell him that?"

"I told him to mind his own business."

"And?"

Helen sighs. "He said I was his business."

She feels cold inside and sort of sick. She knows she won't be staying overnight at Helen's anymore.

"Are you ashamed, Ellie"

"I feel unsafe," she says. "Why? Are you ashamed?"

"I don't know. I can't believe it happened."

"You made it happen," she points out.

"You let it happen," Helen reminds her. "When will I see you again?"

"You'll have to come to Pine Hill, I guess. Don't tell anyone when you're going, or where."

"I won't."

XVI

The doctor put Joey on stronger medication. Ellie heard Mom and Dad talking in the kitchen one evening. Joey was throwing up again, unable to keep even a glass of milk down.

"Next time I'm going to the hospital with you," she said, breaking into their conversation.

They stopped talking and looked at her.

She squirmed under their gaze and felt compelled to explain. "I hate going to Helen's when her dad's home. He scares me." Pure terror washed over her, saying it. If Mr. Lindquist got wind of what she'd just admitted, he'd do something terrible to her. Maybe whatever he did to Helen when he took her away in the night.

"How does he scare you?" Mom asked.

"I don't like playing hide-and-seek with him," she mumbled.

"Hide-and-seek?" Dad inquired. "Where?"

"In the house. They play it at night."

"It sounds like fun," Mom said.

"It's not fun," she replied, remembering the closet.

Her parents looked at each other, puzzled. Then her sister called from the couch and Mom went to her.

"Something funny going on over there?" Dad asked as he had the evening they were weeding.

"It's not funny, Dad."

"I mean strange," he said.

But she didn't know what he was talking about.

The next morning Joey was too ill to go to school, so Ellie waited alone for Helen on her porch. A cool wind rattled the yellowing leaves. Sitting on the swing, she watched Janice and Nancy start toward school.

Helen's red hair caught the breeze and floated behind her on the way. "Do you think your sister's going to die?" she asked.

"No! She's not that sick. She just can't breathe or eat." It sounded pretty serious put that way. She began to feel sorry for herself at the thought of losing her sister so young.

"I wish I could die sometimes," Helen said, jolting her out of her self-pity.

She gave her a startled look. "You aren't sick."

"What's that got to do with it?" she asked, her voice sharp.

"I don't know. I think you have to be sick to die." The subject was too unthinkable.

"Oh, forget it," Helen said with a toss of her head, haughtily dismissing her and her ideas. "I'll tell you a secret if you promise not to tell no one else."

"I promise."

"Junior did it to Janice." Her eyes looked paler in the early light, the color of new leaves.

"Did what?" she asked, puzzled.

"You know," Helen said. "He said he got to first base with her."

She looked blankly at Helen. He was playing baseball with Janice? So what?

"He stuck his finger up her and touched her here." Helen patted her breasts.

Struck dumb, unable to digest this, yet she felt a twinge of excitement. Janice was in sixth grade, Helen's grade. "She's too young," she decided.

"She's twelve, going on thirteen. She's been kept back."

"How old is Junior?"

"Fourteen."

"He doesn't look that old."

"He don't have his growth yet. My dad calls him a runt. If Dad finds out, he'll beat him to a pulp."

She shivered.

At recess she leaned against the fence and studied Janice who, as usual, was hanging around with Helen and her school friends. She realized for the first time that what people do in private doesn't show up like you think it would. Janice looked no different—her hair long and kind of stringy, her skin pale and sort of doughy looking. Her eyes were her best feature, large and a luminous brown, and her mouth was the next best part, sweet and generous.

Janice walked over to her. "Where's your little sister?"

"Home sick."

Janice jerked her head toward the girls clustered with Helen. "Why don't you come over?"

"They don't want me hanging around." She slid down the fence to sit in the sparse grass and wished Joey was there, so she wouldn't feel alone.

"Me neither," Janice said.

She couldn't think of anything else to say and after a while Janice wandered off with a "see ya." The bell rang and they all went inside.

Richard grimaced at her as he took his seat in front of hers. He had brown hair and eyes and clear skin. "You want to play dodgeball at lunch?"

"Sure," she said gratefully. Alone on the playground, she stood out. Without friends, other kids avoided her. They flocked around the popular girls and boys instead. It shamed her to feel so unattractive.

Dodgeball was the only game she was okay at and that was because she was a natural at dodging anything coming at her. She thought Richard wouldn't regret asking her.

She did all right. Once, though, she looked over to see if Helen saw her playing with others and the ball knocked her to the ground. She went down with a thud, scraping her hands and knees but she just brushed them off and continued playing.

When Richard mounted his bike and rode away after school, he waved to her.

"Who's he?" Helen asked.

"He sits in front of me in class."

She smiled, narrowing her sea-green eyes. "Is he your boyfriend?"

"No!"

"What did Janice say to you?" she asked.

She'd forgotten about talking to Janice during the morning recess. "She asked about Joey."

"Why don't you come over when I'm with my other friends?"

She shrugged, unwilling to say she didn't feel welcome. "Want to ride bikes this afternoon?" she asked.

Helen grimaced. "My dad won't let me probably."

She rode by herself, pretending her bike was the Black Stallion. When she saw her dad coming her way, she rode to meet him, got off her bike and walked home with him. She asked him Helen's question. "Dad, is Joey going to die?"

His hand tightened on her shoulder. "Of course not. What makes you ask that?"

"She's sick all the time. Helen says she wouldn't mind dying sometimes." She looked up at him and tripped over the bike's pedal, but not before she saw the worried, sad look on his face.

He steadied her. "Did Helen put that idea into your head?" He was frowning. "Watch where you're going, Ellie."

"She just asked." She chewed on her lip.

"Well, Joey is going to get better. That's what usually happens to kids with asthma. They get over it when they grow up."

"Why, Dad?"

"I don't know but I don't think I want you going to Helen's when her dad's home."

She held her breath, wondering what he knew. "Okay, Dad. I won't. Better tell Joey not to go there either."

Later, she overheard her dad talking to her mother in the kitchen. "Something's going on next door," he said.

"Like what?" Mom asked.

"Why would someone as young as Helen want to die?"

"Her father?"

"I don't know what to do about it. It's just a hunch." Dad's voice was a low growl. "The bastard."

"And to think we made Ellie stay there those nights."

She slipped away before they saw her, wondering what it was her dad guessed about Helen's father and wanting to look up bastard in the dictionary.

"What are they talking about?" her sister asked from her bed on the couch.

"Helen. Dad said we're not supposed to go over there when Mr. Lindquist's home."

"I don't want to anyway."

She stared at her sister. "Are you ever scared, Joey?"

"I'm scared of Mr. Lindquist. He's creepy."

"Did he do something to you?"

"No, but he does things to Helen. Did he to you?"

She shook her head. "What did he do to Helen?"

"Pulled her on his lap and kissed her and stuff. She doesn't like it." Joey's face was pale, her blue eyes nearly black.

"Are you better?"

"Yeah. I'm going to school tomorrow."

"Want to ride on the back of my bike?"

"Sure." Her grin was shaky.

She wasn't really good enough to ride Joey on the back of her bike and neither was Helen. So, they walked most days. She was surprised that Helen would walk with her and Joey when she could ride, but she did.

The rustling leaves turned shades of red and yellow, then fell from the trees in the fall winds. They shuffled through them. The dusty, smoky smells of the season stayed with them till the first snowfall.

On a morning a week before Thanksgiving vacation, winter's first flakes drifted from the overcast sky. The trees stood black and barren, the grass lay brownish and limp, lifeless stalks in the garden shook in the cold wind.

"It's snowing, Joey," she said excitedly, looking out the bedroom window, hurrying into her clothes so that she could help her dad shovel if need be. The snow was melting as it hit the pavement.

She watched the snow falling outside the classroom windows. When they went out for recess, there was some accumulation. She played dodgeball with Richard and his friends. They yelled as they leaped out of the way, dodging the ball but not the dirty slush.

On the way home they scooped snow up in their mittens to taste. It lost its texture on their tongues, turning to ice water.

"Why don't you come over anymore?" Helen asked.

"Why don't you come over to my house instead?" Ellie said, unable to admit that Helen's home was off-limits when her dad was there.

"I'll see what Dad says." Helen slowly climbed the porch steps.

They found Mom in the kitchen, putting away groceries. "Helen wants us to play at her house," Joey said.

"Ask her over," Mom suggested.

"I did," Ellie told her. She missed not being able to spend time with Helen after school but not enough to want to go to her house. "Maybe if you called and asked Mr. Lindquist."

Mom looked at her. "I'll do that," she said and went to the phone. "What's her number?"

Mom calling Mr. Lindquist worked. Helen burst through the front door a few minutes later. The snow had stopped and the elms cast cold, black shadows across the yards as darkness fell. The three of them made popcorn and stretched out on Ellie's bed with a bowl to share.

"Junior broke up with Janice," Helen said. "She was afraid she'd have a baby."

"She's not married," Joey asked. "How could she have a baby?"

"Don't be dumb," Ellie said, hiding her own confusion.

Joey shot back, "I'm not dumb. Mom said you have to be married to have a baby."

"I'm gonna make my boyfriend use rubbers," Helen said.

Ellie pictured the kind of rubbers they wore when it rained and wondered.

Joey looked mystified. "Do you have a boyfriend?"

Helen tossed her hair as she did when she was annoyed. "I'm waiting till I go to junior high next year."

At dinnertime Helen went home. Ellie's dad was scraping the snow off the sidewalk and she went out to help.

Thanksgiving came and went and the month of December crept by. The week before Christmas found her empty-handed with no gifts for anyone. Dad said she and Joey could go in with him to buy a present for Mom but she wanted to find something special for both of them.

Saturday after the movies, she and Helen and Joey stopped at the dime store where the windows were decorated with toys set on fluffy, white stuff that was supposed to look like snow. A bell jingled as they pushed through the door and walked into a wall of warmth. Helen went off by herself, while she and Joey looked on the shelves and countertops for things their parents might like that they could afford.

Helen came by and hissed, "Come on. Let's go."

Down the street, Helen pulled a magazine out of her coat and showed it to them.

"Where'd you get that?" Ellie asked, looking at a picture of Rita Hayworth.

"What did it cost?" Joey squinted at Helen in the hard sunlight.

"Nothing. I took it." Helen tossed her hair.

"That's stealing," Joey said.

Before going home, Ellie and Joey returned to the dime store and bought a bottle of cologne for Mom and shaving cream for Dad. Joey suggested they sneak them out under their jackets but she was too chicken.

Christmas was a high point of the year, partly because they spent it at Pine Hill with their aunt and uncle and cousins. Joey was better in the more sterile atmosphere of winter as long as she covered her mouth against the cold. Their older cousins pulled her up the hill on the toboggan and sometimes took her hand when they skated on the small lake while Ellie jealously watched.

The months dragged after Christmas. They walked to and from school, knocking down and tasting the icicles that hung from the eaves of houses they passed, throwing snowballs at each other or at trees, the wind in their faces or at their backs. By March she was heartily tired of snow and cold, of helping her dad shovel, even of skating on the outdoor rink.

Helen had turned twelve in November. In September she would be in junior high and Ellie worried about whether she would want her for a friend anymore. She'd still be at Roosevelt Elementary.

"You don't come over no more anyway," Helen said, when she asked her. "Think you're too good for my house, don't you?"

"You can come over to mine," she told her, tongue-tied by the truth.

Joey spoke it. "Dad won't let us go to your house because of your dad. He says something funny goes on there."

Ellie grew clammy with horror. "Shut up, Joey."

"Well, it's true," her sister said, and left her standing on the sidewalk with Helen.

Helen's eyes narrowed. It had been months since she'd taken her to the basement, which was all right with her. Just because she couldn't resist didn't mean she wanted Helen to show her the things that men do to women.

"What'd you tell your dad?" Helen asked.

"Nothing." It was the truth.

"Then why don't he let you come over?"

She squirmed under the green gaze until Helen's dad stuck his head out the door.

"What're you doing out there? Come on in."

Mr. Lindquist filled her with fear. "Come over," Ellie whispered before heading on home.

"You come over, girlie," Mr. Lindquist called to her. "It's your turn. We'll play hide-and-seek." He laughed.

Helen didn't come over that afternoon. She watched Helen's room from her parents' darkened bedroom after she put on her pajamas that night. The light switched on and Helen went to the window and looked in her direction. Ellie was sure Helen could see her standing in the dark, spying on her, but Helen pulled the shade and shut her out.

In bed she told Joey she could walk to school herself from now on.

Joey said stubbornly, "I was telling the truth, is all. She wanted to know. Dad said we couldn't go over there when her father was home."

"You don't always tell the truth, you dummy," she hissed into the dimly lit darkness.

"She wanted to know," Joey repeated.

XVII

At Pine Hill, she awakes at ten thirty Wednesday night, startled by the dog's barking and a persistent pounding on the door. Her heart leaps into action, hammering as hard as the person wanting in. She sniffs, wondering if the house is on fire and Lyle has come to warn her.

In her robe, she peers out the small window in the door. Helen looks back at her, making her laugh out loud. She opens to her. "God, you scared me. What a surprise."

Helen kisses her on the mouth. "I came right from work. I was afraid Jay would show up with the kids if I waited till morning."

She glances out the door but she can't see Helen's car.

"I parked by the garage," Helen explains.

"Oh. Do you think Jay might find you?"

"He don't know how to get here."

Wide awake, she asks, "Want something to eat or drink?"

Helen has a small roll-type suitcase with her. "I just want to go

to bed. With you." She pulls it toward the bedroom. "Are you coming?"

"I have to use the john." She wants to brush her teeth. "You go ahead."

"I'll wait. I have to go too."

Helen comes to bed wearing a nightshirt with cats on it.

Ellie grins. "You look so wholesome."

"Don't be fooled by the cats."

In a minute or two, she's looking up at Helen through a curtain of red hair. "You don't waste any time."

"Want me to show you what women do to women or do you want to show me?"

Immediately taken back to Helen's basement, she recalls the hand between her legs, the tongue in her mouth, the disabling excitement. She shrugs out of the memory. She wants to participate, not to observe. Still, part of her watches, amazed that she is in bed with Helen, doing what she's doing.

It's not like it was when they were kids, though. There's a searching tenderness that wasn't there then. No one is going to call them on this right now. No mothers or fathers to answer to. The explaining will be to their children and will come later if the intimacy grows into a relationship.

She asks Helen how they can make this more than a once a week occurrence.

"You can come to my place, that's how."

"Don't you think that's a little risky with Jay already suspicious?"

Helen throws an arm and leg over her. "Let's sleep on it."

However, sleep evades her. She lies awake, trying not to flop around too much. Her thoughts go back to the time Helen lived next door. When Donny came along, Helen latched onto him like a life jacket. It never occurred to her that Helen might be more interested in her some day. Aside from those few times in the basement, which she now understands had more to do with control than sex, Helen seemed headed toward a strictly heterosexual life

and she went on to marry Will. It makes her wonder if this is for real or just an experiment.

She rolls away from Helen and finally falls asleep, only to waken in the morning to Helen's touch. After taking the dog out, she goes back to bed. When they finally get up, it's nearly noon.

"What do you want to do with the rest of the day?" she asks.

"Go back to bed."

She gestures toward the open kitchen window. "It's lovely out there."

"We can see it through the windows."

"Tell me where this is going," she says, when they're again lying on the crumpled sheets.

"Do you mean are we going to live together happily ever after?" Helen asks lightly.

What would her daughters and Jo say to that? What would Helen's sons do?

Helen turns on her side, facing Ellie. "Does it have to go somewhere? Can't it just be?"

"Sure," she says, getting up. "I'm taking Bitsy for a walk. Are you coming?" She jerks on yesterday's clothes, not sure why she's angry, thinking maybe it's because of the cavalier tone.

Helen emits a loud sigh. "Give me a minute." She finds her clothes and pulls them on. "What are you so mad about anyway?"

Faced with a direct question she can't answer, she says, "I'm not. I just want to go outside. So does Bitsy. We've got all night."

Skinny clouds scud across the sky, covering and uncovering the sun, creating sweeping shadows on the ground. It's cooler than Ellie thought. She walks briskly toward the pines on the hill. Waves cross the small lake, pushed by a northwesterly wind, depositing foam on the southeastern shore.

"I need a jacket." Helen heads for her vehicle. "Can I put my car in the barn, just in case?"

"Just in case what?" she asks, her adrenaline kicking in.

"Well, in case Jay finds me. I don't think he knows where to look but he'd make a good detective."

"Why would he be looking?" she asks.

" 'Cause I didn't tell anyone I was leaving. That gets him going."

"Does he tell you every time he goes somewhere?" Sarcasm sneaks into her tone and she wonders if sex gives you rights you didn't have before.

"Hell, no. He doesn't tell me much of anything but I don't ask neither."

"Sure, go ahead." She slides the door open. It softens her when Helen talks like she did when they were girls.

In the pines the wind moans overhead. Bitsy stands down by the lake, lapping water. She sits on the matt of needles.

Helen gently pushes her onto her back, slides cold hands under her sweatshirt and leans over to kiss her.

She turns her head away. "Lyle could show up. I'm not comfortable doing this out here."

"Let's go inside then." Helen sits up and starts throwing pinecones.

"I want to talk a while."

"What about?"

"About what's going on."

"Don't you like it?"

She glances at Helen. "What if Jay finds out?"

"What if your girls find out, or Jo?"

"You said Jay would beat the shit out of Chris and any guy he found him with." Would he do that to her if he knew she was with his mother?

"Not just Jay. Jack, too."

"That makes me want to jump into bed with you."

Helen throws back her head and laughs. "How are they going to find out?"

"Catch us in the act?"

"If we're careful, they'll never know."

"Yeah, sure." She sits up and throws pinecones too. Bitsy catches one and spits it out.

120

"So you don't want to see me anymore?" Helen asks, her jaw set, her head back.

"I just want to know how we're going to manage to keep this hush-hush. I can't go to your place. You have to sneak off to come here. Can't you talk to your sons? Are they really so bigoted?"

Helen shrugs. "They don't trust anyone who's different. Jews, foreigners, gays, environmentalists, you name it. They think like their dad."

"Where were you when they were growing up?"

"I tried. They were sweet till they hit their teens. If they helped around the house, Donny scoffed at them. He knocked them around when they stood up to him. I guess I wasn't tough enough."

"What about Chris and Randy? You said they took your side during the divorce. Didn't he knock them around?"

"Not so much. They pretty much kept their mouths shut and pretended to go along with him. When I told them I wanted out, they said it was about time." She smiles at the memory. "And your girls. What did they say when you left your husband?"

"They didn't understand why and I didn't tell them because I wasn't sure I understood. How do you tell your kids their dad wants out, not because he doesn't love you, but because you don't love him enough?" It depresses her to think about it. She throws another pinecone, this time toward the water. "I'm cold. Let's go back."

After feeding Bitsy, she asks Helen if she wants to go out to eat.

"Are you kidding? I'd eat supper in bed if you'd let us."

At the knock, they jump and the dog rushes to the door. Lyle stands on the porch, a big grin on his face. "Harriet said to invite you to dinner."

"Our dinner is already started. Tell Harriet thanks anyway," she says. "I'll get you a beer, Lyle. You two can talk while I work on dinner."

She hears the murmur of their voices coming from the living room. Lyle brings in his empty bottle and says good-bye before leaving.

"He's something of a pest," Helen remarks when the door closes behind him.

"Want to open a bottle of wine?" She knows how necessary Lyle is. "He plows out the driveway when it snows. He cleaned the gutters for Mom and sometimes mowed the grass. The problem is he just happens to be nuts about you." She wonders if Harriet notices.

"Are you?" Helen asks.

"I'm stunned by this. I have trouble believing it's really happening."

The following morning she watches Helen drive away in a cloud of sandy dust and hugs herself for comfort. Part of her wishes Helen hadn't come back in her life. Then she wouldn't know this ache when she leaves. It doesn't help to realize she'll always be leaving.

It's like a sickness. She can't concentrate on anything. The manuscript lies in her lap where she let it fall after rereading the same page three times. It's a good piece of work, too, from an author whose books she likes.

Sitting on the porch, hearing Lyle's John Deere growling in a field somewhere across the road, she runs to answer the phone.

"Hi, Mom, want some company this weekend?" Liz asks. "I've got someone to take my lab. Katie and I thought we'd drive up tonight. Don't make supper for us. We'll be late. Jo said to tell you she's coming early and wants to go out for fish."

"I haven't heard from Jo."

"She's incredibly busy. At least, that's what she told me."

"It will be wonderful to see you." She hasn't seen either of her kids since the funeral.

"Ditto. I've got to go now if I'm going to see you later."

Pushed to finish the manuscript, she reads it at the kitchen table, a splash of sunlight across the pages. Except for a sandwich and coffee, she doesn't move. When Jo arrives, she stretches and massages her stiff neck, reorienting herself to her surroundings.

"You okay? You look like you're in la-la land. I let Bitsy out. He had his legs crossed he had to pee so bad."

"I'm trying to finish this manuscript. I've got to send it off Monday."

"Want me to leave?" Jo asks. "I'm still packed."

"No. I'm almost done." She remembers the bed in the guest room, the covers pulled over the used sheets, and flushes. "Put your stuff in Mom's room. We'll give the girls the guest room."

"Yes, ma'am," Jo says. "How about a hug?"

Gathering the manuscript, she stuffs it into its box and quickly embraces her sister. "I have to do something."

Hurriedly, she pulls the sheets off the bed in the guest room and throws them in a pile on the floor. Jo comes to the doorway. "Want some help?"

"Sure."

"They can't be very dirty."

"Steven was here."

"He's one of the cleanest persons I know. Showers every day."

She snaps the bottom sheet and it floats above the bed. Jo tucks in the corners on one side and helps with the rest of the making.

"So what's new? Have you just been holed up here?"

"Pretty much. What's new with you?"

"I have another job." Jo's face is telling. Bright when happy, shuttered during bad times.

She hadn't noticed in her rush to cover any telltale tracks. "What? Where?"

"With a magazine called *Wild Wisconsin*."

"What about Pete's magazine?" she asks, momentarily forgetting the name.

"He's moving to Montana. I'm not going."

"Oh, Joey," she says, and Jo's face crumples.

She holds her sister, trying to think of something comforting to say.

"He asked me to follow him to Montana. It would have been a chance for us to start a life together, you know, but his wife and kids are going too."

"I'm so sorry." Even though she thinks Jo should never have begun the affair, she understands the hurt. She comforts her sister until the sobs stop.

Jo plucks a tissue from the box on the bed stand and blows her nose. "I should have listened to you and Steven. Pete is never going to leave his wife and kids and you know, I'm sort of glad about that. I wouldn't have trusted him if he had."

They eat at the Wind Bar and Restaurant where the Wind River flows outside the windows. The trout stream hurries over and around boulders. A fisherman stands in the water, whipping a fly rod.

"I wonder why they never wash the windows," she says.

Jo plays with the straw in her drink. "I feel like a fool, wasting all these years. If he calls, I don't want to talk to him."

She feels a worse fool, getting mixed up with Helen.

Pete doesn't call, nor does Helen. The girls show up around ten, looking surprisingly lively. They enthusiastically tell stories about their lives. She's pleased to know they're happy and apparently on track.

"What about you, Mom? When are you going home?"

"I'm thinking about staying on. It doesn't matter where I live. I can work from anywhere."

Jo says, "I thought you were lonely here."

"What's the difference between being lonely here or at the condo? I'd rather be here in the summer."

"Are you going to sell the condo?" Katie asks.

"I haven't gotten that far yet. I went back to get my mail and more clothes. So much traffic, so much noise, so much light."

They stare at her. Liz says, "I thought you liked the city."

"Sometimes. Do you mind my staying here, Jo?" After all, Pine Hill belongs to Jo as much as to her.

"Nope. Why would I mind? You can take care of the place."

Liz stretches. "Whatever makes you happy, Mom. I'm going to bed."

Katie takes the dog out before following her sister.

"Did we get along so well?" Jo asks when they're alone.

"They fought when they were kids. Remember? I don't think we fought much till you turned thirteen. What was that about anyway?"

"I was rebelling against all that mothering, everyone always worrying about me. You weren't so easy to live with either."

Tripped up by her hormones, she'd snarled in her frustrated sexuality. "I know, and neither were they a few years ago. Liz was stuck on that annoying kid and Katie was boy crazy. I was terrified one or both would get pregnant."

In the night, Jo's crying wakes her up. Turning over, she scoots near and puts an arm around her. "Want me to tell you a story?"

"Like Mom?" Jo asks.

Her heart clenches. "Once upon a time, a girl took a horse from her favorite book and brought it to life. She rode the Black Stallion through the fields behind her house and alongside the car wherever she went. She had a little sister who wanted to ride with her." Her voice disintegrates into sleep.

"Hey, finish the story," Jo says, shaking the arm around her.

Jerking awake, she makes it short. "The girl gave her little sister a leg up behind her and they rode into their dreams." How did her mother stay awake long enough to finish her stories?

"Thanks for taking me with you," Jo murmurs.

XVIII

In the spring, Joey made friends with Janice's younger sister Nancy who became a fixture in Ellie and Joey's bedroom and house. Nancy and Joey skated up and down the block together. Joey no longer tagged after Ellie.

"Nancy's trash," Ellie reminded her one night in bed.

"She's not," Joey said fiercely. "She's my best friend."

Understanding what a best friend was, she said no more.

The school year ended in early June. Helen barely passed and Nancy was held back. Nancy and Joey would be in the same grade in the fall. Ellie moved up to Miss Buxton's sixth-grade class. Miss Albertson said she'd miss her. Richard winked and said he'd see her in Bugsie's room.

The first week after school, she went upstairs to retrieve the gum she'd stuck to the rung of her bed the night before. She'd forgotten the attacks that kept Joey up all night, the medicine that caused her to heave up everything she ate and drank. So she was

startled to see her sitting on the edge of her bed, staring straight ahead, struggling to breathe.

Reluctant to ask, because acknowledging Joey's condition would make it real, she said, "Did you use your atomizer?"

Joey nodded, the look on her face a mix of despair and resignation as if she too had thought maybe the asthma was gone.

She turned and took the stairs two at a time to the living room where Helen waited. "Joey's sick," she told her, picking up the phone to call her mother.

"You can spend the night at my house," Helen said.

She shook her head.

"Maybe I can spend the night at your house," Helen suggested.

She hung up after Mom said she was on her way home. "Think your dad would let you?"

"I'll ask my mom."

"But not unless Joey goes to the hospital," she said. "When Joey's sick, Mom sleeps in our room."

When Mom came home, Ellie and Helen left for their bike ride. There was no enjoyment in it for her, though. They rode to the junior high, which was attached to the high school. At two thirty they started for home, knowing Helen's father would be doing the same.

She climbed the stairs to her bedroom, hoping to find Joey miraculously well but of course, she wasn't. She and Mom were sitting side by side on her sister's bed. Joey's eyes had that hollowed out, anxious look they got when she couldn't breathe.

"The doctor's on his way," Mom said.

A summery breeze swept in one window and out the other. Ellie thought she smelled the new crop of weeds in the garden. Sitting on her bed, she waited with them for the doctor.

Her parents took Joey to the hospital during the night. Mom leaned over her and whispered her name. She told her they would lock the door and she was to stay inside till one of them returned. No one suggested she go to Helen's.

When she woke in the morning, Dad was home getting ready for work.

"How's Joey, Dad?" she asked as he ate a bowl of Wheaties.

He looked out the kitchen window before answering. "Better. Maybe because we didn't wait so long to take her to the hospital this time."

"Next year I can visit her," she pointed out.

He stared at her and she thought she'd said something wrong. "Next year," he repeated.

"Yeah, Dad, after my birthday next summer, I'll be twelve."

He cleared his throat and squeezed her shoulder. "That's right."

"Dad, can Helen stay over tonight? Then you don't have to worry about me when you're at the hospital."

"She can stay over any night as far as I'm concerned." He put his empty bowl in the sink. "Will you hang around the house today, Ellie? I'll be at work, your mother will be at the hospital at least part of the day."

"Sure," she said, surprised. "I weeded yesterday."

"I know. You're a good kid and a big help." He smiled absently and tousled her hair.

She knew his thoughts were with Mom and Joey. She also knew she wasn't good, and worried that he and Mom might discover why.

Calling Helen after Dad left for work, she told her she could spend the night. Helen asked her mother.

"She says yeah. I'll bring my stuff over later."

The day crept by. Mom came home in the morning and went to work for a few hours before returning to the hospital. Ellie dusted, which took about an hour, then lay on her bed and read for another hour until Helen rang the doorbell.

With her was Nancy, looking for Joey.

"I told her Joey was in the hospital," Helen said, "but she wanted to see she wasn't here for herself." To Helen, Nancy was still trash.

"She had a bad attack of asthma," Ellie explained to the little girl with the big gray eyes and snarled brown hair.

"When will she be home?" Nancy asked.

"I don't know. Come back in a few days," she said dismissively.

Carrying a bag with her overnight things in it, Helen pushed past Nancy who turned away. "I'll take this stuff upstairs."

"Can you stay the rest of the day?" she asked, following her to her room.

"Till three, then I have to go home for a while."

For supper that night Dad fixed bacon, lettuce and tomato sandwiches. Helen hadn't returned yet and she asked if he would call her dad and remind him that she was supposed to spend the night at their house.

He said he would. She heard his voice on the phone while she was making herself a peanut butter sandwich for dessert and didn't hear what he said. When he returned to the kitchen with his mouth set, she thought Helen's dad had said no.

"She can't come?" she asked.

"No, she's coming."

"When?" she asked.

"After they eat."

"Will you be here then?" She didn't want Helen's dad walking over here once Dad was gone.

"I'll wait," he said.

After Dad left, she and Helen made popcorn. They forgot to put the lid on the pan and the kernels popped all over the kitchen. Shrieking and laughing, they covered the exploding popcorn and crawled around the floor picking up the escaped pieces.

They ate it while playing cards, War and Eights, in the living room till darkness finally fell. She was thinking that June days go on forever when she heard noises outside, a tapping that moved around the house, a rustling of bushes under the large front window. Spooked, the popcorn turned dry and tasteless in her mouth.

"Do you hear something?" she asked Helen.

"It's probably Junior trying to scare us." Helen looked toward the dining room window where there was a sound like rain on the glass. Only it wasn't raining. It took a ladder to reach that window from the backyard. Neither of them moved to investigate.

Instead, they climbed the stairs to Ellie's room where she pulled the shades and closed and locked the windows. Better to be hot,

she told herself, not finishing the thought. When Helen put on a nightgown, she noticed how her breasts had grown. They were nearly adult-size. Hers were still practically nonexistent. She undressed to her underwear and got into bed without turning off the overhead light.

Helen made no comment. She slipped into Joey's bed and they lay quietly listening. Ellie hoped they were too high for anyone to reach and prayed for her dad to come home. The small alarm clock on the table between the beds read nine thirty.

"Do you ever want to be someone else?" she asked Helen. She longed to be the boy who rode the Black Stallion.

"All the time," Helen said. "Do you hear anything?"

Listening intently, she thought something scraped the side of the house. "Maybe," she admitted, wondering if she should call the hospital. But she'd have to go downstairs to do that.

Paralyzed with fear, she realized someone was coming up the side of the house, and in a moment of self-preservation that unfroze her joints, she jumped up and turned off the light, saying, "Come on."

Helen dove under her bed with her. There was barely room for the two of them to lie side by side, flattened against the cool wood of the floor. She hadn't thought to dust under the bed and felt soft lint balls drifting out of their way.

The scraping became more audible, then something or someone tapped on the window. Helen let out a small, terrified sound. Ellie thought if she started screaming she'd never stop.

Over the pounding in her ears, she heard the neighbors' car in their driveway and someone called, "Hey, that you, Larry?"

And the reply close by, "Yeah. The window jammed."

"Need some help?"

"I got it already. I'm on my way down."

There was the scraping again, the shaking of a ladder and the neighbor's door slamming.

"Didn't sound like Junior to me," she muttered when they felt safe enough to drag themselves out from under the bed. It sounded like Mr. Lindquist instead. In the glow cast by the streetlight, she

saw the look on Helen's face. It was a lot like Joey's expression when asthma had her in its grip.

She fell asleep long after the silence of night settled in and only an occasional passing car broke the quiet.

Waking to footsteps on the stairs, she assumed it was Dad but when their door swung open, she knew it wasn't. She smelled the beer and cigarettes. Helen's dad tiptoed first to her bed and then to Joey's where he shook Helen awake.

He whispered, "Come on now. It won't take long."

But this time she sat up and yelled, "No. Leave me alone. I'm gonna tell."

He left, stumbling down the stairs and out the front door. She heard it close behind him. Without a thought except to lock him out, she swung her legs over the bed and ran downstairs to fasten the dead bolt. Helen was right behind her. They checked the windows on the first floor, which were closed and locked. Neither of them could bring themselves to go down to the basement. Instead, she put a kitchen chair under the doorknob.

Later, she heard the car turn in the driveway, the front door open, footsteps on the stairs. Dad peeked in the bedroom and quietly shut the door. And she fell asleep.

The next morning when she woke up Helen was still asleep. It was strange to see her in Joey's bed. Ellie's dad was already downstairs in the kitchen.

"Hi, kiddo," he said with a tired smile that didn't reach his eyes. "How come there's a chair under the basement door. You kids get scared last night?"

She nodded, tired herself. "How's Joey?"

"Better and better. She'll be home by the end of the week." He put an arm around her shoulders. "This is hard for you, isn't it? Either your mother or I'll be home tonight. Did you have a good time with Helen?"

"Yeah, Dad." Relief made her bold. "Could someone get in the house through the basement?"

"I don't know how, short of breaking a window and squeezing through it or forcing the door. Want to check?"

She nodded, following him down the steep, spider-strewn steps. The walls were made of concrete block, the few windows high and narrow, the black furnace dominated the corner near the back door. Another room adjoined this one. Mom used the shelves that lined its walls as a pantry.

The windows and door were shut and locked. They went back upstairs and Dad stood for a moment in the dining room before walking over to the windows.

"Now one of these is unlocked," he said.

She should tell him, she thought. She would have had he returned home when she'd wished him to last night. If she told him, though, he might never let Helen stay again.

"When's Mom coming home?" she asked, longing to see her.

"Soon as I take her the car."

Helen padded into the room on bare feet, dressed in yesterday's clothes.

After Dad left, Helen asked, "Did you tell him?"

"No."

"Thanks," she said. "You're my best friend."

Suddenly she wished Helen would go home. She was angry with her, with everyone—even Joey, even Mom and Dad.

She leaned into Mom on the couch, wanting to climb into her lap, to feel her heart beating against her cheek, to smell her own particular odor, to know she was safe. She thought she'd heard a high, thinly threaded sound coming from upstairs next door when she'd stepped outside to get the paper for Mom. Rain had begun to fall, and she'd stood on the stoop for a moment before shutting herself safely inside away from any intruding noises.

Helen would get it for telling her dad to leave her alone last night. She'd said she would go home with Helen and together they could tell her mom what had happened, when she saw how fearful Helen was, tense and short-tempered with it. Her mom would believe both of them, she added.

"Ain't you the brave one," Helen had said, her green eyes nar-

rowing and snapping. "You can go home after and leave me to face my dad. You think my mom wants to know about it?"

"But won't she make him stop?" She didn't know what happened when he took her from her bed but she knew instinctively that it was bad, something you didn't talk about.

"She can't make him do nothing. She's scared of him," Helen had said scornfully.

"Mom, could Helen live with us if she wanted to?" she asked, her voice muffled under her mother's arm. Even with the windows shut on that side of the house, she was sure she could hear Helen.

"No, sweetheart," her mother said. "She has a home and parents of her own." She gave her a hug. "And we don't have room."

"Her dad's bad, Mom."

Shifting on the couch, Mom lifted her chin so that Ellie couldn't avoid her eyes. "How is he bad?"

She squirmed, consumed with fear that whatever she said would get back to him. "I don't like him."

"Just because you don't like him doesn't make him bad," Mom said gently. "What did he do?"

"He takes Helen from her bed in the night," she said, holding her breath, waiting for her mother's reaction.

Mom's face colored. "I'll talk to her mother."

"He'll get me, Mom, if he thinks I told." But now that she'd broached the subject, it gushed from her. "He came through the dining room window last night and into our bedroom. She wouldn't go with him and I heard her screaming when I went to get the paper."

Her mother sat very straight and still, staring at her. All the color drained out of her face. "You have such an imagination, Ellie. You probably heard your dad coming home."

"No, Mom, I know when Dad came home. I was awake. It was later." She didn't know which was worse—her mother disbelieving her or Helen's dad finding out she'd talked. Then she remembered the neighbor. "Ask Mr. Hayden. He saw Mr. Lindquist on the ladder by our bedroom window and thought it was Dad."

Getting up, Mom went outside and stood on the stoop in the rain. Ellie went with her, both of them sheltered by the overhang,

133

listening for sounds from next door, hearing none. The rain fell through a windless night, pattering on the walk and roof. She took her mother's hand, felt her answering squeeze.

"It won't help to tell her mother. She won't believe you and she's scared of him too." If Helen lived with them, she'd be safe as long as Mom and Dad didn't go away.

Mom couldn't or wouldn't sit down for longer than a few minutes when they went back inside. She kept looking out the windows at Helen's house and then walking aimlessly around. Ellie wanted to sit next to her on the couch, to lay her head in her lap. She was so sleepy, her eyes closing and snapping open.

"You need to go to bed, honey," Mom said after a while, finally noticing her.

"Come with me," she begged, fear spurting through her. She was sure Mr. Lindquist would know she'd told on him, that he was lurking outside right now, listening.

Her mother looked at her absently and she wondered why she wasn't there in her eyes. "We'll both go to bed," Mom said.

"Don't shut the door," she said, falling asleep with her mother beside her. Mom would leave her bed when Dad came home. There was no sickness to keep her there, only Ellie's fear.

"I won't."

She slept through the night, never hearing Dad's return or Mom telling him what she'd told her. The next morning it was on his face and in his words, though. He was on the phone talking to Mr. Hayden when she stumbled downstairs. And he nodded affirmation at Mom when he hung up. They both looked haggard, their faces sort of caved in.

"Your mother and I think it would be best if you went to stay with Grandma and Grandpa Poole," Dad said.

"Can Helen come with me?" she asked, forgetting that she wasn't going to take Helen to Pine Hill again.

"I don't think so, honey," Mom said. "Joey will be going with you. It would be too much for your grandparents to ask them to look after someone else."

134

XIX

On Sunday, after her daughters and Jo leave, Ellie calls Helen. The phone rings until the answering machine kicks in and she hangs up. Settling down with a new manuscript, she sets a goal of fifty pages. When she looks up the sun has moved to the other side of the house and the living room is dim.

Bitsy whines and she stands and stretches. Outside, she waits on the porch, willing the phone to ring. She's done all she can to settle the estate and has turned it over to the lawyer in Cedar Creek who drew up the will. She's thinking maybe she should live in the Fox Cities—not on Elm Street, though, where she lived next to Helen. There the elms died from disease and were removed to make room for four lanes. She'll look at renting rather than buying. Monday she'll call a realtor friend and list the condo in Shorewood.

When the phone finally rings, it's dark out.

"I called earlier but didn't leave a message," she tells Helen.

"I wondered why I hadn't heard from you. I went to visit my dad."

She stiffens. "Oh."

"He's pathetic, Ellie. He don't know where he is or who I am."

"So why do you go?"

"I don't know. Because I feel kind of sorry for him, I guess, ending up like this. He doesn't have any money left, so it's not a fancy place."

She clams up. Her mind screams, *he abused you*, but Helen knows that.

"How was your weekend?"

"Nice."

"Come on, Ellie. If you'd just go see him with me, you'd understand."

"Understand what?"

"He's not the same man. He has to wear a helmet because he bangs his head against the walls. He keeps asking me who I am. Everyone there asks me who I am every few minutes. They can't hold a thought in their heads." Helen changes tack. "Can you come into town tomorrow?"

"I thought we agreed I wouldn't do that, that you'd come here instead."

"I can't. I'm working during the day tomorrow. I get off at five. You can stay overnight."

Temptation chips at her better judgment. "And what if Jay finds out, or Jack?"

"They won't. I told Jay I won't be able to babysit on Thursdays anymore. He's pretty pissed."

"You could bring the boys here," she says. "I'd show them how to catch snakes and turtles." Not frogs, though. They're too fragile.

"Yuck. Not unless I have to. We won't have any privacy with them around."

"It's a way to see each other and take care of the boys."

"You won't see me if you're catching snakes and turtles."

"Save me the Sunday paper, will you, Helen?"

"I'll have to get one first."

136

"Will you do that?"

"For you anything."

She phones Gloria to tell her of her decision.

"What's his name?" Gloria demands. "Why can't he move here?"

"I'm not moving because of someone else. The Fox Cities are closer to Pine Hill and Pine Hill is too isolated to stay there all the time," she explains.

Unconvinced, Gloria says she knows there is another more compelling reason for Ellie to consider moving and wants to know who it is.

Ellie remains mum. Even though she admits to being rash, to acting on a whim, Gloria's persuasive reasons to put the move on hold fail to change her mind.

She calls Lisa Murchasek, the agent who sold her the condominium, on Monday.

"I'll mail you the contract. You can fill in the blanks," Lisa says after they discuss the terms of the sale. "I need to measure the place. Gloria has a key, right?"

"Yes. You need to tell me what you think I should ask. You know what I paid for it."

"Bridge won't be the same, or Friday night fish. Have you talked to Gloria about this yet?"

"I called her yesterday."

Working into the afternoon, she puts a few things into her backpack around four and throws it in the backseat with Bitsy's bed and the bag carrying his food and bowl. The dog loves riding in the car and jumps in.

She arrives at Helen's small house before Helen does. A truck is parked in the driveway. Continuing around the corner, she parks at the lake a few blocks down the street. The water is dull under a cloudy sky. Waves roll against the shore.

Getting out, she puts the dog on a leash and walks to the water.

Bitsy laps a drink. Sitting on the park bench with a donor's name engraved on the back, she opens up her book. Forty-five minutes pass before she loads the dog in the car and drives to Helen's.

The truck is gone. Helen comes out of the house to greet her. "I thought you weren't coming. I called your house."

"I've been here close to an hour. I went to the lake and read, hoping whoever owned the truck in your driveway would be gone when I came back."

"Jack. He dropped in for a few minutes. I hadn't seen him in a while."

"Four boys and no Donny Junior?" She goes into the house with Helen.

"Jay is a junior but I didn't want to call him Junior like my brother and I didn't want to call him Donny like his dad. Donald seemed too big for him when he was a baby. So I nicknamed him Jay and it stuck."

"No chance anyone else will drop in?" she asks.

"We put both cars in the garage. If we don't answer the door or phone, nobody will know we're here." Helen starts closing blinds.

The darkened room brings to mind Helen's house on Elm Street. "Maybe you could just close the front blinds. I'll take my bag upstairs. I can go there if someone comes." It occurs to her to wonder why she's here if she feels the need to hide.

When she comes downstairs, Helen hands her a drink and the Sunday paper and goes into the kitchen. "Seafood Alfredo okay?" she asks.

"I'll help."

"Relax. Read the paper. I'll be there in a minute."

She turns to the classifieds and scans the columns, checking the apartments that sound attractive and reasonable.

"Don't you get a paper?"

"*The Milwaukee Journal.*"

"Why'd you want this one?"

"I'm apartment hunting."

Poking her head around the corner, Helen stares at Ellie. "You're what?"

"Apartment hunting."

"Here?"

"Yes."

Emitting a little squeal, Helen goes to Ellie and throws her arms around her neck. Her hands smell of the shrimp she has been peeling. "You're coming home? For real?"

"I put my condo on the market today."

Looking astonished, Helen sits on the arm of the chair, her hands now clasped in her lap. "What made you decide to do that?"

"This is closer to Pine Hill than Shorewood." She smiles and shrugs as if this is reason enough.

"We have to celebrate. I'm so excited." Starting toward the kitchen, Helen turns and asks worriedly, "Are you sure this is what you really want to do? I don't want you to be sorry."

"I'm renting, not buying. It'll be easy to move if I don't like it."

"You could live here with me."

"Oh, sure. What would Jay and Jack have to say about that?"

"I'd tell them I could use the rent money."

"I've got a household of stuff. I need a place of my own."

Over dinner, Helen asks, "When are you moving?"

"After the condo sells. Places sell better when they have furniture in them."

"Why'd you want the paper then?"

"Because I want to see what's out there."

After cleaning up the dishes, Helen takes her hand and pulls her toward the stairs. "We can watch TV in bed."

As soon as they're in the bedroom, though, the phone rings. Ellie jumps at the sound.

"Ignore it," Helen says. "The machine can answer."

"I'm not ready to go to bed," she says, but she is. She's just not sleepy. She wants to feel Helen's warm skin against her own so badly that she attempts to hide the desire, thinking it unseemly.

Later, curled around each other, warm and wet and relaxed, they hear the front door open, the shout of the boys, Jay's deep voice.

Without a word, Ellie jumps out of the bed, gathers her clothes

and the dog and dives into the closet, where she struggles to dress among the hanging clothes and shoes lined up on the floor. A thin line of light between the doors and floor provides illumination. Claustrophobic and panicked, as if she's playing hide-and-seek again, she squats to clamp a hand over Bitsy's snout when the door opens.

"Are you sick, Ma?" Jay's voice is accusing. "Why don't you answer the phone?"

"I was napping and don't jump on the bed, boys," Helen says. "Wait downstairs, while I get dressed."

The door closes and the questioning voices of the boys along with Jay's gruff answers fade down the stairs. When she tries to ease a cramp in her leg, Bitsy manages to get a small "woof" out from between her fingers.

Poking her tousled head in the closet, Helen promises, "I'll get rid of them. Are you all right in there?"

"Yes." She swears she'll never come to Helen's house again if she can just leave without Jay knowing she's there.

In the front hall, Helen and Jay argue. Somewhere in the house, the boys shout. "Leave the cat alone, Sonny," Helen calls, then says, "All right, I'll take them Thursday, but you're going to have to spend some time with them yourself from now on. They're your kids, Jay. They need you. Why don't you take them to see Grandpa?"

"I won't take my kids near him and don't you neither. You know what that old man used to try to get me do, Ma?"

There's a hush before Helen says, "No, what?"

"He used to try to get me to suck his dick, that's what."

"Why didn't you tell me?"

Ellie can almost hear the shrug. "I didn't do it."

"And the other boys?"

"He tried Jack. I don't know about Chris and Randy. I never left him alone with them."

"Goddamn him!" Helen wails. "I thought you were safe, being boys. I'm sorry, Jay. You should have told."

"Who would've believed me?"

"I would."

"What'd he do to you, Ma?"

The boys are back, the confessions over. "Come here, guys, give me a kiss. I'll see you on Thursday."

The front door opens and shuts. Helen's lighter tread comes up the stairs. Her hand is clamped over her mouth when she enters the bedroom.

Ellie has managed to get into her clothes. She opens her arms.

"My boys, even my boys," Helen says, her voice toneless.

"Let's go to a motel," she urges, holding Helen close. "We can talk there." Tightly strung, her heart hammers everywhere.

Bitsy whines, bringing her back to reality. Hotels and motels don't allow dogs. "I forgot about the dog. We have to stay." She mutters, "I can't do this again. We'll have to meet at Pine Hill."

Helen gives her a blank stare, as if she hasn't heard. She plunks down on the double bed. "I left my boys alone with him. What was I thinking?"

"That they were safe because they were boys. It wasn't your fault. A pedophile is a pedophile. Sometimes it doesn't matter what sex the child is."

"I wanted him to love me." Helen looks at her, her green eyes imploring. "He never loved anybody, did he?"

Ellie shakes her head. Sitting next to Helen, she rocks her.

XX

Mom talked to Mrs. Lindquist. Ellie didn't know what she told her. Helen said nothing changed. But Mom went out of her way to be nice to Helen, asking her to stay to dinner, to sleep over. If Helen couldn't live with them, then the next best thing was for her to spend time at their house instead of her own and this is what Mom did for her.

Ellie asked Helen the day after she heard the thin screaming if she'd gotten it.

Helen tossed her head and said, "There's ways to get out of punishments."

"How?" She asked for future reference.

"Not for you. You don't know what it is to get it," she said with disdain.

This was when Mom was talking to Helen's mom. Ellie and Helen sat on Ellie's stoop in the warm sunshine and watched the two women on Helen's porch. Mom's arms were clasped across her chest as if she was holding herself together. Mrs. Lindquist's hands

fluttered up and down, sometimes flying to her mouth. The two of them looked toward her and Helen and back at each other.

"What are they talking about?" Helen asked.

"Last night," she answered.

Helen turned her emerald gaze on Ellie. "You told?"

She shrank from her expected anger.

Instead Helen sighed. "It won't do no good."

Dad stayed with her after work that night while Mom went to the hospital. He and Mom had talked earlier about confronting Mr. Lindquist. Ellie pressed up against the door frame, listening. Dad said he couldn't let Helen's dad get away with breaking into the house and scaring Ellie and Helen half to death.

"If you want to help Helen, you won't make him mad because he'll take it out on her," Mom replied.

She knew he was thinking about what to say because he picked up the phone and put it down again. Finally, he dialed.

"Mr. Lindquist, this is Larry McGowan. My daughter says someone was trying to get into the house night before last when your daughter stayed over. I thought you should know that I notified the police."

"Did you, Dad?" She asked when he hung up.

"Of course," he said. "Mr. Hayden said he saw someone on a ladder and thought it was me. But we don't know for sure who it was, do we?"

"No," she said in a small voice. Even though she'd told Mom it was Mr. Lindquist, she hadn't actually seen him on the ladder.

"The police will give Mr. Lindquist a call."

Would they call her too, she wondered.

"You won't be alone anymore, Ellie," Dad said, going back to his paper, snapping it open. A lock of hair hung over his forehead.

Joey came home on Friday. She looked so fragile next to Nancy. Nancy stood in the living room, sturdy and already brown, pulling nervously on her fingers.

"Can you play?" she asked Joey, who had gone straight from the car to the couch and gazed at them out of huge eyes.

"Something quiet," Mom suggested.

"I'll get the paper dolls." Ellie found them in a box under Joey's bed and took them to her. "You can have mine too." She'd outgrown any kind of dolls.

"Thanks," Joey said.

There was a knock on the door and thinking it was Helen, Ellie went to answer. A policeman stood on the stoop.

"Mom, Dad," she called.

Ellie and her dad went outside to talk to the policeman who asked her questions about the night Mr. Lindquist was sneaking around the house.

Her heart thudded like a wild thing, banging against her ribs, causing her breath to come in gulps.

"It's all right, Ellie," Dad said with alarm, patting her on the back, which made her feel worse.

"It must have been pretty scary," the officer said to her. "Do you have any idea who it might have been?"

She shook her head. She'd never tell, knowing what she knew now—that no one could protect Helen from her father, not even Mom and Dad. Nor would they always be able to shield her from Mr. Lindquist. It was late morning, so Helen's dad wasn't home yet.

"I talked to your friend, Helen. She didn't know who it was either," the policeman said. "Good thing your neighbor came home. Too bad he thought it was you on that ladder, Mr. McGowan."

Dad nodded but he looked at her as he shook the policeman's hand. As the police car backed out of the driveway, Dad said, "Your mother told me Mr. Lindquist came to your room."

"Yes," she whispered. "He comes for Helen. Can't you stop him, Dad?"

"Not unless Helen tells, and even then, maybe not." He sat on the stoop and patted it. "Your mother's right."

"How, Dad?"

144

"The more time Helen spends with us, the less she's at home." He smiled at her, but his eyes remained serious. "She's lucky to have you for a friend."

She stayed on the stoop when he went inside to eat lunch before going back to work. For once she wasn't hungry.

When Helen came over, the first thing she asked was, "Did you tell the cop?"

"Tell him what?"

"That you thought it was my dad climbing around on a ladder. He's not that stupid. He came in the front door."

"The front door was locked. He climbed in the dining room window."

"You didn't see him," she said, her freckled face red and angry. "It was too dark."

"I heard him."

"That's not the same as seeing him." She was at her haughtiest and her blind defense of her dad drove Ellie crazy.

She jumped to her feet, wishing she had told on Helen's father. "Next time I'll tell."

Helen backed down, her anger suddenly gone. "Want to go in the basement?"

"No." Although her legs went weak as always, she was too angry to give in. "I want to go for a bike ride."

She and Joey avoided Helen's house when Mr. Lindquist was home, and Mom and Dad never left them alone at night.

Helen came over one morning in late June to confide that she had a boyfriend, a friend of Junior's.

"I didn't know Junior had any friends," she said jealously, not wanting to share Helen.

"He's sixteen."

"A junior in high school!" So much older than Helen!

Helen made a scornful sound. "Donny don't go to school. He works in the mill. I'm going to quit as soon as I can too."

Sometimes Ellie pretended an indifference to learning,

although she knew without actually being able to say why quitting school was not an option for her, that she would finish high school and go on to college. It was the first serious rift between them, one that appeared to be insurmountable.

"He's got a brother you might like," Helen went on. "Want to meet him? He's not that old."

"How old?"

"Fourteen maybe."

She wasn't even eleven and not interested in boyfriends. She wanted to be a boy, so that she could do all the things that boys do. Too many doors slammed shut if you were a girl. But the thought of Helen leaving her behind was unbearable. She shrugged. "I guess."

They rode their bikes to the cemetery at the edge of town where the two boys waited, sitting on the grass next to a motor-bike.

Donny was the older of the two, the one interested in Helen. He wore a torn, black T-shirt and faded jeans over his scrawny body. His hair, which he flung back periodically in a sullen fashion, hung over shifting eyes and acted as a veil to hide bad skin. His ears stuck out and a cigarette hung from his lips. He stared so intently at Helen's breasts when he asked her what took us so long, that Ellie followed his gaze. She couldn't imagine what Helen saw in him.

"I don't have a motorbike," Helen said in a sappy way, tossing her hair so that the red highlights caught the sun. "Want to give me a ride?"

Before Donny roared off with Helen behind him, her arms clutched around his waist, Helen introduced Allen to Ellie.

Ellie panicked, wondering what she would say to Allen.

The boy sat in the grass, pulling it out by the handfuls, glaring at her. He took a pack of cigarettes from the pocket of his T-shirt, shook one out and lit it.

"Where do you go to school?" she asked.

"I hate school. I'm gonna quit soon as I can," he said sullenly,

then asked suspiciously as if he'd somehow been tricked, "How old are you anyway?"

She considered lying, but didn't. "Almost eleven."

He scoffed and smoke trickled from his lips. "You're just a baby." Jerking his head in the direction the bike had taken, he added, "So is she."

"She's twelve and a half," she told him, indignant for Helen.

"Yeah. So? I'm fourteen." His hair was lighter than his brother's, but just as lank, and his skin erupted with pimples.

"Big deal. It's just a number." She couldn't help her age. "I rode here with Helen to keep her company. That's all."

He gave her an appraising look. "Yeah? Do you like to kiss?"

She'd never kissed anyone except her parents, grandparents and Helen. She sure didn't want his tongue in her mouth, if that's what he meant. "I only kiss people I really like," she said, trying to sound convincing. She stood with one leg over her bike.

He flicked the stub of cigarette into the gravel driveway, leaned back on his elbows and laughed. "You ain't never kissed anyone except your mom and dad, I bet."

"It's none of your business."

Unfolding himself, he stood up. Even shorter and skinnier than his brother, he was taller than she was. She put one foot on the pedal, ready to flee, but he did nothing but stretch, revealing a protruding belly button.

"I suppose they're necking somewhere," he said with disgust. "I shoulda stayed home." He stomped around in a little circle. "Want to look at graves?"

That was the first interesting thing he'd said. "Sure." There was nothing better to do.

"My grandpa's buried here," he told her, and before she could think of something sympathetic to say, he said, "Somebody shoulda shot the bastard. Served him right."

"What'd he do?" A sliver of shock rippled through her. She knew what a bastard was now, after looking it up in the dictionary.

"He used to beat my grandma and my ma when he drank. Ain't

a day go by he didn't get drunk." He sounded angry, his bad grammar tangling his tongue.

"Is your grandma alive?" she asked.

"Yeah. She married someone else who beats her now. So did my ma."

"She's not married to your dad?"

"My ma? Nah. He run off when I was little. No-good son of a bitch. We ain't seen him since."

"Where's your grandpa's grave?"

"Here." He kicked a marker at their feet. It read Lyle Norman and under it 1895–1939.

"He wasn't very old," she said for lack of anything else to say. Her grandparents were in their late fifties. "You weren't very old."

"I remember him beating on my ma and grandma and my uncle threatening to kill him."

"Did he kill him?"

"Didn't have to. He dropped over dead the next week." He looked toward the road. "Where are them two?"

"I better go. Tell Helen I went home."

"She ain't safe with him." He grabbed her arm. "You know what he'll do?" He pulled her to him and gave her a sloppy kiss, which smelled of cigarettes.

She pushed on his chest and stumbled backward, wiping her mouth, her heart beating wildly with alarm. "Don't."

The motorbike purred into view, Helen's red hair floating behind her as she clutched Donny. Ellie heard her laughter.

"I'm going home now, Helen," she told her when Donny turned off the engine and they could hear again.

As if she'd forgotten all about keeping track, Helen asked, "What time is it?"

Donny looked at his wrist. "Almost two."

"I've got to go." She looked scared.

He reached for her. "What's the rush?"

Pulling free, she righted her bike. Ellie was already on hers, waiting for Helen to push off.

"See you. Thanks for the ride."

They started off with Donny and Allen keeping abreast, the motorbike wobbling at a slow speed as Donny and Helen shouted to each other over the noise of the engine.

"Meet you tomorrow," Donny said.

Helen stood up, pumping to gain momentum. "Okay."

"You coming too, buddy?" Donny asked his brother.

"You?" Allen shouted at me from his perch behind Donny.

"I don't know. Maybe." Allen had said Helen wasn't safe alone with Donny.

Helen stopped her bike for a few minutes to tell Donny to meet her at River Park, but Ellie kept on riding.

"You gotta go with me," Helen said as they stood on the lawn the next morning. "I told them you was coming."

She had sort of said she was coming too. "Okay, but just this one time."

When they reached River Park, Donny and Allen were sitting on a bench near the entrance. Beyond the expanse of trees and mown grass flowed the river, lazy and wide at the mouth to the lake.

"Come on, Red," Donny said, taking Helen's arm and propelling her across a high, little bridge to a small island where they disappeared from sight.

"Don't waste your time watching them. They're laying in the grass behind a bush. He's gonna try to feel her up."

Angrily, she asked, "How do you know?"

"He told me."

She ached at the thought of Donny's hands on Helen. Although she didn't know what "feeling her up" meant exactly, she knew it was what Junior did to Janice.

A cluster of swings and seesaws and a large sandbox stood nearby. Allen sauntered over to a swing and sat down, idly kicking the dirt underneath, moving back and forth.

She sat on one of the corner seats of the sandbox. Somebody had left a small rusted shovel and a bucket behind. She began making a mound of sand.

Allen filled the bucket with water from a nearby hand pump and poured it over the pile.

"Hey," she protested.

"Now you can do something with it," he said.

Together they constructed a castle with turrets and a moat. They took their shoes off and she dug her toes into the sand, feeling the heat of it.

With a cigarette dangling from his lips, his jeans rolled up, Allen carried water to keep the sand wet enough to mold. By the time Helen and Donny returned, they'd built a small town around the castle's moat.

Donny waded into the sandbox and kicked it apart. "Time to go, kids."

"What'd you do that for?" she protested.

"I ain't no kid," Allen said, sounding sullen again.

"Well, you act like one."

She knew then and there she hated Donny. Brushing her hands off, she said a pointed good-bye to Allen, got on her bike and rode off.

"Hey," Allen called after her. "You coming back?"

She pumped furiously, speeding toward home. Helen never caught up.

Helen always wanted to be with Donny, even though he lost his temper when Helen was late or said she couldn't meet him. He said if she loved him she'd be there no matter what.

Why Helen loved a scrawny, bad-skinned, bad-tempered, not-very-smart boy escaped Ellie's understanding. Helen said she knew he loved her and that's why she loved him. When Ellie asked her how she knew, she said it was because he wanted her to spend all her time with him.

"He's not even cute and he's not going anywhere. He won't even finish high school," Ellie argued, rephrasing her dad's words—"No one goes anywhere in life, not without a high school diploma."

"He is too cute and he wants to marry me," Helen said hotly.

"He's only sixteen and you're twelve." She felt desperate, knowing she would lose Helen forever if she married Donny.

Helen tossed her hair in annoyance. "We'll have our own place. You can visit."

"I won't come. I don't like him." He wasn't any better than Helen's father but she didn't say that.

"I thought you were my friend, my best friend."

She gave in a little. "Well, maybe when he's at work I'll come."

Helen began regularly meeting Donny at the park and going off with him on his motorbike. She went with Helen when she knew Allen would be there.

"Where do they go?" she asked worriedly one morning in late July when Helen had been meeting Donny for over a month.

Allen shrugged. "Don't know."

"What do you think they do?" she persisted, as they were stood on the island throwing stones in the river.

Allen looked at her like she was stupid. "What d'you think?"

"I don't know. Kiss?" She felt she had to know.

"More than kiss. Don't she tell you nothing?" His black eyes were flat.

Her pulse caused her face to flush. "She wouldn't let him." If Helen didn't want her dad to do whatever he did, why would she want Donny? Why would it be different? She thought of Helen kissing Donny's pimply face, of him pushing her against a wall and sticking his tongue in her mouth and his hand between her legs, and her throat filled with her breakfast. "I don't believe it," she said.

Allen shrugged. "It don't matter what you think."

XXI

She tells herself this is a mistake, that they'll never be safe together. She has lesbian friends who hide their relationships from their families but not because they fear for their safety. Lying in bed, holding Helen, she finally stops listening for a key in the door and begins to doze.

"Nothing changes, does it?" Helen says, startling her. "It's like we're kids again."

"We're still in the basement," Ellie responds sleepily, knowing that she still feels the need to hide.

"But it's the way we are, Ellie."

"Are we? Really?" She is so sure at times and so unsure at others.

Helen turns toward her, throwing an arm over her. "I am."

"Are you sure it's not because of your father and your marriage?"

"Hell, no. When I lost you after I married, it was like losing my

arm or something. I'd dream of lying in bed with you instead of Donny and his stinking feet."

She laughs. "Because my feet don't smell bad?"

"Because I missed you. You were part of me. I feel peaceful when I'm with you."

"That could define best friends." Ellie wishes she were as sure of this. Instead, she's on a seesaw—missing Helen when she's gone, questioning what they're doing when they're together, wondering why the sex is so exciting, knowing it will be almost impossible to give up. Peaceful doesn't describe the way she feels around Helen. She wants to talk to Steven.

Anxiously listening for a truck in the driveway, a key in the door, she sleeps lightly. Whenever she wakes up, Helen is awake too.

"Why did you give them keys?" she asks when the clock reads four and the sky starts to lighten.

"Don't your girls have keys to your place?" Helen begins a half-hearted caress.

But neither is willing to risk getting caught in the act. "Yes," she admits, "but my girls aren't going to beat you up."

Helen giggles. "I don't think my boys would hurt you either. They'd holler a lot, is all."

She feels a chill and pulls the blanket over her.

Before driving home she makes a call and looks at several apartments. Most have cheap dark woodwork, small kitchens, brown carpeting and no space for a washer and dryer. The hallways smell of cooked meals and few have covered parking, much less a garage.

"There is a place I think you'd like." The rental agent—a slender, carefully made-up woman with dyed blond hair whose high heels sink into the carpeting—makes Ellie feel frumpy. "It's recently vacated and hasn't been repainted yet but it's almost a thousand square feet."

The apartment building holds twelve units and is set among

trees on a quiet street. It requires a key to open the front door. No food smells linger in the hallways.

The manager unlocks the door and they step into a sun-flooded room with French doors that open onto a balcony. A counter separates the kitchen from the living room. There is space for a table and hutch along the wall. The two bedrooms are across from each other down a hallway, along with a large bathroom.

"There's room for a stacked washer and dryer in the bathroom but there are large coin-operated ones downstairs." The tall, pale, curly-haired manager glances at his watch. "I live here. It's very quiet. Will you lock the door when you leave? I have to go."

"We won't be long." The rental agent promises, then turns to Ellie. "They'll want the first and last month's rent."

"Let me think about it," she says after going through the rooms again, trying to imagine her furniture in them, knowing that it won't all fit.

"Sure. Give me a call anytime. A month's rent will hold the place for thirty days."

During the drive to Pine Hill, she wonders if she made a mistake suggesting Helen bring the boys with her.

"Don't tell Jay how to get there," she warned, shivering as she imagined him showing up on her doorstep.

"I have to tell him I'm taking the boys away."

"Do you have to tell him where?" As a parent, she knew she would want to know where her kids were.

"I'll just say it's a place where I used to go when I was a kid and that it's a surprise. He doesn't care as long as he doesn't have to take care of them. You said we should come, that you'd take them turtle and snake hunting. Remember?" Helen made a face.

"I know, and I will, but . . ." She didn't finish the sentence. She has already said it.

⁂

She calls Steven that evening. "I've got to talk to someone and you're the only one who knows."

"Wait. Let me change clothes, pee and fix a drink. I'll call you back."

The phone rings a few minutes later. Flopping in the chair in the living room, she answers. "That you, Steven?"

" 'Tis me, sweetie. I'm all ears."

She fills him in on what has happened. "What do you think?"

"I think you should run, not walk, away from all this. It isn't worth the hassle."

"Helen's coming on Thursday with her grandsons. I can't just call it off. Last time I tried to slip away to Shorewood, she came here and it all began. We ended up in bed."

"So that's how it is," he says.

"She thinks she loves me."

"Are you sure it's not lust on both ends?"

"I don't know if I'm in love, in lust, or if I just love her as a friend. Anyway, I don't quite believe any of it. It seems unreal when I'm away from her but sort of natural when we're together."

"What about her sons? How dangerous are they?"

"They're scary. How can we build something on top of all that stacked baggage? It'll fall down on itself."

"That's what usually happens, Ellie. Are you ready to tell the girls and Jo?"

"No." She's ashamed, like she was when she was a kid. "I don't know how. They don't have a clue."

"Well, invite Helen when they're around, so they can get to know her."

"She works on the weekends. Maybe during the summer." Perhaps by then it'll be over. "I put the condo up for sale."

"You what?"

"I looked at apartments when I was at Helen's this weekend."

"Before or after you hid in the closet from her son?"

"After." She smiles, waiting for his next words.

"I don't know, Ellie. Moving is a big decision. Are you thinking or just chasing your dick?"

"I don't have a dick."

"Look, this is all new to you, give it some time to develop. Make sure it's the real thing. What have you got in common anyway?"

Were they interested in any of the same things? "I can't find that out if I don't spend more time with Helen." She changes the subject. "How's Leonard?"

"Boxing my stuff."

"Why didn't you call?"

"And tell you what? That it's time to leave before his boyfriend moves in? That's what I mean by not getting in too much of a hurry. Leonard and I jumped into bed on the first date and moved in together after the first month."

"Yeah, but that was years ago."

"I know. I'm coming Friday to see if you're still alive."

Helen and the boys arrive around one. Sonny clutches a toy dump truck and Scott holds a shovel and pail. All three are wearing shorts.

"I see you guys are prepared to move some sand." She smiles at Helen, so glad to see her. "Did you stop for lunch?"

"Yep. We're ready to go."

"Yeah," Sonny says. "Where's the lake?"

Scott falls to his knees to pat the dog, which licks the ketchup off his mouth. "Can Bitsy swim?"

"All dogs know how to swim. Do you?"

Both boys shake their heads.

"Let me grab a sandwich and I'll show you how Bitsy swims."

Swimming, however, isn't one of Bitsy's priorities. She throws pinecones in the water for the dog to fetch. He wades in up to his belly and laps water. "Guess it's too cold for him today."

Carrying a couple of lawn chairs to the shore, she and Helen sit and talk while the boys play on the sandy beach.

"Did Jay ask where you were going?"

"Nope. I told him I'd drop the boys off at his place when we got back. That's all he cared about."

When the boys tire of moving sand, she takes them to the swampy wetland at the end of the lake. At first, they squeal when frogs jump out of their way but soon they're trying to catch them and put them in the bucket. She tries to show them how to gently grasp the amphibians but the boys pull their hands back after the first touch.

Bending over to pick up a small garter snake, she holds it toward them. They reach out with small, sandy fingers, hesitate, pull back. When they finally touch the snake, they jump back with shrieks.

"Look how small it is and how big you are. It's probably scared to death of you."

"We should kill him," Sonny says.

"Why would we do that?" She's horrified.

"Dad would."

"He has a right to live too. I'm going to let him go now." The snake disappears into the tall grass next to the beach. "There's a turtle on the log. See it?"

"Can we catch it?" Scott asks.

She wades into the water, the mucky bottom swirling around her feet but the turtle slides off the log and dives long before she gets there. "Too late."

The boys look relieved. She leads them back to Helen, who eyes the ground worriedly. Ellie laughs.

"We touched a snake and a frog," Scotty yells.

"You didn't!" Helen exclaims.

"The frogs jump out of the pail," Sonny adds.

The day flies by. Still talking about frogs and turtles and snakes, the boys nearly fall asleep over dinner. Helen cleans them up and puts them to bed, while Ellie finishes up in the kitchen. Outside, the sun's rays poke through the pines, giving the trees an ethereal look.

Helen sneaks up behind her and grasps her around the waist. Setting down the dishtowel and pan, she turns around.

157

"Lyle could be watching." She nods toward the window next to the table, seeing a pair of cardinals at the feeder.

"Then he'll leave me alone, won't he?" Helen releases her suddenly when the doorbell rings.

They stare at each other. Ellie expects Jay is at the door and sees that Helen does too.

Should have figured, Ellie thinks when she sees Lyle's head distorted through the rectangular window. "Come in, Lyle. We just finished eating. Would you like a beer?"

"No, I have to get on home." He looks hot and sweaty. "I saw the boys and wondered if they'd like a ride on the tractor tomorrow." He looks past Ellie at Helen.

"Sure," Helen says. "They'll love it."

"Okay, then." He looks pleased. "See you tomorrow."

"Want to sit on the porch and finish off the wine?" Ellie asks as they watch Lyle mount his John Deere and chug for home.

"Let's go to bed," Helen urges.

"Can't we wait till dark?" she says with a teasing smile.

A pool of sweat lies between them. Ellie feels it spreading from her navel to her breasts and belly. The top sheet and coverlet lie heaped at the end of the bed. The bottom sheet is damp beneath them. They strain to close any gaps between them. When they fall away, the suction breaks with a liquid sound. Cooling, Ellie pulls the sheet over their bodies.

"Happy now?" she asks.

"For the moment."

Reaching for the wine bottle, she pours what's left in two glasses and hands one to Helen. The red liquid matches the sky. The sun is a huge orb framed in the windows. It sets the horizon behind the pines ablaze as if the trees are burning.

The doors are dead-bolted, the windows closed and locked, except in their bedroom where they are open. Pine Hill was her only safe place when she lived on Elm Street. She needs it to be a haven, not a stronghold. Leaning back on pillows, she sips.

"When you have your apartment, we can meet there," Helen says.

That will keep Pine Hill hidden.

The next morning Lyle takes each of the boys for a ride on the John Deere, just as he took Helen and Ellie and Joey long ago. Only this time the boys sit on the seat, while he stands on the running board near the clutch. In first gear, the tractor lurches down the driveway and across the road to a field of alfalfa. It circles the perimeter and returns for Scotty. Sonny importantly passes on information to his brother.

"You gotta stay on the dirt road. You can't drive over the hay. That's hay over there."

Afterward, Lyle takes the boys to the barn to show them around. Before they leave, Harriet asks them in for freshly baked cookies.

When it's time to leave, the boys beg Helen to stay. They gaze longingly out the window as she buckles them in the car.

"They're going to want to come back," Helen warns as she hugs Ellie good-bye.

"I know. We'll talk about that later." Of course they'll want to return.

Driving in with the top down on the Mustang, his short hair standing on end, Steven brakes when Bitsy races to bite the tires. "Want to go for a ride?" he calls before getting out.

Sitting on the porch, reading a particularly absorbing manuscript, Ellie looks over her reading glasses at him and smiles. "Later, when we go out for fish."

"How about a drink?" He opens the screen door.

"A glass of water, please. We drank a bottle of wine last night. I'm kind of drunk out and very thirsty."

"You and Helen?" His eyebrows arch in question.

"She brought her grandsons."

"Grandmas in love. That makes a compelling picture."

"Go fix your drink. I'm not a grandma, as you well know, but anyone can be a grandma at a young age, as you also know, especially when she starts having babies in her teens."

He returns and settles in next to her, putting his feet on the railing. "Are you getting a lot of work done?"

"Enough. And you?"

"I've got the client from hell."

"I saw that in the paper. He's a real scumbag. Killed his girlfriend because she was pregnant. Was that the one you hoped would fire you?"

"Yep. So much for defending the poor and innocent."

"He's poor, isn't he?"

"Yeah. Let's not talk about him. Do you discuss everything with Helen?"

"What do you mean everything?"

"The usual. Politics, books, the economy."

"I'll take that drink now." She has never seen Helen read nor heard her talk about politics or the economy except in reference to how many people are traveling.

He fixes her a vodka and tonic. "Did you and Leonard talk a lot?"

"Sure, but not politics or books. He doesn't read much. Just the newspaper and magazines like *People*. He's a little shallow but that's not why I was with him."

"Why were you with him if he's shallow and you didn't have sex?"

"We had lots of sex at first. Don't expect sex to bind you for very long. When the allure is gone, and it goes pretty quick once you're together, you have to have something else to hold things together." He swirls the ice in his empty glass. "Are you hungry? I'm starved."

In the car she throws her head back to the warm wind washing over her. "Were you really worried about me?"

"I think you've lost all reason, selling the condo to live near Helen and her bigoted sons."

She silently agrees. "I have to give it a try, Steven. I don't even know why."

"You're a lustful wench. That's why." He grins.

"No more lustful than you, cousin." She has never thought of herself that way till now.

XXII

"Where do you go with Helen?" Mom asked one day.

"To the park," she said, knowing immediately something was wrong. Mom's back was too straight, her voice too stern.

"I hear Helen has a boyfriend and that her boyfriend has a brother."

"Who told you that?" she asked, dumbfounded.

"It doesn't matter. What does matter is you're too young to be meeting boys. How old are these boys?"

Uncertain about how much Mom knew, she decided it was safer to be honest. "Helen's boyfriend is sixteen."

"Helen is only twelve, isn't she?" Mom asked, looking her in the eye.

She nodded and hung her head, hoping her mother wouldn't ask Allen's age, but she did.

"I don't know for sure, maybe fourteen," thinking he didn't seem any older than she was. All they ever did was talk. Out of the

corner of her eye she saw movement in the dining room. She swiveled but Joey slipped out of view.

"You're not even eleven," Mom said. "You can't see this boy."

That would give her an excuse to say no when Helen wanted her to go to the park, but, perversely, she suddenly wanted to do just that. "Mom, we just talk." She didn't want to admit to playing in the sandbox and swinging and throwing stuff in the river.

"He's too old for you." Mom's lips were two thin lines of disapproval.

"He's just a friend."

"This isn't a discussion, Ellie. I'm telling you you can't see this boy anymore." She went back to putting away groceries. "Now, don't you have something to do?"

Weed, she thought bitterly. Why did she have to do all the work? "It's not fair, Mom. I'm not a little girl anymore." She stood at the kitchen door, one hand on the knob, consumed with self-righteous anger.

"You're not old enough to make those decisions," Mom said.

She knew better than to press her mother. Allen was off-limits, giving him an allure where before she only tolerated him. She stomped out the door and down the steps to the backyard.

Because of the dry spell, the tomato and bean plants looked spindly, the corn dwarfed but the weeds grew in healthy profusion. Crawling along the rows, she ripped at their heads with a vengeance, knowing they'd be poking out of the soil again the next day. The thing about weeds was they adapt, Dad said. Look at dandelions, which hug the ground after they've been mowed a few times. They were the survivors. Every year they planted vegetables but last year's weeds spring up on their own.

Yet she thought dandelions were pretty and loved the wildflowers that grew in the ditches in profusion—the orange daylilies, the blue vetch, the wild roses and all the others she couldn't identify. No one planted them but who could call them weeds. Weeds were unwanted.

She sensed Joey before she saw her standing at the end of the row, waiting. Ellie rocked back on her heels.

"What are you doing here? You want to help?" she said sarcastically.

"You've got a boyfriend?" Joey asked, eyeing her with wonder.

"You got it wrong, tattletale. Helen's got a boyfriend, not me." She was probably kissing him right now, she thought, wondering what time it was. "How did you find out?" she asked savagely.

Joey toed the ground. "Junior's been following you."

"Why didn't you tell me, instead of Mom? Go play with Nancy and leave me alone?"

Tears crept down Joey's cheeks. "She's helping her mother."

"Well, that's what you should be doing." She ripped at a thistle without looking and drew her smarting hand away. "Damn."

"I won't tell Mom you swore," Joey said.

"Tell her," she told her. "I don't care."

"You're mean," Joey said.

"Go away," she yelled.

When she went inside, she looked at the clock and saw it was past two. Helen would be home soon. She made a peanut butter sandwich and went out on the stoop to look for her.

Helen rode up the sidewalk with a grin on her face. "Guess what I got?" She dropped her bike on the grass between their houses and slipped a hand in the pocket of her pedal pushers, drawing out a pack of Lucky Strikes. "Donny gave me them."

"What for?" she asked.

"To smoke, you dummy."

"And where are you going to do that?"

"In the basement."

"Are you crazy? Your mom will smell it." She wanted to walk away but of course, she didn't.

"Behind the garage then." A falling down building that stood in thistles and ragweed at the end of her sloping, weedy driveway. "Here, take these. We'll smoke them later. I got stuff to tell you." Helen pushed the cigarettes into Ellie's hand. "My dad will be home soon."

"What am I supposed to do with them?" she asked, looking down at the pack of cigarettes, knowing if she was caught with them, she was in for it.

"Bury them in the garden."

She dug a hole between the rows of corn and stuffed the pack in the hole, marking the spot with a stick.

After supper, her dad took her aside and told her she couldn't see Allen anymore. She wandered outside and sat on the stoop. Helen came over and asked if she wanted to smoke.

"Where's your dad?" she asked.

"He had to go to a union meeting."

They went around the side of the house, down the steps and through the backyard to the garden where Ellie crawled down the rows of corn, looking for the stick. She found the spot and dug. Brushing off the pack, she gave it to Helen. Helen opened it and lit a cigarette. The tip glowed when she inhaled. Shaking out another, she handed it to Ellie and lit a match to it.

Ellie breathed in and choked on the smoke that burned her throat. It didn't taste near as good as it looked cool. When she finally caught her breath, she lay back on the poking weeds and gazed at the sky. The stars were first appearing and lightning bugs flickered in the garden.

She told Helen she couldn't go to the park with her anymore, that her parents had found out about Donny and Allen.

"Allen likes you," Helen said, blowing smoke in her direction.

"He's okay."

"I kissed Donny a hundred times," Helen told her.

She knew she'd never catch up with a hundred kisses.

Helen tossed her head and her hair spread out around her shoulders. With arms wrapped around her bent knees and a cigarette between her fingers, she looked glamorous.

The distance between them was widening into a chasm so deep Ellie would never be able to cross. She made an attempt to close the gap. "Want to go to Pine Hill again and see Lyle?"

"Lyle's just a baby," Helen said scornfully.

"He's not a baby. He drives a tractor and takes care of the cows and puts up hay." Even she thought she sounded stupid.

Helen's laughter tinkled like chimes in the night. "Donny has a motorcycle and works in a mill."

Crushed by Helen's disdain, she fell silent. Taking a puff on her cigarette, she choked back another cough.

"We go to his house in the mornings when his parents are working."

"What do you do there?" she asked, her heart thudding loud enough to hear.

"We lay on his bed. He rubs against me like we're married."

She wanted to ask Helen if Donny touched her where she had touched Ellie but she was afraid Helen would say yes. Her crotch tingled.

Hearing a rustling at the edge of the garden, they flattened, hugging the dirt.

"Are you there, Ellie?"

Crushing their cigarettes, they waved away the telling smoke.

"I'm coming." Scrambling to her feet, she made her way out of the garden.

Joey stood on the tracks with Nancy.

"You've been smoking." Joey sounded as if she could hardly believe it herself. "Dad will kill you."

From behind her Helen said, "He don't know and you won't tell him."

"I can smell it," Joey said.

Ellie pulled a package of Juicy Fruit gum out of her pocket, put a piece in her mouth, and gave another to Helen. Then she breathed on Joey. "See, no smoke. What does Mom want?"

"She wants to know where you went. It's after nine."

How had it gotten so late, she wondered. It was dark already. The corn whispered behind them as if it concealed someone else.

In the house she went immediately upstairs, brushed her teeth and got into bed. Mom came into the room with Joey and Ellie's heart beat out her guilt, an uncontrollable staccato against her ribs.

"Don't you feel well, honey?" Mom asked.

Joey grinned knowingly at her.

"Yeah, Mom, I just wanted to read my book some."

"I thought you read all the Black Stallion books."

"I'm reading them again." She wished there were more.

When Mom was gone, Joey turned to Ellie and whispered, "You were smoking, weren't you?"

"Shut up," she said fiercely.

"I want to smoke too."

"Are you crazy? You've got asthma. You can't smoke."

"I don't care."

"Don't be stupid," she said. "Go to sleep."

Helen left to see Donny before ten o'clock in the morning, after she helped her mother around the house. She no longer met him at the park, but around the corner. Hearing the motorbike roar off with the two of them on it, just out of sight, Ellie wondered what Helen told her mother.

She sat disconsolately on the front stoop in the already hot sun, bored. Joey was down at Nancy's house, playing with their new kittens, one of the many batches from their mother cat, which ran wild. She knew she should weed.

Some chores get so tiresome they make you lazy after a while. The ground was rock hard and she took the hoe to it, digging up the package of cigarettes by accident. They fell apart in her hand, and she knew she should have put them in a tin. Sensing someone behind her, she turned quickly. Janice stood at the edge of the garden.

"Your sister's sick. I brung her home. She can't breathe."

She'd never seen Joey like this. All her energy was tied into breathing. Her eyes were popping, her chest heaving, her neck stretched taut. She wheezed and gurgled with every breath.

"She gonna be all right?" Janice asked as Ellie dialed Mom's work number.

"Yeah. She'll be okay. You can go."

Janice left and it seemed like hours, not minutes, till Mom got home. "She must be allergic to cats," she said as she came in the door.

"I'm sorry." Ellie had given Joey her atomizer to use but it hadn't helped much.

Her mother gave her a quick hug and dropped to her knees in front of Joey. "You didn't know. I'll call the doctor."

She rode with them to the hospital where a nurse wheeled Joey away in a wheelchair. Mom, walking alongside, threw a smile over her shoulder. Ellie watched till they got on the elevator, wishing she'd stayed home. The waiting room was painted a yellowish white and orange-covered chairs were arranged in groups. No one else was there and she felt lonely.

When Dad burst through the doors, she jumped to her feet. "Dad," she called as he went to the desk.

"Hi, pumpkin," he said. "What happened?"

"Joey was playing with Nancy's kittens. Can I go home?" The hospital was only ten blocks from the house.

"Sure," he said, cupping her face. "Straight home. You can have Helen over but no one else."

"Thanks, Dad."

Outside, the wet heat slapped her in the face. She wished she had brought her skates. It would have been quicker. She knew Helen was home, because her dad's car was in the driveway. These days she almost welcomed Mr. Lindquist being home because that meant Helen would be too. She couldn't go off with Donny when her dad was around. Maybe he would let her come over.

Hungry, Ellie went inside and made a peanut butter sandwich. The house was quiet and she wandered through the empty rooms, eating. When the doorbell rang, she jumped.

Helen didn't wait for her to open the door. She slipped inside and into the hall closet with a finger to her lips.

Ellie stood staring, her mouth full of peanut butter, her heart full of dread. A pounding on the door made her jump anew. She peeked outside and understood.

"Where is the little cunt?" Mr. Lindquist said, pushing his way into the house.

"Who?" she asked, her mouth too dry to swallow.

"You're just as bad, hiding her, knowing she snuck off to see that guy."

"I'm gonna tell my dad."

He laughed as she stared up at him, unable to move, rooted to the floor. His mouth was wet and twisted, his hands huge and half-curled. He wore slacks and an undershirt and nothing on his feet as if he'd run out of the house in a hurry.

"Are you gonna tell him you hid my daughter from me? Where is she, girlie?"

He threw open the closet door and pushed the coats around, while Ellie held her breath. But he didn't find Helen. He was in too much of a hurry. There was a mound of winter hats and mittens and boots and the blankets they carried in the car in the winter lying in one corner. She tried to keep her eyes off it, because she was sure Helen was crouched under those things. He slammed the door shut.

Glaring at her, he demanded, "Tell me where she is."

Flinching, she shrank against the wall.

He took the stairs two at a time and she heard him rummaging around up there, through those closets, dropping to his knees to look under beds as he had when he'd made them play hide-and-seek. She listened, still rooted to the spot. It never occurred to her to run or to call the hospital.

He thudded down the stairs and clamped a huge hand on her shoulder. "Damn you, where is she?"

She shook her head, unable to think or speak, and he threw her aside with disgust and began a search through the rest of the house.

When she heard him in the basement, she thought Helen might come out of hiding, but she didn't. Maybe she couldn't move either.

Suddenly she realized that she should have left, gotten on her

bike and ridden away, because now he was coming upstairs from the basement. She heard his feet on the wooden steps, in the dining and living room, and then he was standing in front of her, his face red and angry.

"You come with me, girlie," he said, grabbing her by the arm. "I ain't a bad man. I won't hurt you none." Then he yelled, "Will I, Helen? I never hurt you."

She tried to squirm away and found her voice. It came out in a squeak. "I'm not going. I'll tell my dad."

Jerking her off balance, he took her next door. Her feet barely touched the ground. She tried to break away but he tightened his grip till her arm ached.

The shades were pulled as they always were when he was home and he threw her on the couch. She looked around for Junior, hoping for once that he'd be nearby.

Mr. Lindquist stood spread-legged in front of her, his arms crossed. "Who's the son of a bitch she's seeing?"

She swallowed and looked at the door, praying Dad or Mom would suddenly materialize. When they didn't, she said in a high-pitched voice, "I don't know. Let me go."

Suddenly he sat down heavily on the easy chair and waved toward the door. "Go on. Get out of here."

Her legs lost their paralysis and she ran—out the door, down the steps, away from her house toward Janice's. There were usually some kids on her porch, but not today. She hammered on the door, a scream in her throat.

It creaked open and Janice's mother stared at her. "What's wrong? Your sister?"

"Can I come in? Please?" She was sure he was right behind her.

Their living room was strewn with toys and clothes and shoes and empty dishes. Even through her terror, the mess impressed her. A hint of pee hung in the air.

"Janice, your friend's here," her mother yelled.

Janice and Nancy appeared in the doorway. "What's wrong, Ellie?"

Their little brothers danced around Ellie, shooting toy guns.

Cuffing the boys as she left the room, their mother said, "Behave now."

She went from being scared to death to being embarrassed. "I'm okay. Sorry."

Nancy asked about Joey.

"I don't know," she said.

"What happened?" Janice asked.

"Helen's dad came looking for her. He went through our house and made me go with him to his."

"He's just mad 'cause she's seeing Donny," Janice said. "My dad gave me a good whipping over Allen. Now I can't see him."

"Why? 'Cause he's too old?"

"No. My dad don't want me to see any boys. I'm his little girl, he says."

She stared at Janice. "Can you come home with me? Just for a minute?"

When they got there, Helen was gone from the front hall closet. Janice waited while she dug frantically through the blankets in the corner.

"I can't stay long," Janice said.

She decided to get on her bike and ride back to the hospital. It would be safe there.

XXIII

When the phone rings in the night, she drops the receiver and scrambles for it in the darkness. " 'Lo."

"Hi, it's me," Helen whispers into the line. "Did I wake you up?"

She glances at the clock on the bedside table. "It's after one, Helen."

"Sorry. I had to talk to you. It feels so lonely. Are you alone?"

"Steven's here. He's in the other bedroom."

"I don't know if I can wait till next Thursday to see you."

"I don't know if I can either," she says honestly. "You could come Wednesday night."

"Maybe I will. It'll be late but it'll give us two nights."

"Is something wrong?"

"The boys have been asking to come back and Jay wants me to babysit Thursday."

She figured that would happen. "Bring them with you." Totally awake now, she senses something wrong.

"Jay said if I'm going to take the boys to your place, he wants directions."

"You didn't tell him how to get here, did you?"

"No. I said if he didn't trust me I wouldn't take the boys anywhere, that he'd have to find another babysitter."

"Is he there, Helen?"

"Randy's here. He doesn't live in town anymore and he's got a construction job here."

"Why doesn't he stay with Chris? I thought they were close." She swallows a nervous yawn.

"Chris already has a roommate. I feel sort of trapped."

"You are. We both are. We can talk when you get here. Okay?" She stares at the ceiling for a long time after hanging up, thinking she may as well have stayed on the line for all the sleep she's getting.

Wednesday, when light sweeps the driveway and Bitsy barks, Ellie goes out into the warm night. The frogs are still in full chorus. Overhead, the black sky holds zillions of stars. A new moon slides toward the west.

Headlights focus eerily on the barn and Ellie hurries to slide open the hanging door. The Cutlass pulls into the open area meant for machinery and stops next to the riding lawn mower. Helen cuts the engine and douses the lights before stepping out of the car into Ellie's embrace.

"No kids?" Ellie says quietly.

"No kids. They'll be disappointed and Jay will be looking for me."

Outside, Ellie slides the door shut. "Did you tell him you'd be gone?"

"I told him I had plans."

"Good for you." She puts an arm around Helen and they walk toward the house.

Helen carries her bag to the bedroom. "I always feel so free here—and safe. It's like a hideaway."

"Let's keep it that way. Want a glass of wine or something?"

"No. I just want to go to bed."

Ellie turns out all the lights before climbing between the sheets. Already there, Helen gathers Ellie into her arms. "What are these?" She plucks at Ellie's undershirt and panties.

Laughing softly, Ellie takes them off.

The ringing doorbell early in the morning sends Bitsy scrabbling toward it in full bark. Ellie pulls on shorts and a sweatshirt and follows him. Thinking it must be Lyle but unable to imagine why he's there, she closes the bedroom door behind her.

Instead, Jay stands on the porch, the boys tugging on his hands. "Come see the lake, Dad. Look, it's over there behind the barn."

Jay doesn't respond. His eyes bore into Ellie's, sending adrenaline racing through her.

Her thoughts go to the bedroom where Helen lies and then scatter. "What are you doing here?"

"Looking for my ma. She's supposed to take care of my boys."

"Don't you ever take care of them yourself?" Her voice shakes.

He points a finger in her face and Bitsy begins to bark again. "That's not your business."

"Come on, Dad. You said you'd go see the frogs and snakes." Sonny pulls on his dad's hand.

"Let go and shut up." Jay jerks his arm away and cuffs Sonny on the side of the head. The boys stare at him, their eyes wide and fearful and disappointed. Silent tears course down Sonny's face. His nose begins to run. "Don't you go bawling, you hear?"

Sonny wipes his face dry with his arm and licks his upper lip.

"Shut that stupid dog up and go get my ma," Jay orders.

Dressed in yesterday's clothes, Helen pushes past Ellie. "Leave the boys and go home Jay, before I call the sheriff."

"You wouldn't do that, Ma," he says.

"Yes, I would." She shelters the boys under her arms.

"I will," Ellie says.

When the sheriff drives in, Jay is long gone. This is nuts, Ellie thinks as she tries to explain what has happened.

Not long after he leaves, Helen backs her car out of the barn and loads her suitcase and the boys into it. She leans out the window, her face closed and determined. "It won't work, Ellie. I see that now. Jay won't change. He won't leave us alone. The boys need to be protected."

Leaning on the door, Ellie urges, "Why don't you stay the night?"

"Yeah, Grandma. Let's stay." The boys shout from the backseat.

"No. Let it go, Ellie." Helen is crying. The boys are crying and Ellie realizes she is crying too. "Don't call."

She stands in the driveway, watching Helen drive away, knowing she's right, that it will never work, and wondering at the same time what she will do with the pain. It's a physical thing, twisting her insides as it did when she lost Helen all those years ago.

Jo and the girls and Steven arrive on Friday for the Fourth of July holiday. The condo is being shown and Ellie has gone to the Fox Valley to look at apartments but she has made no attempt to see or call Helen, nor has Helen phoned.

"So, you're moving back home," Jo says. They lie side-by-side, careful not to touch, in their mother's bed. The night is hot, the covers piled at the foot of the bed. The girls are upstairs and Steven is in the guest room, the one she and Helen slept in.

"It's closer to Pine Hill. I can't stay here all the time."

"Why not?"

"It's often lonely. I wonder how lonesome Mom was."

Jo says quietly, "You gloss over it all during the funeral, like you're at a reunion or something. Then all of a sudden it hits you, that you'll never see her again, never have another conversation, never be able to pick her memory, never have the chance to tell her how much you loved her." Here the words splinter.

Ellie's throat chokes with tears. What Jo has said fills her with

unspeakable sorrow. "She knew you loved her. Don't cry. You'll get all stuffed up."

"Should we spread her ashes this weekend?" Jo turns on her side, away from Ellie.

"It's the time of year she loved best."

Steven finds her alone in the kitchen the next morning. He knows about Jay's appearance with the boys and Helen's abrupt leaving. He pours himself a cup of coffee and leans against the counter. "Why don't you cancel the sale of the condo?"

"I want to live nearer to Pine Hill, Steven." She slept poorly, awakening many times during the night. Exhaustion runs through her veins.

"You want to live near her."

"It's not that small an area. I won't see her."

"I worry about you now that her son knows how to get here."

"There's no reason for Jay to come here if she's not here."

They take their coffee to the lake where the sun lays a golden path on the flat surface. Sitting on the short pier jutting into the water, she calls back Bitsy who starts after a little green heron working its way along the shoreline. The bird squawks and flies anyway.

"Was there someone you really loved, Steven?"

"Do you care that much about Helen?"

"I did when we were kids. This was just confusing. I can't convince myself she's gay."

"Why?"

"I have a preconceived notion of who she is, I guess."

"You probably have trouble convincing yourself that you're a lesbian," he says, and she knows it's true.

"Answer my question."

"Years ago I did," he admits. "He was an attorney, too, but married with kids. We got together at conferences. I suppose he was my great love but he cared more about his reputation and his kids than me."

"Not his wife?" She feels the sun on her shoulders, already hot although it's not yet nine.

"He loved her too. He was one confused guy, like you." He pushes her off the pier into the knee-deep water and jumps in after her. "It's going to be a scorcher."

At the house, Jo and the girls are mulling around the kitchen, discussing breakfast.

"I'm cooking," Steven announces, "and I'm fixing cakes and bacon. Katie, you're my sous chef. You can have that honor tonight, Liz."

"I know you're moving because you want to be closer to Pine Hill, Mom," Liz says late in the day. She and Ellie and Katie are treading water in the lake, throwing a tennis ball back and forth. Bitsy, who has been coaxed into the water, swims from one to the other, following the ball. "But all your friends are in Milwaukee. You don't know anyone where you're going."

"She knows Helen and that other woman who came to Grandma's funeral." Katie spits out water and throws Bitsy the ball. "You have to let him get it some of the time."

The dog swims toward shore with his trophy and drops it in the shallows. Retrieving the ball, Liz tosses it to Ellie. Bitsy plunges back in and swims between them.

"I'm getting out." Gravity drags at Ellie as she emerges from the water. She's been tired since Helen left, spending the nights either lying awake or wandering through the house.

Joining Jo and Steven who are sitting on lawn chairs in the shade, she picks up the book she's reading. But even a good book has lost its power to save her from her thoughts and she stares at the page without comprehending the words.

"Are we going to do it?" Jo asks.

"What?" Steven says.

"Spread Mom's ashes."

"Are we?" They both look at Ellie.

"Let's."

When everyone is dressed, Ellie takes down the urn that has rested on the mantel since the funeral. Again she is surprised at its

177

weight. She holds it out to Jo who shakes her head. "Does anyone want some ashes to save?"

"Can we?" Katie asks. "I've got a locket. It would be like having a part of Grandma with me."

In the end, all but Steven take some of the ashes. Staring at the contents, Ellie tries to resurrect her mother in her mind.

"Maybe we should bury the urn in her garden," Steven suggests.

She remembers Midnight, how Joey said he couldn't breathe with all that dirt on him, how she half-believed her. "We spread Dad's. She'd want to be with him."

They stand around the garden. Weeds and grass grow where the tomato plants and beans and corn once flourished. There should be flowers, she thinks. Her mother loved flowers.

"It's a wonderfully hot day at Pine Hill, Mom, the kind you loved best. We're spreading your ashes so that you can be with Dad. If you're here somewhere, you know my heart. It's where I keep you," she says softly. Taking a handful, she lets them sift through her fingers. The ashes settle on the ground and she holds the urn out to Jo.

Jo flings hers, which also fall at her feet. She whispers but Ellie hears. "We'll be around, Mom. I love you. I miss you."

Across the road, Lyle is cutting hay. The sound of the tractor, so familiar, is somehow reassuring.

Katie takes her handful to the lake and throws it on the water. Liz sprinkles hers in the wetlands. Ellie is not privy to their comments.

When it's Steven's turn, he empties the urn on the garden and Pine Hill. "We'll plant flowers in your garden," he says. "That's what we come down to, fertilizer. I miss you more than I ever imagined."

They bury the empty urn in the garden, marking the spot with her mother's garden fork. "We should get a stone made with Mom's and Dad's names on it," Ellie says, hugging her daughters. Letting go is the hardest thing to do, she thinks. It doesn't matter if it's your lover or your children or your mother.

XXIV

"I thought you went home." Dad was shaking her shoulder in the hospital waiting room.

Ellie sat up. "How's Joey?"

"Better," he said. It was his standard answer. She almost wished she were safe in a hospital bed with her parents watching over her.

Dad put her bike in the open trunk and drove home. Sitting next to him on the front seat, she wondered whether she should tell him about Helen's dad. But he might say Helen couldn't come over anymore. Her main worry, though, was that Mr. Lindquist would come after her.

At home, Dad told her to go pick some lettuce while he warmed up last night's dinner of macaroni and cheese. It was the hour between day and night and she absentmindedly tore the lettuce and put it in a bag. She wondered where Helen had gone when she left the closet.

"What are you doing?" Junior asked from behind her.

She let out a little screech and stood up. "Do you know where Helen is?"

"Dad's beating on her. Hey, don't look at me like that. She asked for it. Better her than me anyway. He don't like her seeing someone else."

"Can't you protect her?"

"She's always been his little girl. He beat me for fun. Not no more, though. He knows I'd beat him back." He gave her a funny look. "Want to go down to the lumberyard?" It was down the tracks where the gardens ended.

"What for?"

"I'll show you a good time." He put a hand on her chest and she slapped it away.

"My dad's watching."

Glancing up at the lighted windows, he gave a nasty laugh. "Your dad don't watch all the time."

She hurried toward the house, entering the kitchen through the side door. Washing the lettuce, she put it in a bowl.

Dad was taking a pan out of the oven and turned to smile at her. "Let's eat."

She wasn't hungry, though, and pushed the macaroni and cheese, a little crisp at the edges and dried out now, around her plate, taking occasional bites.

"What's the matter, Ellie?" Dad frowned, his fork poised in the air.

"Nothing, Dad." She forced herself to take a mouthful. "Dad, you're not going back to the hospital, are you?"

"Don't talk with your mouth full," he said. "I have to pick up your mother when she calls."

"Can I go with you?"

"Sure." He looked at her, actually seeing her, and she squirmed. "Something happen today, Ellie?"

"No, Dad."

In the dimly lit waiting room at the hospital, she sat again on

one of the orange chairs while Dad went to Joey's room to say good night and get Mom. When he called her, she ran to Mom and buried her face in her softness.

"What's wrong, honey?" Mom asked.

"Mom, can I go to Grandma and Grandpa's?"

Mom hugged her so close that her nose was squashed. She knew Mom was looking at Dad. "Why?"

She could barely breathe and still couldn't get close enough. "I like it there. Lyle lets me drive the tractor and milk the cows. I help Grandma with the garden and Grandpa when he delivers mail. You won't miss me."

"Let's get out of here," Dad said, leading the way outside into the warm, pungent night. Everything was growing like mad, engulfing them in a heady sweetness. When she again brought up spending the rest of the summer at Pine Hill, he said, "Your mother and I'll talk about it. It's only a couple weeks till school starts."

"Joey has to come too," she said. Joey couldn't be home alone when Mom was at work.

"We'll miss you," Mom said. "You sure you want to go?"

She heaved a sigh of relief, knowing they were as good as gone.

When Joey was released from the hospital, the doctor sent a syringe and a small bottle of adrenaline home with her. No longer would she have to be rushed somewhere else for a shot or would the doctor have to come over to give her one. But Mom looked at it askance.

"Maybe they better not go to Mother and Father's," meaning Pine Hill. "Who's going to give Joey a shot if she needs one?"

"Don't sell your parents short, Beth. They can do it," Dad said.

"I won't need a shot," Joey said from the backseat. Ellie ignored them because she was riding the Black Stallion alongside the car and didn't want to be interrupted. She'd asked Mom the night before if she could have a horse and keep it at Grandma and Grandpa's, and received an incredulous look.

"Who would take care of it?" Mom had asked.

"Lyle would and I could during the summer. Maybe it could graze with Lyle's cows."

"Maybe we should just forget this conversation."

"We don't even have a dog, Mom," she'd pointed out.

"Joey's allergies."

"She's not allergic to Midnight." Briefly she'd blamed Joey but Joey wanted a dog too.

When they drove up the driveway, Grandma and Grandpa were waiting on the porch as usual but Midnight wasn't with them.

"He died last week. Just went off behind the barn and lay down. We found him there." Tears ran down Grandma's face and dripped off her chin. She was hugging Joey and she hung on longer. Ellie had never seen her cry.

There were tears in Grandpa's eyes, too, and his voice quavered more than usual. "He was a good old dog. We buried him there."

As soon as they could, she and Joey went to see Midnight's grave. They picked the wildflowers that grew too close to the barn for Grandpa to mow and placed them on the raw earth covering the dog. Grandpa had nailed a couple two by fours together and pounded them into the ground to mark the place. Already tiny threads of green stuck up through the dirt.

"I don't want to be put in the ground," Joey said.

"You don't care if you're dead." She hoped that was true.

"What if you wake up? You won't be able to breathe."

"The Indians put their dead in trees. Crows and buzzards pecked their eyes out. Would you like that better?"

"Let's put him in a tree," Joey said. "He can't breathe under all that dirt." She got down on her knees and began digging with her hands.

Lyle came around the corner of the barn. "What are you doing?"

When Ellie told him, he looked at Joey like she was crazy.

Ellie said, "She thinks he can't breathe."

"He wasn't breathing when we put him in the ground. I helped." He looked incredulous. "He'll stink by now, be starting to rot. Come on. Let's go for a swim."

"Yeah, Joey."

When Joey looked like she might cry, Lyle said, "Animals pick the places they want to die. This is where Midnight wants to be."

That convinced Joey.

They spent their afternoons in the water. Ellie helped Lyle with his chores. She worked with her grandma in her garden. And she and Joey went with Grandpa on his mail route. The days flew by, hot and humid and filled with the smells of summer—cut hay, rank weeds, wildflowers like joe-pye weed and sweet clover.

She missed Mom and Dad and Helen, especially at night, but she was safe here.

Mom and Dad returned for them on Labor Day weekend. Monday evening Ellie was sitting on the stoop outside the house when Helen came over. School was starting the next day. She hadn't seen Helen since she'd hidden in the closet.

Helen's freckles had grown darker and bigger. Her eyes flashed a light, clear green. She tossed her red hair and Ellie loved her again, although she didn't want to. "You went away because of my dad, didn't you?" It was an accusation.

She asked, "Where'd you go when you left the closet?"

"Home," she said. "He woulda found me anyways. You ran off and left me."

She felt guilty but she knew she'd run away again. She wasn't brave enough to stand up for Helen. "You weren't afraid?"

Helen sat down next to her. "It don't do no good to be scared. It makes you do stupid things."

"Like run away?"

"I shouldn't have gone and hid in your house. It only made him madder."

"Did you tell Donny?"

"He's gonna marry me soon as he can."

She opened her mouth and shut it again. It didn't do any good to hurt inside when Helen said things like that but she did. She couldn't change Helen. She couldn't change anything.

"I don't blame you for going away," Helen said. "Brought you something for your birthday." She pulled a small package out of her pocket.

They'd celebrated her eleventh birthday at Pine Hill. She unwrapped the gift, a tube of bright red lipstick. Mom would be horrified but she was thrilled because Helen had remembered. "Thanks." She wondered if Helen had stolen it from the dime store.

"You're old enough. Put it on."

"I can't see myself," she said.

"I'll do it." Helen took it away from her. "Look at me."

She raised her face and Helen carefully made up her lips. "You look grown up. Want to go inside and see?"

She was afraid her mom or dad would catch sight of her but Helen dragged her upstairs to the bathroom. Ellie thought she looked like someone had slashed her across the face with a crayon.

"You don't like it," Helen said with obvious disappointment.

"I do," she protested. "I can't believe it's me, is all."

They went into Ellie's room and lay on her bed to catch up on things. Helen told her that Donny was going to take her to school on his motorbike, if she went to school at all. But now his father was working the three to eleven shift, so they couldn't go to his house anymore. She said Allen wanted Ellie to meet him in the park next weekend when she met Donny.

"Mom and Dad won't let me see Allen. He's too old."

"They don't need to know. It'd be fun, the four of us on a double date. Donny's saving up to buy a car. Then we can go anywhere."

She could put up with Allen, he was okay, but she hated Donny. "No."

Helen got up from the bed. "Suit yourself. Maybe Janice wants to go."

"I thought Janice's dad made her break up with Allen."

"He don't want her to be with boys either."

"Why?" Although her parents wouldn't let her see Allen, they never objected to Lyle. It made no sense.

"He don't want to share her," Helen said matter-of-factly.

"Ask her." She almost changed her mind but didn't, even though it hurt to tell her no.

Tuesday on her way to school, she saw Helen meet Donny around the corner and ride off on the motorbike behind him. As she and Helen grew further and further apart, she felt helpless to close the distance between them.

She was again seated behind Richard, who whispered a loud hello.

Miss Buxton, a tall, bosomy woman with hair swept off her neck into a bun, thick eyebrows that met over her nose and startled brown eyes, was their teacher. Her most identifying feature was her overbite. The kids called her Bugsie.

In the afternoon, after Ellie finished writing the required essay about what she did last summer, she pulled her book out of her desk and read it in her lap. She was lost in the story when Bugsie tapped her on the shoulder and held out her hand.

As she gave her the book, snickering rose across the classroom. Richard leaned over his desk, writing diligently. Bugsie wiggled her fingers.

"Your essay, please."

She handed over the sheet of paper, which held her most eloquent writing about Pine Hill with a few lines about taking care of the garden at home. Burning with embarrassment, she stared at her lap.

Bugsie set the book on her desk and tapped it with her fingers. "A good book, Eleanor. It's a wonderful hobby, reading. Keep it up."

She slid down in her seat while Bugsie gathered up the rest of the essays.

After school as she walked to her bike with Richard, the kids in their class passed them in waves.

"Good hobby," one of them said.

"Keep it up," another added.

She ignored them. She liked Miss Buxton but her nickname stuck in her mind. She thought of her as Bugsie.

The next day when Bugsie asked them to read from their essays, Ellie thought she'd die, that she'd melt into a red puddle on the floor. When it came to her turn, the kids snickered. The words on the page blurred.

Miss Buxton came to her rescue. "I'll read it," she said.

She listened, knowing everyone was hearing about Joey's asthma, weeding the garden, putting up hay with Lyle, milking the cows. She wanted to disappear.

"Good essay, Eleanor," Bugsie said. She put the paper on her desk. A big, red A leaped off the page.

On the way out of class, the same two kids who'd made comments yesterday said, "Grab that bale, milk that cow."

"Forget them," Richard said. "They're dopes."

One of the most popular girls bumped her as she passed and sniffed. "Smell a little like a barn around here?"

Stricken, she watched the girl pass with her retinue of giggling girlfriends.

"They'd like you better if Bugsie didn't," Richard told her.

She was glad when Friday arrived. She had no friends at school except Richard. It didn't seem to matter what she did. Bugsie liked it.

Riding home through the dusty smells of fall, Monday seemed a long way away. A few fallen leaves skittered across the road and crunched under her tires. She looked for signs of Helen as she coasted past her house and braked in the driveway. The shades were drawn in her living room.

XXV

Ellie puts money down on the apartment the rental agent was sure she'd like, the one in the twelve-unit building. There isn't enough room in it for all of her things. Some she takes to Pine Hill, some she gives to her girls and Jo and Steven, some to Goodwill. The rest she moves to the apartment.

Gloria makes no secret about her unhappiness with Ellie's move. She thinks it's a mistake and says so but she organizes a good-bye dinner with friends.

The next morning, slightly hungover, with both elbows on the table, clutching a cup of coffee, Ellie tells her friend it's only a separation in miles. "You can visit, I can visit, we can e-mail and phone each other."

"A separation in miles opens a rift that only gets wider with time. Visits and e-mails and phone calls can't close the distance."

Ellie sighs.

"Tell me why you're really going and I'll shut up."

"No, you won't, because no one's in the picture anymore. The truth is that I'm going back home, even though there is no one there anymore. It sounds silly, doesn't it, but I have to figure some things out, things that happened when I was a kid and stuff that happened recently."

She sees the cogs turning behind Gloria's eyes and sighs. "All right, I'll tell you, but you can't tell anyone else," she says, knowing Gloria won't. Still, she gives a spare narrative, leaving out a lot of details.

If the telling shocks her, Gloria doesn't show it. She says, "I understand now. Thanks for sharing."

"What do you understand?"

"You have to finish the story. It keeps getting interrupted."

They box her things in silence for a while, before Gloria suggests they ask some friends over to help. Later, they go out for another good-bye dinner.

She and Steven and one of his friends load the rental moving truck. He drives it and she and the friend follow in their vehicles. After unloading and setting up the apartment, Steven and his friend leave.

"I'd stay the night but he has to get back," Steven says. The friend is waiting in his car. He flashes a grin and gives her a quick kiss. "It's a nice apartment. I approve of it."

She spends the rest of the week emptying boxes and putting things in order. Before she leaves for Pine Hill, she decides the time is right to see Mr. Lindquist. She needs to know if it is true, as Helen claims, that he's paying for what he did or if Helen is just defending her dad again. Mr. Lindquist looms large as the bogeyman of Ellie's childhood. To dispel that image, to know that he can never scare her again, she has to see him. On Friday, she drives to the nursing home where she has located Mr. Lindquist by making phone inquiries.

Weaving between the occupied wheelchairs, she heads for the front desk. One elderly lady with wild white hair grabs her arm with arthritic fingers.

"What's your name, honey?" she asks, her rheumy blue eyes fixed on Ellie.

"Ellie," she says and tries to move forward but the woman hangs on. "What's yours?" she asks.

The woman looks puzzled and let go of her arm but calls after her, "What's your name, honey?"

At the front desk, still surrounded by the elderly, some with walkers, some in wheelchairs, she asks the woman on duty for Mr. Lindquist's room number.

"He's in the Alzheimer wing. Are you a relative?" The woman's smile doesn't quite reach her eyes.

She says, "He's my best friend's father."

"Helen?" She nods. "An attendant will go with you. Mr. Lindquist can be violent."

The attendant, a burly man named Dan, leads her past the people in wheelchairs that line the hallway. The years they've spent living, loving, working no longer distinguish one from another. Some look at her with interest, others have fallen asleep and drool dribbles down their chins.

Her heart began an erratic beat when she parked outside Hopeful Care Center. Now as she follows Dan, she thinks the only thing these people have to be hopeful about is a quick death. She wants to be in control of where she dies, not left to languish in a place like this. When they pause for Dan to unlock the door to the Alzheimer unit, her heartbeat accelerates.

A wailing greets her ears, along with a hammering sound. The halls aren't lined with wheelchairs here. Most patients are in their rooms. Dan pauses at a door and nods at her to go inside. She does.

Mr. Lindquist is sitting on a chair by the window, looking at his hands. He is dressed in gray pants and a gray shirt and wears a helmet. His body is wasted, his skin sallow.

"You have a visitor, Bill."

Mr. Lindquist looks at them vacantly, a frown etched between his brows. His mouth twitches.

She would have recognized him. "Ellie McGowan. I used to be your neighbor."

He gets out of the chair and begins to bang his head against the wall. "Fuck," he yells over and over.

She steps backward.

"Go, go, go," he shouts, still banging his head.

"Come on, Bill," Dan says. "Knock it off." He takes a syringe out of his breast pocket and administers a shot quick enough to avoid the helmet Mr. Lindquist aims at him. Putting his arms around Lindquist, he wrestles him to the bed. "Lie down and rest a while. Your daughter will be here soon."

They go out and shut the door. She looks at Dan. "Will his daughter be here soon?"

"Maybe. Soon is meaningless to him. Most of these people are just bewildered, not recognizing anyone, but some are self-destructive. We have to protect them from themselves."

When she leaves, the wheelchairs fill the hall outside the dining room. She supposes meals are the high points of the day.

She drives away quickly, not wanting to run into Helen. What lingers in her mind is the Mr. Lindquist of her childhood, the tall, muscular man with red chest hair tufting out of his undershirt, a cigarette perpetually dangling from his lips. She compares him to the pathetic person in the helmet and feels no sense of satisfaction. He's still scary, still violent.

Picking up Bitsy at the apartment, she drives to Pine Hill. Spiderwort and vetch bloom in the sandy ditches. Orange and yellow hawkweed carpet whole fields. She waves to Lyle, who is cutting hay across the road.

Changing into her swimsuit, she walks to the lake with a beach towel around her and a book in hand. Grabbing a lawn chair from the barn, she carries it with her. The sun is hot and she drops everything onto the small pier and walks into the cool water. It's

190

early in the afternoon, shortly after three. Steven and Jo won't arrive till around seven.

Thankful that her concentration has returned, she buries herself in books and manuscripts. They are her refuge. When the sun begins to hover over the western end of the lake, she gathers her things and walks back to the house.

That is when she sees the truck parked in front of the house and someone sitting on the porch steps. Bitsy jumps into a running bark, flying toward the intruder, whom she assumes is Jay.

Lyle's tractor is gone from the field. No help there. A glance at her watch confirms that Jo and Steven won't be arriving in the next few minutes. She calls Bitsy, who ignores her. The man dangles his hand in front of the dog and Bitsy shuts up. She walks slowly toward them.

When she's close enough to see the red hair, the man stands up. "Hi. Chris Ebertson, Helen's son. We met at Mom's house."

"I remember. What brings you here?" She can't imagine.

He shrugs. "I was in the area. I wanted to apologize for Jay's visit."

"That was weeks ago." It can't be the reason he's here now.

He looks down at his tennis shoes. His face flushes. "Yeah, well, we're not all like Jay, Randy and I ain't anyway. Jay's ex-wife took the kids and moved to Indiana where her folks live. Jay and Jack are working in Milwaukee." He shuffles his feet, stirring up dust, and Bitsy barks. Hunkering down, he runs a hand over the dog's back. "Protective of you, ain't he?"

She laughs, surprising herself. "More likely, protective of himself. Want something to drink? It's hot."

"Look, I don't mean to butt in. I just wanted to say I'm sorry my brother broke up yours and Mom's friendship." His green eyes meet hers for the first time and she aches for Helen.

"Thanks, Chris. How is she?"

"Okay, I guess."

Before she can ask more, Jo and Steven drive in.

He says, "I better go. You got company."

"You're company, Chris. They're relatives." She introduces him.

Steven's eyes light up as he pumps Chris's hand. "Where'd you come from?"

"This is Helen's son," she says, warning him off.

"You look like your mom," Jo points out. "Where is she?"

"Home, I think. I just came to see her friend here, Mrs . . ."

"Call me Ellie."

"Want to go out for fish with us?" Steven asks. "We can all squeeze into my Mustang."

"I have to go," Chris says, taking a few steps backward. "Nice to meet you." He nods at Jo and Steven. "Bye, ma'am."

"Say hello to your mom," she says.

He climbs in his truck, starts the engine and backs past the other two vehicles and onto the road.

"I think you scared him off," she says to Steven as Jo goes inside.

"He's a hunk. Why was he here anyway?"

"To tell me his brother, the one with the kids, is working in Milwaukee and that the kids moved to Indiana with their mother and that he's sorry his brother broke up my friendship with his mother."

"You haven't talked to Helen?"

"No."

"Well, that's best, isn't it?" Steven takes a long pull of the beer Jo hands him.

"Am I missing something here?" Jo asks.

He sits down and puts his feet up. "You'll have to ask your sister."

Jo turns to her. "Well?"

"There's nothing to miss, nothing to tell." She too sits down. She thinks it odd that Chris showed up at all and wonders how innocent the visit was. Maybe he thought he'd find his mother here.

"Why did you move, Ellie, when all your friends are in Milwaukee?" Jo asks, handing her a drink.

192

"Thanks."

"You told Steven something you didn't tell me, something about Helen." Jo sounds aggrieved. "Is it more than a friendship?"

"It's not even a friendship anymore. Her oldest son showed up and she left. He's a bigoted bully, just like his father."

"But was it more than a friendship?"

She's being talked into a corner.

"Were you lovers?" Jo leans forward and peers into her face before she can look away. "That's what all those trips to the basement were about."

"God, no. Those were her way of acting out the abuse her father inflicted on her."

"Hey, it's okay, Ellie. I just wonder why you came down on me about Pete, when you were having an affair with a woman."

"I wasn't having an affair with a woman." She almost adds "then."

"Don't lie to me, Ellie."

"Then mind your own business."

Jo knows her too well and chips away at her until she puts the story together. "I suppose you knew about this all along, Steven."

"I am in a unique position to be a confidante in this situation," he admits.

"Bullshit. I'm her sister. Siblings are closer biologically than anyone."

"Okay, enough. There never was much going on and there's nothing now, so let's just go to supper and forget it. Can't anyone have any privacy around here?"

"I'll drive," Steven says.

Ellie sits in the back, even though she hates the way her hair blows in her face when the top is down. She can't hear a word they're saying up front.

XXVI

Helen's thirteenth birthday fell the day after Thanksgiving. Ellie took some of her allowance, which had been building up, and on a Saturday rode her bike to the dime store. The leaves were long gone from the trees, burned up in piles along the curbs or caught in the long grass in vacant lots. Her eyes watered from the cold.

She found a gold compact that held rouge on one side and a mirror on the other. Taking it to the checkout counter, she paid the same woman who'd waited on her and Joey last Christmas.

She said, "I remember you. Is this a present?"

"For my best friend," she told her. "She's going to be thirteen."

"Does she have red hair?" She was smiling.

"Yes."

The clerk sighed. "I know her too."

Sighing made Ellie uneasy. When her mother sighed, she thought she'd done something wrong. Now she was sure Helen had been pocketing things from the dime store.

She gave her gift to Helen the Sunday before Thanksgiving on a cold, sunny day as they sat on Ellie's bed. Ellie and her family were going to Pine Hill the Wednesday before Thanksgiving and she wouldn't see Helen on her birthday.

Helen turned the package over in her hands, looked up and smiled brilliantly. "You're my very best friend," she said.

They'd seen little of each other since school began. Helen seldom came over after school, on Saturday mornings she usually managed to slip away to meet Donny.

Helen opened the compact and smiled with delight. Looking in the mirror, she put some rouge on her cheeks. Ellie liked her better without makeup but Helen wore lipstick regularly now. Ellie looked like a little girl next to her.

"I love it," Helen said. "Thanks."

"What are you doing Thanksgiving?" she asked.

"My uncle and aunt and their kids are coming."

"Do you like them?"

She shrugged. "My uncle and my dad get drunk and grab us girls."

"What do your mom and your aunt say?"

"They say it don't mean anything, that they're just drunk and don't know what they're doing."

"Want some popcorn?" she asked.

They went downstairs. Mom and Dad were sitting in the living room reading the Sunday paper.

"Wait here," Mom said and went into the kitchen.

Dad put his section of the *Milwaukee Journal* down, looked at them over the top of his glasses and smiled. When Mom came through the dining room and into the living room, singing "Happy Birthday" and carrying a cake with thirteen candles blazing on top, Ellie was as surprised as Helen.

Helen's lower lip quivered. She blinked away tears and grinned shakily. "Thanks."

Mom gave her a hug and said, "Come on, let's have a piece."

They were sitting at the dining room table, eating cake in the middle of the afternoon, when Joey and Nancy came in.

"Hey, you didn't wait for me," Joey said indignantly.

"Join us then, both of you," Dad spoke up.

Helen and Nancy stuffed their mouths and talked around the food but Dad said nothing. Ellie and Joey looked at each other and said nothing either. The rules were only for them—no talking with your mouth full, no large bites, no singing at the table, no reaching.

"Want to take the cake home?" Mom asked Helen.

"No," Helen said hurriedly, "but thank you."

"You're an official teenager now," Dad commented.

"You can come over whenever you want a piece. You don't have to ask, just take it. It's your cake," Mom told Helen.

The cake disappeared piece by piece over the next couple of days.

When she and Richard lit the cherry bomb and threw it out the classroom window, Ellie thought she would be suddenly popular. But it didn't work that way. She stopped being teacher's pet and became a troublemaker. The cliquey girls still didn't want to have anything to do with her. The popular boys shunned both her and Richard.

Her parents were called to school to confer with Miss Buxton and the principal. She hung her head, knowing she'd caused them shame. It was better to be teacher's pet and now she never would be again.

"May I talk with Eleanor alone?" Bugsie asked at the beginning of the conference.

Her head came up in panic but there was nothing to do but follow Bugsie to an empty classroom next to the principal's office.

"Sit down, Eleanor," she said, pointing to a miniature version of the desk she leaned against. This was a first grade classroom.

She stared at the blackboard behind her teacher and stammered, "I'm sorry, Miss Bugsie."

It slipped out, she never meant to say it, and her mouth dropped a little in distress when she realized she had.

196

Bugsie crossed her arms and looked down and then at her. "Why did you do it, Eleanor?"

Maybe because she'd accidentally called her Miss Bugsie, she whispered the truth. "I thought the kids would like me if you didn't." Her eyes flickered to Bugsie's soft, brown pools and quickly away. She didn't know whether the hurt she saw was for the spoken nickname or because of what she'd just told her.

"And do they like you better?" Bugsie asked quietly.

"No." Tears quivered on her eyelids and she willed them back into her eyes.

"Don't do something you shouldn't to please others. It usually backfires. Please yourself instead." Bugsie straightened up and Ellie started to stand. "Stay here for a while. You can read your book. We'll call you when we're ready."

She didn't know what Bugsie told the others but she went home with her parents a humbler kid. Dad grounded her for two weeks and she didn't care. She wanted to crawl into her room and hide from everyone.

She would have given anything to get back in Miss Buxton's good graces and she tried hard not to think of her as Bugsie. Miss Buxton moved Richard to another desk. Ellie worked hard at anything the teacher asked them to do and managed to get As in everything but arithmetic, and a B in that. But Miss Buxton seldom looked at her anymore. Most of the time, she acted as if Ellie wasn't there.

She felt very sad going home from school in the cold with blue shadows from the trees already stretching across the sidewalks and yards. Once Richard turned up Oak Street, she was alone. Now that the girls were talking to her, she no longer cared. She'd found out how boring they were. All they talked about was boys. She no longer dreaded school, though, because all the kids in her class were friendly to her. She guessed the cherry bomb incident, which she so regretted, had done the trick.

It hadn't worked for Richard. He wasn't popular. Some of the boys called him a sissy. He wasn't, though. Nothing scared him. Why else would he have set off a cherry bomb? All she'd done was hand him the matches.

Helen looked different going into spring that year, older, of course, with a body Ellie envied. Ellie still wore her hair in braids, and her chest was nearly flat. It wasn't just the physical difference that separated them, though, there was a gulf of knowing she couldn't bridge and only sensed. The thought of what was behind it she found vaguely exciting and lonesome. Helen was her only girlfriend.

They lolled on Ellie's bed talking one Sunday afternoon. She told Helen about ice skating with Richard. The winter before she and Helen had skated on the rink near the library. Helen was grace on ice but she had spent her free time with Donny this winter.

"Do you like Richard?" Helen asked.

"Yeah, he's okay. He makes me laugh."

"You're such a kid," Helen said, a corner of her mouth curving upward.

She'd said the wrong thing again. "You're just jealous because Donny's no fun." She'd never seen him smile. Instead, he sneered at everything.

"He is too." Helen frowned and picked at the tufts on the quilt. "What do you do that's fun?"

She tossed her hair. "Ride in his car. We go out on the ice and do spins. Skating is for kids." Donny had bought an old Plymouth Coupe that winter.

She didn't want to talk about Donny. "Did you like Miss Buxton?"

Helen shrugged as if she was bored. "Bugsie? She was better than them stupid teachers at junior high, except Novotski. He reads to us all the time. He read this scary story about a monkey's paw that gave wishes and another about some count stuck in jail."

"Richard and I threw a cherry bomb out the window when Miss Buxton wasn't there." She'd told no one who didn't already know about the incident.

Narrowing her eyes, Helen said, "You wouldn't do nothing like that."

She nodded. "I did."

Helen looked impressed. "What happened?"

"We got in trouble. Miss Buxton really liked me before that. Now she doesn't and the kids do."

"Yeah?" Another shrug. "They probably thought you was a brown nose. None of my teachers ever liked me much."

"It was Richard's idea."

"Is he a fairy?"

"What?" she asked.

"You know. A fairy. A boy that likes other boys. Does he ever kiss you?"

"No." Lots of boys hung around together. "I don't want to kiss him."

Mom called up the stairs. "Helen, you're supposed to go home. Your dad called."

"Want to come over?" she asked.

"I got homework to do," she said, wishing Helen could stay, wanting her to be like she was before she met Donny.

"I don't do homework," Helen said. "Sometimes I don't even go to school."

"Dad says everyone needs to finish high school so you can get a job if you have to."

"My mom didn't finish high school, neither did my dad." Her hand was on the doorknob. "I don't need no diploma to get a job. I can work in the dime store."

"You have to be able to add and subtract and stuff," she pointed out.

"I can do that easy." She opened the door. Joey was standing on the other side. "You listening to us?"

"No." Joey went into the bathroom and shut the door.

She didn't know why she asked. "Helen, does your dad still come and get you at night?"

"What d'you care? You won't even come over."

"Is your mom home?"

"Yeah," she said.

"Okay, I'll come."

Helen smiled, her pug nose crinkling, her teeth straight like her dad's, only white.

They ran to her house through a cold drizzle. The shades were up, Mrs. Lindquist called hello from the kitchen. Mr. Lindquist sat in his easy chair, dressed in slacks and an undershirt, smoking a cigarette and drinking beer, listening to the same football game her dad was. He grabbed at Helen as they walked past him but she spun out of reach.

"Hey, girlie, who said you could come over?"

Helen's mother appeared in the doorway. "He's teasing, Ellie."

"Both you come sit in my lap. Cute, ain't they, Ruth?"

"He don't mean nothing," Helen's mother said. "You girls go on upstairs."

She breathed easier when Helen closed the door to her room. "Where's your brother?" She seldom saw Junior anymore.

"He ain't home much. Want a cigarette?" Helen pulled some Lucky Strikes out of her pocket.

"Won't your mom and dad smell the smoke?" she asked.

"I'll open the window. I do it all the time. My dad can't smell it because he smokes. My mom never says nothing."

Hers would, though, if she smelled it on her. She'd brush her teeth quick when she got home. Taking a cigarette, she puffed when Helen lit it and nearly choked.

Helen laughed. "You don't smoke much." She walked to the open window and looked outside. Rain slid down the glass and dripped on the sill. Her hair hung thick and bright around her shoulders.

"I wish I had hair like yours," she said.

Helen turned. "Let me fix them for you. Sit here." She patted the old wood chair in front of her desk and handed Ellie a mirror to hold.

Helen's fingers pulled at Ellie's hair as she unbraided it. It was black and kinky from being twisted and was as long as Helen's. Shivers ran down her back as Helen brushed it out. She gazed at

her reflection, liking the way she looked, thinking she would ask her mother to let her hair hang loose.

"I like them better this way," Helen said, the cigarette dangling from her lips so that the smoke made her squint as it drifted past her eyes. "You're too old for braids."

Ellie puffed on her Lucky Strike, thinking they both looked cool.

The door opened and they froze. Helen's dad filled the frame, smiling one of those non-smiles. "Caught you. You're big enough to smoke, you're big enough for other things. Give us a kiss. You too, girlie, or I'll tell your dad on you."

Helen crushed out her cigarette in a dish on the desk. Ellie burned her fingers before she did the same. Pulling Helen close, he kissed her on the mouth. Ellie jumped to her feet and tried to squeeze past them but he grabbed her.

"You want a kiss now, girlie?" He smelled like stale beer and the cigarette Ellie had just put out.

Freed from his grasp, Helen jerked on his arms, saying, "No, Dad, no." He let go of Ellie long enough to send Helen flying with a swat to the head but she scrambled to her feet and tugged on his arms again. "Stop, Dad, stop."

He shoved Ellie away then and took hold of his daughter. "Okay, if that's what you want."

Ellie ran, stumbling down the stairs, meeting Helen's mother on the way up. Mrs. Lindquist put her arms out.

"What's wrong, Ellie? What happened?"

"Helen. He's got Helen." She pushed past her, heading for the door. Yanking it open, she slipped on the porch steps, sprawling onto the sidewalk. She was running before she got up, taking off like a runner in a race.

Joey was coming out the front door as Ellie went in.

"Ellie?" she said.

"Don't go to Helen's." She galloped up the stairs to the bathroom. Locking the door behind her, she brushed her teeth until her gums bled and scrubbed her face till it hurt.

Mom knocked on the door. "Ellie? Let me in, honey."

"I'm on the toilet, Mom," she said. "I'll be downstairs in a minute."

Drying her face and combing her hair, she breathed into her hand to check for the smell of cigarettes and went down the steps. Dad looked up from *Life* magazine and smiled vaguely at her. She walked past him through the dining room to the kitchen.

"Need some help, Mom?" she asked.

"You can peel potatoes," Mom said, and she thought it was going to be all right but then Mom asked, "Something wrong, Ellie?"

"No, Mom," she lied.

"Then why are you shaking?"

"I'm cold," she said, willing her hands to be steady.

After supper, which she hardly tasted, she went upstairs, locked the bathroom door and filled the tub with water so hot it took her a while to lower herself into it.

Mom was sitting on her bed when she got to her room. "You don't seem yourself, honey."

She couldn't look at her, so she stared at the window. It wasn't even dark yet. No wonder Mom was wondering if she was okay.

"I'm swell, Mom." That was the word everyone was using at school. "I wanted to read in bed."

"You look boiled. You're all red. Look at me when you talk to me, Ellie."

Mom shifted toward her and wrapped her in her arms. Her face, suddenly wet with tears and snot, was mashed against soft, warm breasts. Mom smelled of the lilies of the valley cologne she and Joey had given her. Ellie longed to be little again, safe in her embrace. But her mother would release her soon, and tomorrow she would return to school and maybe see Helen afterward.

The tears dried, the sobbing lessened, even though she tried to sustain both. She guessed a person naturally stops crying sooner or later. Her mother leaned back and wiped her face with a handkerchief.

Mom was smiling at her. "Growing up isn't easy, Ellie, and the worst part is you have to do most of it on your own. But Dad and I are always here to help you when you ask. You have to trust us enough to talk to us."

It wasn't that she didn't trust them. She'd learned they couldn't protect her from most things. Not from Mr. Lindquist, not from school and what went on there, not from losing Helen to Donny. Just like they couldn't keep Joey from having asthma.

XXVII

Asters and chicory brighten the ditches, while goldenrods and sunflowers nod in the fields. The sun's rays lengthen and mellow as the nights grow shorter and cooler. Ellie spends weekdays at the apartment in town, where she meets Alison McDonald who lives in an apartment downstairs.

Tall, on the heavy side, and younger than Ellie by ten years, Alison begins a conversation one day while they're opening their mailboxes.

"Do you get any interesting junk mail? Mine is always so boring. Coupons for oil lubes, carpet cleaning, Bill's Exercise Gym. Hey, do you exercise? It might be more fun to go with someone."

"When I'm in town, I do. I belong to the Y. Are you a member?"

The foyer traps hot air and Alison's upper lip is damp. "Not since I was a kid but I've been thinking about joining. Hey, speak-

ing of calories, want to go to a wine tasting tonight? It's fun and only costs ten bucks."

"Sure," she says, having nothing else to do.

"I'll reserve a couple spaces. We can order food there."

That night they get a little tipsy and laugh so hard trying to unlock the door to the apartment building, they keep dropping their keys.

Following that night out, Alison knocks on Ellie's door nearly every day after school. She teaches sixth grade and loves the kids, whom Ellie is sure love her back. She and Ellie exchange novels. Because Alison's favorite teacher loved to read, Alison wanted to teach. When she says, "Odds are I can make readers out of some of the kids who pass through my classroom. I already have," Ellie remembers Miss Buxton.

She recalls hanging around the empty playground on the last day of school, waiting to say good-bye to Miss Buxton. When her teacher came outside, Ellie gave her the already wilting lilacs she'd torn off a nearby bush.

Miss Buxton smiled, exposing a touch of red lipstick on her front teeth. "Thank you, Eleanor. I love lilacs. They're so fragrant."

Ellie threw a leg over her bike and blurted, "I'll miss your class." A red flush crept up her neck to her face.

"I'll miss you. It's not every year I have a reader. Reading is good for the soul."

Now she asks Alison if she has favorite students.

"Oh, yes, although I try not to show it. They make up for the little bastards who try to make my life miserable. They have a nickname for me. Want to guess?"

"We had a teacher we called Bugsie."

"She had an overbite, I assume."

"Yes, I called her Miss Bugsie to her face once by mistake. I was forever sorry."

Alison laughs. She has a great laugh, full bodied and genuine. "I'm Big Mac."

Ellie remembers Big Al and thinks how little has changed.

Alison joins the Y and meets Ellie there after school three days a week. They walk on the treadmill, talking to pass the time. Alison perspires profusely. Ellie's eyes sweat. After a half hour, they progress to the upper and lower body machines. Sometimes they eat together afterward.

The leaves turn and fall, dry and dusty underfoot. She walks through them with Bitsy twice a day. On weekends, she drives to Pine Hill if the girls or Jo or Steven are going to be there. Otherwise, she stays in town.

She tries not to think of Helen but knows she's looking for her whenever she's out and about. She expects to see her in the grocery aisles, at the gas station or the Y, on the street, at the mall. She has conversations with her every day, sometimes in her head, sometimes aloud. She wonders if Helen is looking for her around every corner and storing up things to tell her.

Thanksgiving eve arrives on a cold, windy day. Gloria has come as well as Steven, Jo, Liz and Katie. Ellie shopped in town on Monday and drove to Pine Hill from the grocery store. Everyone else arrives Wednesday evening to the smells of bread baking, a fire burning in the fireplace and the sounds of Beethoven's *Ninth Symphony* on public radio.

Congregating in the steamy kitchen, they make drinks and talk. Ellie leans on the counter near the stove, sipping vodka and tonic and listening to snippets of conversation. Liz and Katie vie for her attention, as does Gloria.

Her master's degree achieved, Liz is job hunting. She has an offer with the State Department of Natural Resources, a low-level job in shoreland management.

Katie has been offered a position with the university's literary publication but she's so busy with the professor's research that she doesn't know whether to take it.

With a laugh, Gloria says, "I'll stand in line, Ellie. God knows I

don't have anything exciting to impart. We can catch up on things later."

Attempting to eavesdrop on Jo and Steven's heated discussion, fearing that somehow Pete is at the root of it, she nearly loses the thread of Liz's job worries.

Refocusing, she suggests, "Why don't you accept the offer? Won't it be easier to change jobs from the inside?"

"I was thinking that myself."

"So was I," Katie interjects.

"And why don't you go for the job that gives you the most experience in your field, Katie, the one you really want?"

"Because the research pays."

"What does your dad say?"

"Same as you do. Go for it."

"Then do just that."

Jo and Steven leave the room. Liz and Katie don jackets and take the dog out. She gives herself over to Gloria, who says, "What's new, girlfriend?"

Lying in their mother's bed with Jo, she asks what Jo and Steven were discussing. Gloria is in the guest room. Steven and the girls are sleeping upstairs. It's wonderful to have so much distraction, she thinks, as she puts the screws to Jo.

"He saw me with Pete at a restaurant."

"I thought Pete was moving out west," she says.

"We were having a farewell dinner. Pete introduced me to a friend of his, a really nice guy, but he's recently divorced and I just ended a relationship."

Ellie jumps in. "Go out with him if he asks. You don't have to leap into bed with him. Get to know him."

"I was kind of thinking that but Steven thought I was seeing Pete again. Pete just wanted to say good-bye."

"And how did that go, saying good-bye?"

"How do you think?" Jo begins to cry. "I love him."

"Do you, really?"

"Of course. Why would I have put up with all the bullshit if I didn't?"

"I don't know. It was easy, comfortable, familiar."

"It wasn't easy. Every holiday he spent with his wife and kids. They came first. I fit in when it was convenient."

She and Steven had pointed that out from time to time but she refrained from saying it now.

"Do you miss Helen?" Jo asks.

The wound never heals, only scabs over. Maybe that's how Jo feels about Pete. "Yes," she says into her pillow.

Jo throws an arm around her and sobs quietly into her back until they both fall asleep.

On Thanksgiving, the falling snow creates a picture postcard outside the windows. They bundle up and walk through it as it melts under their feet. Ellie is not ready for another winter.

When everyone leaves on Sunday, she finishes up the cleaning and drives to her apartment. Her heart somersaults at the flashing light on her answering machine but it's only Alison. She returns the call. "Why don't you come up for supper, if you can stand Thanksgiving leftovers."

"I love other people's leftovers," Alison says. "Someone was at the door asking if you lived here when I got home. A guy with a pickup truck. Kind of cute but a little young for either of us."

"Redhead?" she asks.

"Actually, there were two of them but the other stayed in the truck. He gave me a card for you."

She opens it as if it might contain anthrax. On the outside is a drawing of a tail-wagging dog. Printed on the inside are the words *Thank You For a Doggone Good Time*. At the bottom are handwritten XXXs and OOOs followed by Sonny and Scott's names, each letter written in a different color.

She laughs and shows the card to Alison.

"Friends of yours?" Alison smiles.

"I guess so." The card is postmarked Indianapolis with Ellie's

name and Helen's address on the envelope. Warmth floods her. As tenuous as it is, it's a connection.

She spends Christmas with family at Pine Hill—cross-country skiing, eating, drinking and talking.

Jo has taken up with Pete's friend Nathan, a divorced man without children, and she glows in his attention. They sleep in the guest bedroom, leaving her alone in her mother's room. Feeling as if her life stopped when Helen left, she knows it's time to re-start it.

She endures the winter—the cold, snowy walks with Bitsy, waking up to darkness, watching TV when she is tired of reading or working on manuscripts. Alison brings together two friends to make a foursome for bridge, which they play once a week. She also joins Alison's book group. The women range in age from thirties to seventies and meet in each other's homes.

Late on a windy, cool March day, she stops at Woodman's to pick up an avocado, a bag of chips and a bottle of wine. The bridge group is meeting at her apartment in two hours and she's in a hurry.

Over the avocados, she looks up and sees Helen on the other side of the display, looking back. A sensation akin to an electric shock burns through her.

"Hi," she says.

Helen gives her a wry smile. "I knew we'd run into each other one of these days."

"It would have been easier and quicker to call."

"Yeah, but that would start things up again."

A man comes up behind Helen. Tall, wide-shouldered and dark, he's too old to be a son. "Find what you're looking for?" he asks.

Ellie feels nauseous and lightheaded.

Putting a hand lightly on the man's arm, Helen introduces him. "Ellie, this is Rudy."

Rudy reaches over the avocados to shake her hand. "Rudy Gilliam."

His grip is rough. "Ellie McGowan," she responds, and looks at her watch. "I'm running late. I've got to go."

"Nice to meetcha," Rudy says as she puts an avocado in her cart, never mind that it's too hard.

"Same here. Bye."

She checks out near the door where she entered, relieved that Helen and Rudy are nowhere in sight.

That night, distracted, she loses track of the trump count, forgets what has been played and only manages to make her bid because she has an unusually good hand.

"Got something on your mind?" Alison asks as she uncorks the wine.

"I'm sorry. I'll do better. I promise."

Their partners are two gay men, who discuss every hand in detail after it's over.

"You don't have to be kind," she says, setting down the snacks while Alison pours wine. "I ran into an old flame today."

"That is *sooo* hard," Ken says, squeezing her hand. "Was he friendly?"

She laughs. "She, and yes. She was with a man." It amazes her how easy it is to own up to what she has hidden so well.

"Oh, that's even harder," Jerry sympathizes. "No wonder you've been playing like shit."

She laughs again, catching the astonished look on Alison's face. "I promised Alison I'd keep better track of the cards."

"I'm sorry too," Alison says.

Fighting back tears, she gulps a little wine. "Yeah, so am I. Let's play bridge." She has no wish to talk about Helen and Rudy. She's been fighting to dispel an image of Rudy's rough hands on Helen's smooth skin.

When Ken and Jerry leave, Alison lingers to help clean up. Ellie senses she wants to say something about Helen, like how it's

fine with her, but Ellie doesn't want this discussion. Talking would make Rudy more real than he already is.

When the phone rings in the night, she doesn't answer. Her message comes on after four rings, and whoever is on the other end hangs up. Sitting in the darkened room, she looks out the balcony doors. The lights around the parking lot blot out the stars. A sliver of moon, visible in the southwest, hangs over the highway. Tomorrow she'll shop and go to Pine Hill. Why hang around here anymore?

That's what she's been doing, making a life for herself, hoping that Helen will move back into it. She takes Bitsy outside for a nightly tinkle and stands on the blacktop while he sniffs around the bushes at its edge.

She feels a fool for moving here. The breeze lifts her hair, finger-light on her scalp. Whatever is twisting her guts takes another turn. Calling the dog, she goes inside.

XXVIII

Summer was divided into three parts. The headiness of June with three months vacation ahead, dissolved into the long, lazy days of July that continued into August. But after Ellie's birthday, the days slid by with amazing speed and she became a little desperate to enjoy them before school started. It was no different the summer she turned twelve.

On a hot and breathlessly humid day when Mom was at work and Joey was at Nancy's, she got the mower out of the garage. Dad had asked her to cut the front lawn. It wasn't easy pushing the mower, even on flat surfaces, and you had to shove it fast enough or it wouldn't clip the grass. She leaned into it to get more leverage, thinking that Joey could never do this. She'd be puffing and panting in no time.

Helen came outside and together they pushed the mower, giggling over how silly they must look. It was early afternoon when they finished and went inside to make peanut butter sandwiches.

They ate on the front stoop, the peanut butter sticking to the roof of Ellie's mouth.

Crickets chirped in the grass and the aroma of the roses Mom had planted out front a couple years ago wafted their way, sweet in the heat of the day. It was hard to catch a breath of air.

"Let's go up to your room," Helen said, when they finished eating.

It was hotter in her room under the eaves but a fitful breeze blew through one open window and out the other. Ellie turned on the fan and they lay on her bed, their hair stirring where it wasn't stuck to their skin.

"School's gonna start soon," she said.

"I won't be going back for long," Helen replied. "I'll tell you a secret, if you promise not to tell no one."

"I promise," she said, cold inside despite the heat. If Helen said nothing, nothing would change and then everything did.

"I think I'm pregnant." Helen's green eyes clouded over.

"Did you tell your mom?"

She shook her head. "I didn't tell Donny neither. You're the first."

"How do you know for sure?" Maybe she was mistaken.

"I missed my period. I never missed it before."

She hadn't either since hers had begun. She picked at a thread on the bedspread as the hot air from the fan blew on her neck. Then she rolled over and stared at the ceiling. "What will your dad do?"

"I won't tell him nothing," she said. "I won't even tell Donny till I'm sure. Don't you tell no one."

"I won't," she promised again. Her heart beat slow and steady and already she was thinking about who would take Helen's place. Maybe Richard would be her best friend or she'd meet another girl at school. "What was it like?"

"Doing it?" Helen said.

"Yeah. Doing it."

"We take all our clothes off and while we kiss, we touch each

other all over. He gets a hard-on and puts it inside. It don't take long."

"What's a hard-on?"

Helen smiled a little, her green eyes crimping at the corners. "You don't know nothing, do you?" But then she told.

Ellie tried to picture her dad with a hard-on but she'd never seen him without some clothes on, so she had no starting point. She asked, "Does it hurt?"

"Only when I'm not ready. I like the touching and kissing but he can't hold off, and it's over so fast. Then he don't touch or kiss me no more."

Ellie wondered what she meant by not ready, and asked.

"You get wet down there when you're ready."

It sounded mysterious and unbelievable but so had the curse at first. Bodies were pretty disgusting and she told herself she wasn't going to do that stuff ever. But then she remembered following Helen to the basement and Helen touching her down there and her legs getting weak with excitement. And she knew she wasn't above anything.

A couple weeks later, Helen took Ellie aside. "I told my mom and she's real upset. She don't know how to tell my dad. I begged her not to till after the wedding but she thinks he's got to sign the papers so I can get married."

Sometimes, she felt herself getting smaller and smaller till she almost disappeared. This usually happened at school when she was in class. It was going on now. She was tiny, nearly to the vanishing point, and her voice sounded high and tinny. "How did you tell your mom?"

"I said, 'I'm gonna have a baby.'"

"What did she say?"

"She cried. She don't think I'm old enough and she's scared of what Dad will do when he finds out."

"Aren't you?" She was. She didn't want to be nearby when that happened.

"We'll live with Donny's parents and sleep in his room."

That didn't sound fun to her. Why move at all, if you couldn't have your own place? "You can't live alone?"

"Not right away."

"What'll you do all day if you can't go to school?" Pregnant girls were expelled.

"I don't know. Sleep, help his ma around the house."

She was trying to imagine what her mother would say if she just came out and told her Helen was pregnant. Then she wondered how much time she had left with Helen and she could hardly breathe around the pain. "When are you gonna get married?"

"On my birthday."

Less than three months away.

September turned into October. The last rain had driven away the hot weather and the leaves started to fall in earnest. The color wasn't good because it had been dry so long, Dad said. She rode the bus to junior high school and home again and Helen went with her during the weeks Donny worked days. Otherwise, he picked her up and took her away.

She would have stopped time had she known how. She still hadn't told Mom Helen was pregnant. The words stuck in the back of her throat whenever an opportunity arose to speak them. Nor had Helen's mother told Mr. Lindquist.

Mom and Dad were looking for another house and had found one they liked on a corner across from a park on the river. She had seen the outside of the house and the neighborhood. It was a different park from the one where she and Helen had met Allen and Donny.

She was ready to move, knowing Helen wouldn't be living next door much longer. It would get her away from Mr. Lindquist and

215

Junior. On a Saturday near the end of October, her parents made an appointment to look at the inside of the house.

"Can Nancy come too?" Joey asked.

"I don't see why not," Mom said. They were at the kitchen table, eating oatmeal and toast.

"I'm staying home," she told them. "Helen's coming over." She hoarded time alone with Helen. There was so little of it left.

"We'll be back in an hour or two."

Helen walked over as Dad backed the car out of the driveway. Ellie closed the door behind her. She didn't think to lock it. Mom and Dad wouldn't be gone long, and they never locked it, except at night or when they left town or when they were all away for the day.

"Come on. Let's go to your room," Helen said, grabbing her arm. She was sick some mornings but today she looked pretty good.

She and Helen were lying across her bed when the front door opened. At first, she thought her parents had come back for something they forgot but then Mr. Lindquist started yelling.

"Where are you, you goddamned slut? I'm gonna beat that bastard out of you." He thudded around downstairs before thumping up the steps.

Ellie stared at Helen, seeing the panic mirrored in her eyes.

"Mom told him," Helen whispered.

They did what they'd done when Mr. Lindquist put a ladder under Ellie's window and climbed it. They crawled under the bed.

The bedroom door slammed open, hitting the wall with a crash. Ellie held her breath and prayed as she only did when things like this happened. *Please, please, don't let him find us.*

His worn, black shoes stopped next to the bed. His pants slid up his legs as he bent over, exposing thick red hair above his white socks. Lifting the bedspread, he peered in at her and Helen.

Coughing a laugh that spewed out the stink of cigarettes and beer, he said, "Get out from under there, you little bitches."

Helen scrabbled further away.

Ellie noticed the fair hair and freckles that covered his long,

thick forearm as her wrist disappeared in his hand and he dragged her out. His touch loosened her terror enough for her to scream and not stop till he slapped the sound away. It rang in her ears along with the booming of her heart.

"My dad's coming home any minute," she said in a high, scared voice as she struggled to get out of his grip.

He shook her. "You won't be hiding and lying for her no more. I ought to whip you good."

"My dad will put you in jail." Once she started talking, the words slipped out unbidden.

He sneered. "Your dad never done anything. He ain't going to do nothing now."

"That's 'cause I never told him," she said, surprised she could talk past the fear.

Helen crawled out from under the bed and started easing past them toward the door. His back was to her and Ellie thought she might get away and go for help, but he must have seen her because he stopped hitting Ellie and grabbed Helen.

"Thought you was going to get away, didn't ya?" He threw Ellie on Joey's bed and Helen down next to her.

With one hand on Helen's chest to hold her down, he fumbled with his pants. Ellie tried to get up but he pushed her back on the bed. That's when she started screaming again and Helen joined in. They made such a racket, she failed to hear the front door open or her dad taking the stairs two and three at a time. Mr. Lindquist must have heard, though, because he let go of Helen and pulled his pants together.

"What the hell is going on?" Dad yelled.

Mr. Lindquist stood his ground. "I didn't hurt them none."

"Get out of here. I'm calling the police." Dad shouted in Mr. Lindquist's face.

"Oh, my God," Mom said, standing in the doorway. Ellie threw herself at her mother, nearly knocking her over. Mom put a protective arm around her and reached out for Helen, who also flew to her.

"She's my daughter. She got herself knocked up. I got a right to punish her," Mr. Lindquist said, edging toward the door.

"Not in my house you don't," Dad shouted.

"Come on, Helen. We're going home." Mr. Lindquist took hold of Helen's arm and she flinched.

"Don't let him take her, Dad," Ellie hollered, burrowing into Mom.

"Take your hands off her." Dad shook with anger. He was scary to look at.

"You can't keep her here." But Mr. Lindquist was going down the stairs. "You hafta send her home."

"I'm calling the police," Dad announced as Mr. Lindquist slammed out the front door.

"I think you should call Helen's mother first," Mom said.

Dad called both. When the police came, Mrs. Lindquist was at the house.

"Tell the officers what happened," Dad urged Helen and Ellie.

"I'm going to live with my boyfriend's family," Helen said, her mouth set in a stubborn look. She tossed her hair back and Ellie's heart turned over with grief.

The policemen looked at Helen's mother for answers.

"It might be better if she don't come home," Mrs. Lindquist said in a soft voice, tears in her eyes.

Ellie had never seen her father so angry and figured he must be mad at her too for not really telling him anything. But when he spoke to her, his voice was gentle and apologetic.

"What happened, Ellie? Why were you screaming?"

"It don't matter. He wasn't after her. He was after me. If I ain't there, he can't get me," Helen said.

Ellie looked at the two policemen, both big enough to beat up Mr. Lindquist but who wouldn't be around when he came back. She'd be the one here. She remembered Mr. Lindquist saying her dad never did anything which was her fault because she never told him enough.

"I'm sorry, Dad," she murmured.

Dad pulled her hard against his chest. He blinked several times and she thought he was ashamed of her.

"I'm the one who's sorry, Ellie. I just didn't know." He held her tight, mashing her nose sideways against his shirt. She smelled his aftershave mixed in with the familiar odor of his skin.

"Oh no, Dad. You didn't do anything."

That's when Joey came in the house with Nancy and stood staring at Dad. She looked puzzled, frightened. "What's wrong, Daddy?" She still called him that sometimes.

"I'm so sorry," he said, taking both girls in his arms.

Joey patted him on the shoulder. "It's okay, Daddy." But, of course, she didn't know what was wrong in the first place.

He smiled a little, making Ellie feel better.

Ellie caught Helen staring at them and saw the longing in her eyes. She smiled at Helen but Helen turned back to her mother, leaning against her so that Mrs. Lindquist put an arm around her.

Mrs. Lindquist went home with one of the policemen to pack Helen's things. The other policeman stayed. While he and Mom and Dad talked quietly, Joey and Nancy went upstairs.

Ellie sat next to Helen on the couch and Helen reached out to touch the side of Ellie's face. "Does it hurt?"

Ellie put her hand over Helen's. "Can you tell?"

"Yeah. It looks like mine did after he caught us smoking." Helen took her hand away and looked at the floor. "He don't love me, does he?" she whispered shakily.

Ellie shook her head but Helen couldn't see.

She didn't have to tell her mother that Helen was pregnant after all. Helen married Donny on her birthday in November. Ellie attended the ceremony at the courthouse with her mother. They sat with Mrs. Lindquist. Allen and his mother, a thin, tired looking woman, took seats across the aisle.

Before he sat down, Allen asked how she was. He wore a shirt and tie and shabby black pants. His hair was slicked down except for a cowlick, which poked up from the crown of his head.

When the judge was talking, Helen turned and grinned at her

as if this was a lighthearted event. She smiled back, hiding the ache that filled her chest. She hadn't seen Helen since she moved into Donny's house and she knew her getting married would change everything.

Mr. Lindquist, who had disappeared for a few days, went home after being warned by the police and Ellie's dad to keep away from Helen and Ellie. Mom was staying home from work till they moved into the house they bought, the one across the street from the park. The house on Elm Street was sold.

Mom hadn't lectured her about Helen being pregnant nor had she scolded Ellie for not telling her. She seemed more concerned about Helen, saying instead, "Poor girl. She never had a chance. I wish we'd done more."

Donny looked like a scrawny boy next to Helen, not someone who was about to become a husband and a father. But Dad said it didn't take brains to marry and have kids. Mr. Lindquist was a father and husband and had failed miserably at both. Donny reminded her of Junior, someone else who wasn't there for the wedding. There were only Ellie, Mom, Mrs. Lindquist, Allen and his mother to witness Helen and Donny's marriage.

They moved a month later. There were huge walk-in closets in the large bedrooms. Hers had two and for months after they moved in, Joey slept in Ellie's room with its twin beds, because she was terrified of the long closet in her bedroom.

Helen came over one day during that first Christmas vacation. You could tell she was pregnant by then and Joey stared at her till Mom made her leave the room. Mom brought cookies on a plate and sat down with Ellie and Helen for a few moments.

Helen talked a little about her new life, which sounded boring and lonely to Ellie. When she asked if they were spending Christmas at Pine Hill and Mom told her they were, she said, "Say hello to Lyle. Wish I was going with you."

For a moment, Ellie wished she were too.

When Mom went out of the room, leaving them alone, Helen said quietly, fiercely, "You promised to come over when Donny wasn't around. Remember? You're still my best friend. We can pretend we're married. It'll be more fun with you."

Although Ellie's legs betrayed her by going weak, she didn't want to know what Donny did with Helen. She realized with a pang that the Helen she loved was gone, that it would never be the same between them again and if it couldn't be like it was, she didn't want to see Helen. "Okay," she said, knowing she wouldn't go.

XXIX

Planning to leave for Pine Hill in the afternoon, Ellie goes to the Y early the next morning. After working out on the treadmill and swimming laps for a half hour, she steps into the hot tub and back into Barb's life.

As she gingerly lowers herself into the swirling hot water, she barely glances at the woman sitting across from her until she asks:

"Ellie, is it?"

Half smiling, she looks across the foaming water. She knows other women here, casual acquaintances, who exercise when she does. Her smile fades with recognition. "Barb? What are you doing here?"

Two other women are lowering themselves into the hot tub. Barb wades through the water and sits next to Ellie. "I could ask the same of you."

"I moved back a few months ago. This is where I grew up."

"What a coincidence. I found a job here after my divorce was

finalized." Barb touches her arm. "Good to see you again. I'm free now. Are you?"

Just when she was going to flee to Pine Hill, this happens. It amazes her. "Yes." Her heartbeat accelerates. With angst? With excitement? She doesn't know.

"I have to go to work now but maybe we could have a drink afterward. I could meet you somewhere."

She sneaks another look at Barb. "I don't even know your last name."

"I'll write it down for you, and my phone number."

Before leaving the locker room, Barb scribbles her full name, phone number and e-mail address on a scrap of paper. Ellie feels she has to do the same, even though her better sense cautions her to go slow here. After all, the woman disappeared after three meetings more than five years ago. It's astounding that she's run into her again at another Y in another city.

When her phone rings at five fifteen, she's working on a manuscript. Her packed suitcase stands in the living room. Worn out from waiting, Bitsy sleeps on the rug in front of the door, determined not to be left behind.

" 'Lo," she says, picking up just before the answering machine clicks on.

"Hi. It's Barb Mahoney. What are you doing?"

"Working. And you?"

"Getting ready to leave work. Want to meet at the Martini Place?"

She hates martinis.

"You don't have to drink one. Maybe we can go to the Wine Bar for dinner. I'll call and see if we can get in at seven."

She hesitates before saying, "Give me a half hour."

"There's free parking behind the Wine Bar."

"I know." She's up looking through her wardrobe for something appropriate. "See you." Putting on black slacks and a red silk blouse, she runs a brush through her thick hair. Gray streaked and slightly wavy, it falls back in the same place. Dabbing on mascara

223

and lipstick, she briefly studies her image in the bathroom mirror. It'll have to do.

Barb is sitting on a bar stool with a martini in hand. "I love martinis. Just this one and we'll go the Wine Bar. What would you like to drink?"

She loves margaritas but doubts they'll make a good one here. Nevertheless, she orders and is pleasantly surprised. "Where do you work?"

"I'm teaching computer classes at the Tech. What were you doing when I called?"

She tells her.

"I'm not surprised. You always look like you're thinking about something else."

She nearly spits out a mouthful of margarita. "Last time I saw you, you didn't want to know who I was or what I did."

Barb eyes her appraisingly, her dark eyes unreadable. "Right. I had an abusive husband. I kept my affairs hidden for my sake and those involved."

She briefly wonders how many women entered Barb's life like she did and departed after a few meetings.

They cross the street in the relatively warm evening, dodging vehicles. Seating them at a table near the front windows, the hostess hands them menus and recites the specials—which Ellie misses completely because she spots Helen and Rudy at a table for two near the back. It makes her wish she'd gone to Pine Hill. She wonders how long it's going to hurt to run into Helen.

The waitress brings their glasses of wine and Ellie downs a slug before she orders.

"Somebody you know?" Barb asks, following her gaze after the waitress leaves.

"Yes." Helen hasn't given any indication that she's seen her.

"The redhead? She works at a travel agency, doesn't she?"

"Do you know her?"

Barb nods and arches an eyebrow. "Quite well, actually."

Ellie's heart pauses on its treadmill to give a little leap. "How well?"

"Let's just say we met a few times, like you and I did."

She likes this woman less and less. "When was that?"

"Weeks ago. I don't know why she's with that man, unless he's gay."

Ellie hasn't thought of this. "He was shopping with her."

Barb shrugs. "Oh well, you never know."

The food is good but rich. After the meal, Ellie excuses herself. Helen's table is being bussed when she passes it. Ellie thought that they had left but when she walks in the bathroom, Helen is drying her hands.

"Don't go with her." Helen throws the paper towel in the wastebasket.

"You did." She takes in the green eyes and freckles hungrily.

"I was trying to get you out of my system."

"I guess it worked. Now you have Rudy. That's a switch."

Helen laughs. "I don't know what I'd do without him."

Heading for the farthest stall, she says, "Go away, Helen."

The outer door closes just before Ellie becomes very sick. There'll be no going home with Barb tonight.

Before she gets into her car, though, Barb invites her for dinner the next night. In a hurry to get away, she agrees.

She drives there the following evening, determined to stay out of Barb's bed. Barb's apartment looks a lot like her own, which she finds a little unsettling. Barb hands her a margarita out of the freezer. The song playing on the CD player is "Time To Say Good-bye." It makes her want to cry.

"Hope you like Mexican as much as margaritas. Have some chips and dip."

"Whose CD?"

"Chris Botti." Barb tosses the salad and puts it aside.

After dinner, when Barb pats the sofa next to her, Ellie eyes it warily. "I have to leave soon."

"Not before we finish the wine."

She sits down at the far end of the couch.

Barb closes the distance between them and before Ellie can think of a reason not to, they're kissing. From there it is only a short trip to the bed.

The sex is very physical. "Come on," Barb protests, when she tries to slow her downward trend.

"It tickles."

"Does this?"

At the touch of tongue, she gasps and gives in.

Afterward, she falls into a wine-and-margarita-soaked sleep. Awakening in the night, at first disoriented by the dark apartment, she quietly dresses and leaves.

Bitsy is waiting at the door, desperate to go outside. She takes him for a walk under the streetlights before falling into bed, where she lies awake. Knowing it was a mistake to go to Barb's apartment, that she'd gone because Helen told her not to, she loads the car and leaves for Pine Hill before six.

Passing Lyle, who is tilling the young crop in one of the fields across the road, she waves and turns into her driveway.

A sense of well-being settles over her. Pine Hill has always been her haven. Only here she found safety from Helen's father. Here she grieved when her own father died and when she divorced. And here she stayed during and after her mother's death. It is her safe place.

The lack of sleep catches up with her after a shower and she lies down. Waking to the sound of someone pounding on the door, she pulls on jeans and a T-shirt. She assumes Lyle will be on the other side of the door.

Instead, it's Helen. Alone. Bitsy launches himself at her and she leans over to pat him. "How's it going?" she asks, as if months haven't passed since she drove away, as if she hadn't introduced Ellie to Rudy in the grocery store two days ago, as if that little exchange in the Wine Bar's bathroom had never taken place.

"I was asleep." Ellie runs her fingers through her hair, wondering how she looks.

"Late night?"

"Yeah. How did you know I was here?"

"I asked this woman named Alison. She said you left her a note. Can I come in?"

"Guess so. You came this far." She shuts the door behind Helen.

"Do you have any coffee?"

"I'll make some. I could use a cup too."

Helen follows her into the kitchen. "I shouldn't have laughed when you said 'now you have Rudy.' I should have told you when I introduced him that Rudy is my Steven."

It takes her a minute to digest this. "He's your cousin?"

"He's gay. I didn't switch."

"Barb said—"

Helen waves a hand. "Forget Barb. She was a flash in the pan as they say."

The aroma of coffee fills the room as it drips into the pot. She takes down a couple of mugs.

"Look," Helen says. "I thought I was doing the right thing when I drove away with the boys. I really didn't think it would work, but you know what?"

"What?" she asks guardedly.

"It doesn't work without you either. I thought maybe we could try again. I know there's a lot of baggage between us, our kids and all, but we can't change that."

Ellie puts down the coffee pot and takes Helen's hand. Her legs are weak, mushy actually. "Come on. We've wasted enough time."

The sun covers them as they lie on her mother's bed, which will be their bed at Pine Hill. Ellie gazes at Helen with something like awe. She hardly believes she's here, willing to take this risk. When they make love, she tries to prolong it, knowing it will never be quite like this again, replete with the wonder of renewal.

Publications from

BELLA BOOKS, INC.

The best in contemporary lesbian fiction

P.O. Box 10543, Tallahassee, FL 32302
Phone: 800-729-4992
www.bellabooks.com

OUT OF THE FIRE by Beth Moore. Author Ann Covington feels at the top of the world when told her book is being made into a movie. Then in walks Casey Duncan the actress who is playing the lead in her movie. Will Casey turn Ann's world upside down?
1-59493-088-0 $13.95

STAKE THROUGH THE HEART: NEW EXPLOITS OF TWILIGHT LESBIANS by Karin Kallmaker, Julia Watts, Barbara Johnson and Therese Szymanski. The playful quartet that penned the acclaimed *Once Upon A Dyke* are dimming the lights for journeys into worlds of breathless seduction.
1-59493-071-6 $15.95

THE HOUSE ON SANDSTONE by KG MacGregor. Carly Griffin returns home to Leland and finds that her old high school friend Justine is awakening more than just old memories.
1-59493-076-7 $13.95

WILD NIGHTS: MOSTLY TRUE STORIES OF WOMEN LOVING WOMEN edited by Therese Szymanski. 264 pp. 23 new stories from today's hottest erotic writers are sure to give you your wildest night ever!
1-59493-069-4 $15.95

COYOTE SKY by Gerri Hill. 248 pp. Sheriff Lee Foxx is trying to cope with the realization that she has fallen in love for the first time. And fallen for author Kate Winters, who is technically unavailable. Will Lee fight to keep Kate in Coyote?
1-59493-065-1 $13.95

VOICES OF THE HEART by Frankie J. Jones. 264 pp. A series of events force Erin to swear off love as she tries to break away from the woman of her dreams. Will Erin ever find the key to her future happiness?
1-59493-068-6 $13.95

SHELTER FROM THE STORM by Peggy J. Herring. 296 pp. A story about family and getting reacquainted with one's past that shows that sometimes you don't appreciate what you have until you almost lose it.
1-59493-064-3 $13.95

WRITING MY LOVE by Claire McNab. 192 pp. Romance writer Vonny Smith believes she will be able to woo her editor Diana through her writing . . .
1-59493-063-5 $13.95

PAID IN FULL by Ann Roberts. 200 pp. Ari Adams will need to choose between the debts of the past and the promise of a happy future.
1-59493-059-7 $13.95

ROMANCING THE ZONE by Kenna White. 272 pp. Liz's world begins to crumble when a secret from her past returns to Ashton . . .
1-59493-060-0 $13.95

SIGN ON THE LINE by Jaime Clevenger. 204 pp. Alexis Getty, a flirtatious delivery driver is committed to finding the rightful owner of a mysterious package.

1-59493-052-X $13.95

END OF WATCH by Clare Baxter. 256 pp. LAPD Lieutenant L.A Franco Frank follows the lone clue down the unlit steps of memory to a final, unthinkable resolution. 1-59493-064-4 $13.95

BEHIND THE PINE CURTAIN by Gerri Hill. 280 pp. Jacqueline returns home after her father's death and comes face-to-face with her first crush.

1-59493-057-0 $13.95

18TH & CASTRO by Karin Kallmaker. 200 pp. First-time couplings and couples who know how to mix lust and love make 18th & Castro the hottest address in the city by the bay.   1-59493-066-X $13.95

JUST THIS ONCE by KG MacGregor. 200 pp. Mindful of the obligations back home that she must honor, Wynne Connelly struggles to resist the fascination and allure that a particular woman she meets on her business trip represents.

1-59493-087-2 $13.95

ANTICIPATION by Terri Breneman. 240 pp. Two women struggle to remain professional as they work together to find a serial killer.   1-59493-055-4 $13.95

OBSESSION by Jackie Calhoun. 240 pp. Lindsey's life is turned upside down when Sarah comes into the family nursery in search of perennials.   1-59493-058-9 $13.95

BENEATH THE WILLOW by Kenna White. 240 pp. A torch that still burns brightly even after twenty-five years threatens to consume two childhood friends.

1-59493-053-8 $13.95

SISTER LOST, SISTER FOUND by Jeanne G'fellers. 224 pp. The highly anticipated sequel to No Sister of Mine.   1-59493-056-2 $13.95

THE WEEKEND VISITOR by Jessica Thomas. 240 pp. In this latest Alex Peres mystery, Alex is asked to investigate an assault on a local woman but finds that her client may have more secrets than she lets on.   1-59493-054-6 $13.95

THE KILLING ROOM by Gerri Hill. 392 pp. How can two women forget and go their separate ways?   1-59493-050-3 $12.95

PASSIONATE KISSES by Megan Carter. 240 pp. Will two old friends run from love? 1-59493-051-1 $12.95

ALWAYS AND FOREVER by Lyn Denison. 224 pp. The girl next door turns Shannon's world upside down.   1-59493-049-X $12.95

BACK TALK by Saxon Bennett. 200 pp. Can a talk show host find love after heartbreak? 1-59493-028-7 $12.95

THE PERFECT VALENTINE: EROTIC LESBIAN VALENTINE STORIES edited by Barbara Johnson and Therese Szymanski—from Bella After Dark. 328 pp. Stories from the hottest writers around.   1-59493-061-9 $14.95

MURDER AT RANDOM by Claire McNab. 200 pp. The Sixth Denise Cleever Thriller. Denise realizes the fate of thousands is in her hands.   1-59493-047-3 $12.95

THE TIDES OF PASSION by Diana Tremain Braund. 240 pp. Will Susan be able to hold it all together and find the one woman who touches her soul?

1-59493-048-1 $12.95

JUST LIKE THAT by Karin Kallmaker. 240 pp. Disliking each other—and everything they stand for—even before they meet, Toni and Syrah find feelings can change, just like that. 1-59493-025-2 $12.95

WHEN FIRST WE PRACTICE by Therese Szymanski. 200 pp. Brett and Allie are once again caught in the middle of murder and intrigue. 1-59493-045-7 $12.95

REUNION by Jane Frances. 240 pp. Cathy Braithwaite seems to have it all: good looks, money and a thriving accounting practice . . . 1-59493-046-5 $12.95

BELL, BOOK & DYKE: NEW EXPLOITS OF MAGICAL LESBIANS by Kallmaker, Watts, Johnson and Szymanski. 360 pp. Reluctant witches, tempting spells and skyclad beauties—delve into the mysteries of love, lust and power in this quartet of novellas. 1-59493-023-6 $14.95

ARTIST'S DREAM by Gerri Hill. 320 pp. When Cassie meets Luke Winston, she can no longer deny her attraction to women . . . 1-59493-042-2 $12.95

NO EVIDENCE by Nancy Sanra. 240 pp. Private Investigator Tally McGinnis once again returns to the horror-filled world of a serial killer. 1-59493-043-04 $12.95

WHEN LOVE FINDS A HOME by Megan Carter. 280 pp. What will it take for Anna and Rona to find their way back to each other again? 1-59493-041-4 $12.95

MEMORIES TO DIE FOR by Adrian Gold. 240 pp. Rachel attempts to avoid her attraction to the charms of Anna Sigurdson . . . 1-59493-038-4 $12.95

SILENT HEART by Claire McNab. 280 pp. Exotic lesbian romance. 1-59493-044-9 $12.95

MIDNIGHT RAIN by Peggy J. Herring. 240 pp. Bridget McBee is determined to find the woman who saved her life. 1-59493-021-X $12.95

THE MISSING PAGE A Brenda Strange Mystery by Patty G. Henderson. 240 pp. Brenda investigates her client's murder . . . 1-59493-004-X $12.95

WHISPERS ON THE WIND by Frankie J. Jones. 240 pp. Dixon thinks she and her best friend, Elizabeth Colter, would make the perfect couple . . . 1-59493-037-6 $12.95

CALL OF THE DARK: EROTIC LESBIAN TALES OF THE SUPERNATURAL edited by Therese Szymanski—from Bella After Dark. 320 pp. 1-59493-040-6 $14.95

A TIME TO CAST AWAY A Helen Black Mystery by Pat Welch. 240 pp. Helen stops by Alice's apartment—only to find the woman dead . . . 1-59493-036-8 $12.95

DESERT OF THE HEART by Jane Rule. 224 pp. The book that launched the most popular lesbian movie of all time is back. 1-1-59493-035-X $12.95

THE NEXT WORLD by Ursula Steck. 240 pp. Anna's friend Mido is threatened and eventually disappears . . . 1-59493-024-4 $12.95

CALL SHOTGUN by Jaime Clevenger. 240 pp. Kelly gets pulled back into the world of private investigation . . . 1-59493-016-3 $12.95

52 PICKUP by Bonnie J. Morris and E.B. Casey. 240 pp. 52 hot, romantic tales—one for every Saturday night of the year. 1-59493-026-0 $12.95

GOLD FEVER by Lyn Denison. 240 pp. Kate's first love, Ashley, returns to their home town, where Kate now lives . . . 1-1-59493-039-2 $12.95

RISKY INVESTMENT by Beth Moore. 240 pp. Lynn's best friend and roommate needs her to pretend Chris is his fiancé. But nothing is ever easy.   1-59493-019-8 $12.95

HUNTER'S WAY by Gerri Hill. 240 pp. Homicide detective Tori Hunter is forced to team up with the hot-tempered Samantha Kennedy.   1-59493-018-X $12.95

CAR POOL by Karin Kallmaker. 240 pp. Soft shoulders, merging traffic and slippery when wet . . . Anthea and Shay find love in the car pool.   1-59493-013-9 $12.95

NO SISTER OF MINE by Jeanne G'Fellers. 240 pp. Telepathic women fight to coexist with a patriarchal society that wishes their eradication.   1-59493-017-1 $12.95

ON THE WINGS OF LOVE by Megan Carter. 240 pp. Stacie's reporting career is on the rocks. She has to interview bestselling author Cheryl, or else!

1-59493-027-9 $12.95

WICKED GOOD TIME by Diana Tremain Braund. 224 pp. Does Christina need Miki as a protector . . . or want her as a lover?   1-59493-031-7 $12.95

THOSE WHO WAIT by Peggy J. Herring. 240 pp. Two brilliant sisters—in love with the same woman!   1-59493-032-5 $12.95

ABBY'S PASSION by Jackie Calhoun. 240 pp. Abby's bipolar sister helps turn her world upside down, so she must decide what's most important.   1-59493-014-7 $12.95

PICTURE PERFECT by Jane Vollbrecht. 240 pp. Kate is reintroduced to Casey, the daughter of an old friend. Can they withstand Kate's career?   1-59493-015-5 $12.95

PAPERBACK ROMANCE by Karin Kallmaker. 240 pp. Carolyn falls for tall, dark and . . . female . . . in this classic lesbian romance.   1-59493-033-3 $12.95

DAWN OF CHANGE by Gerri Hill. 240 pp. Susan ran away to find peace in remote Kings Canyon—then she met Shawn . . .   1-59493-011-2 $12.95

DOWN THE RABBIT HOLE by Lynne Jamneck. 240 pp. Is a killer holding a grudge against FBI Agent Samantha Skellar?   1-59493-012-0 $12.95

SEASONS OF THE HEART by Jackie Calhoun. 240 pp. Overwhelmed, Sara saw only one way out—leaving . . .   1-59493-030-9 $12.95

TURNING THE TABLES by Jessica Thomas. 240 pp. The 2nd Alex Peres Mystery. *From ghosties and ghoulies and long leggity beasties* . . .   1-59493-009-0 $12.95

FOR EVERY SEASON by Frankie Jones. 240 pp. Andi, who is investigating a 65-year-old murder, meets Janice, a charming district attorney . . .   1-59493-010-4 $12.95

LOVE ON THE LINE by Laura DeHart Young. 240 pp. Kay leaves a younger woman behind to go on a mission to Alaska . . . will she regret it?   1-59493-008-2 $12.95

UNDER THE SOUTHERN CROSS by Claire McNab. 200 pp. Lee, an American travel agent, goes down under and meets Australian Alex, and the sparks fly under the Southern Cross.   1-59493-029-5 $12.95

SUGAR by Karin Kallmaker. 240 pp. Three women want sugar from Sugar, who can't make up her mind.   1-59493-001-5 $12.95

FALL GUY by Claire McNab. 200 pp. 16th Detective Inspector Carol Ashton Mystery. 1-59493-000-7 $12.95

ONE SUMMER NIGHT by Gerri Hill. 232 pp. Johanna swore to never fall in love again—but then she met the charming Kelly . . .   1-59493-007-4 $12.95

TALK OF THE TOWN TOO by Saxon Bennett. 181 pp. Second in the series about wild and fun loving friends.
1-931513-77-5 $12.95

LOVE SPEAKS HER NAME by Laura DeHart Young. 170 pp. Love and friendship, desire and intrigue, spark this exciting sequel to *Forever and the Night*.
1-59493-002-3 $12.95

TO HAVE AND TO HOLD by Peggy J. Herring. 184 pp. By finally letting down her defenses, will Dorian be opening herself to a devastating betrayal?
1-59493-005-8 $12.95

WILD THINGS by Karin Kallmaker. 228 pp. Dutiful daughter Faith has met the perfect man. There's just one problem: she's in love with his sister.
1-931513-64-3 $12.95

SHARED WINDS by Kenna White. 216 pp. Can Emma rebuild more than just Lanny's marina?
1-59493-006-6 $12.95

THE UNKNOWN MILE by Jaime Clevenger. 253 pp. Kelly's world is getting more and more complicated every moment.
1-931513-57-0 $12.95

TREASURED PAST by Linda Hill. 189 pp. A shared passion for antiques leads to love.
1-59493-003-1 $12.95

SIERRA CITY by Gerri Hill. 284 pp. Chris and Jesse cannot deny their growing attraction . . .
1-931513-98-8 $12.95

ALL THE WRONG PLACES by Karin Kallmaker. 174 pp. Sex and the single girl— Brandy is looking for love and usually she finds it. Karin Kallmaker's first *After Dark* erotic novel.
1-931513-76-7 $12.95

WHEN THE CORPSE LIES A Motor City Thriller by Therese Szymanski. 328 pp. Butch bad-girl Brett Higgins is used to waking up next to beautiful women she hardly knows. Problem is, this one's dead.
1-931513-74-0 $12.95

GUARDED HEARTS by Hannah Rickard. 240 pp. Someone's reminding Alyssa about her secret past, and then she becomes the suspect in a series of burglaries.
1-931513-99-6 $12.95

ONCE MORE WITH FEELING by Peggy J. Herring. 184 pp. Lighthearted, loving, romantic adventure.
1-931513-60-0 $12.95

TANGLED AND DARK A Brenda Strange Mystery by Patty G. Henderson. 240 pp. When investigating a local death, Brenda finds two possible killers—one diagnosed with Multiple Personality Disorder.
1-931513-75-9 $12.95

WHITE LACE AND PROMISES by Peggy J. Herring. 240 pp. Maxine and Betina realize sex may not be the most important thing in their lives.
1-931513-73-2 $12.95

UNFORGETTABLE by Karin Kallmaker. 288 pp. Can Rett find love with the cheerleader who broke her heart so many years ago?
1-931513-63-5 $12.95

HIGHER GROUND by Saxon Bennett. 280 pp. A delightfully complex reflection of the successful, high society lives of a small group of women.
1-931513-69-4 $12.95

LAST CALL A Detective Franco Mystery by Baxter Clare. 240 pp. Frank overlooks all else to try to solve a cold case of two murdered children . . .
1-931513-70-8 $12.95

ONCE UPON A DYKE: NEW EXPLOITS OF FAIRY-TALE LESBIANS by Karin Kallmaker, Julia Watts, Barbara Johnson & Therese Szymanski. 320 pp. You've never read fairy tales like these before! From Bella After Dark.
1-931513-71-6 $14.95

FINEST KIND OF LOVE by Diana Tremain Braund. 224 pp. Can Molly and Carolyn stop clashing long enough to see beyond their differences? 1-931513-68-6 $12.95

DREAM LOVER by Lyn Denison. 188 pp. A soft, sensuous, romantic fantasy.
1-931513-96-1 $12.95

NEVER SAY NEVER by Linda Hill. 224 pp. A classic love story . . . where rules aren't the only things broken. 1-931513-67-8 $12.95

PAINTED MOON by Karin Kallmaker. 214 pp. Stranded together in a snowbound cabin, Jackie and Leah's lives will never be the same. 1-931513-53-8 $12.95

WIZARD OF ISIS by Jean Stewart. 240 pp. Fifth in the exciting Isis series.
1-931513-71-4 $12.95

WOMAN IN THE MIRROR by Jackie Calhoun. 216 pp. Josey learns to love again, while her niece is learning to love women for the first time. 1-931513-78-3 $12.95

SUBSTITUTE FOR LOVE by Karin Kallmaker. 200 pp. When Holly and Reyna meet the combination adds up to pure passion. But what about tomorrow?
1-931513-62-7 $12.95

GULF BREEZE by Gerri Hill. 288 pp. Could Carly really be the woman Pat has always been searching for? 1-931513-97-X $12.95

THE TOMSTOWN INCIDENT by Penny Hayes. 184 pp. Caught between two worlds, Eloise must make a decision that will change her life forever.
1-931513-56-2 $12.95

MAKING UP FOR LOST TIME by Karin Kallmaker. 240 pp. Discover delicious recipes for romance by the undisputed mistress. 1-931513-61-9 $12.95

THE WAY LIFE SHOULD BE by Diana Tremain Braund. 173 pp. With which woman will Jennifer find the true meaning of love? 1-931513-66-X $12.95

BACK TO BASICS: A BUTCH/FEMME ANTHOLOGY edited by Therese Szymanski—from Bella After Dark. 324 pp. 1-931513-35-X $14.95

SURVIVAL OF LOVE by Frankie J. Jones. 236 pp. What will Jody do when she falls in love with her best friend's daughter? 1-931513-55-4 $12.95

LESSONS IN MURDER by Claire McNab. 184 pp. 1st Detective Inspector Carol Ashton Mystery. 1-931513-65-1 $12.95

DEATH BY DEATH by Claire McNab. 167 pp. 5th Denise Cleever Thriller.
1-931513-34-1 $12.95

CAUGHT IN THE NET by Jessica Thomas. 188 pp. A wickedly observant story of mystery, danger, and love in Provincetown. 1-931513-54-6 $12.95

DREAMS FOUND by Lyn Denison. Australian Riley embarks on a journey to meet her birth mother . . . and gains not just a family, but the love of her life.
1-931513-58-9 $12.95

A MOMENT'S INDISCRETION by Peggy J. Herring. 154 pp. Jackie is torn between her better judgment and the overwhelming attraction she feels for Valerie.
1-931513-59-7 $12.95

IN EVERY PORT by Karin Kallmaker. 224 pp. Jessica has a woman in every port. Will meeting Cat change all that? 1-931513-36-8 $12.95

TOUCHWOOD by Karin Kallmaker. 240 pp. Rayann loves Louisa. Louisa loves Rayann. Can the decades between their ages keep them apart? 1-931513-37-6 $12.95

WATERMARK by Karin Kallmaker. 248 pp. Teresa wants a future with a woman whose heart has been frozen by loss. Sequel to *Touchwood*. 1-931513-38-4 $12.95

EMBRACE IN MOTION by Karin Kallmaker. 240 pp. Has Sarah found lust or love? 1-931513-39-2 $12.95

ONE DEGREE OF SEPARATION by Karin Kallmaker. 232 pp. Sizzling small town romance between Marian, the town librarian, and the new girl from the big city. 1-931513-30-9 $12.95

CRY HAVOC A Detective Franco Mystery by Baxter Clare. 240 pp. A dead hustler with a headless rooster in his lap sends Lt. L.A. Franco headfirst against Mother Love. 1-931513931-7 $12.95

DISTANT THUNDER by Peggy J. Herring. 294 pp. Bankrobbing drifter Cordy awakens strange new feelings in Leo in this romantic tale set in the Old West. 1-931513-28-7 $12.95

COP OUT by Claire McNab. 216 pp. 4th Detective Inspector Carol Ashton Mystery. 1-931513-29-5 $12.95

BLOOD LINK by Claire McNab. 159 pp. 15th Detective Inspector Carol Ashton Mystery. Is Carol unwittingly playing into a deadly plan? 1-931513-27-9 $12.95

TALK OF THE TOWN by Saxon Bennett. 239 pp. With enough beer, barbecue and B.S., anything is possible! 1-931513-18-X $12.95

MAYBE NEXT TIME by Karin Kallmaker. 256 pp. Sabrina has everything she ever wanted—except Jorie. 1-931513-26-0 $12.95

WHEN GOOD GIRLS GO BAD: A Motor City Thriller by Therese Szymanski. 230 pp. Brett, Randi and Allie join forces to stop a serial killer. 1-931513-11-2 $12.95

A DAY TOO LONG: A Helen Black Mystery by Pat Welch. 328 pp. This time Helen's fate is in her own hands. 1-931513-22-8 $12.95

THE RED LINE OF YARMALD by Diana Rivers. 256 pp. The Hadra's only hope lies in a magical red line . . . climactic sequel to *Clouds of War*. 1-931513-23-6 $12.95

OUTSIDE THE FLOCK by Jackie Calhoun. 224 pp. Jo embraces her new love and life. 1-931513-13-9 $12.95

LEGACY OF LOVE by Marianne K. Martin. 224 pp. Read the whole Sage Bristo story. 1-931513-15-5 $12.95

STREET RULES: A Detective Franco Mystery by Baxter Clare. 304 pp. Gritty, fast-paced mystery with compelling Detective L.A. Franco. 1-931513-14-7 $12.95

RECOGNITION FACTOR: 4th Denise Cleever Thriller by Claire McNab. 176 pp. Denise Cleever tracks a notorious terrorist to America. 1-931513-24-4 $12.95

NORA AND LIZ by Nancy Garden. 296 pp. Lesbian romance by the author of *Annie on My Mind*. 1-931513-20-1 $12.95

MIDAS TOUCH by Frankie J. Jones. 208 pp. Sandra had everything but love. 1-931513-21-X $12.95

BEYOND ALL REASON by Peggy J. Herring. 240 pp. A romance hotter than Texas. 1-9513-25-2 $12.95

About the Author

Jackie Calhoun is the author of *Obsession*, *Abby's Passion*, *Woman in the Mirror*, *Outside the Flock*, *Tamarack Creek* and *Off Season*, published by Bella Books; ten books published by Naiad Press, some of which are being rereleased; and *Crossing the Center Line*, published out by Windstorm Creative Ltd. Jackie lives with her partner in northeast Wisconsin.

Dedicated to my parents and sister.

Acknowledgments

Joan Hendry, my first reader
Anna Chinappi, my editor
Linda Hill and the staff at Bella Books

Bella Books, Inc.
P.O. Box 10543
Tallahassee, FL 32302

Printed in the United States of America on acid-free paper
First Edition

Editor: Anna Chinappi
Cover designer: LA Callaghan

ISBN-10: 1-59493-092-9
ISBN-13: 978-1-59493-092-8

The
EDUCATION
of ELLIE

JACKIE CALHOUN

Bella
BOOKS
2007

Visit

Bella Books

at

BellaBooks.com

or call our toll-free number

1-800-729-4992

She opens the door and looks at Helen through the screen. The dog shuts up and the silence seems as loud as the barking.

"Can I come in?"

"I'm packing."

"I thought so." Helen opens the screen and lets it slap shut behind her. Never breaking eye contact, she shuts and locks the door before gently backing Ellie into the nearest wall.

The wainscoting cuts into Ellie's hips as Helen presses her against it. Her legs lose their strength. Her arms lie uselessly at her sides. She is once again ten years old.

Helen's green eyes seem to ask permission as she slowly leans forward. Her lips are pliable, her tongue almost a query.

Ellie's heart beats wildly in her throat. She feels as if she's melting into the wall. She can't breathe and develops a sudden headache. If this is excitement at its most extreme, she will die from it. She pushes Helen away enough to free her mouth. "I can't—"